YOU
AUTO~COMPLETE
ME

Katie MacAlister

FAT CAT BOOKS

This book is for all those readers, young adult and just young at heart, who have grown a bit older but still love shenanigans, dishy British men, and Emily.

EMILY'S HANDY TIPS TO READING THIS BOOK

The author, in what she calls her "wisdom," has decided to recount my story in the series of texts in which they were originally written. Because it would be weird to make the whole book a series of my phone screens, she stripped out the text and slapped it straight into the book.

I know. I told her to do it differently, but will she listen to me? No, she won't. Authors, man!

Anyhoo, in case you get confused by who's saying what, here's a key:

EM Emily (AKA me)
DRU Dru (my bestie)
FANG Fang (my friend with benefits. Kind of. It's complicated…)

There you go! You should be set. Oh, and you might want to read the author's note at the end of my fabulous story just in case a few parts of the book sound familiar. It turns out the author has been writing about my life for years! I feel so violated! Also, kind of famous.

Emily Williams, heroine

CHAPTER ONE

EM Well, I'm here.

DRU Emily! There you are! Wait … what the hell is this? Why aren't we using WhatsApp? Why can't we use pictures?

EM I refer you to Brother.

DRU What's he done now?

EM Allow me to tell you. Brace yourself, I'm using voice-to-text because my thumbs would drop off if I tried to type this all out to you.

First of all, my room is haunted. And not just haunted by any old run-of-the-mill ghost—oh, no, my ghost is an underwear pervert.

DRU Wow. That's … wow.

EM I know, right? Dru, Dru, dear, sweet Dru, I can't begin to tell you just how awful my life is. Well, OK, I can, and since I'm having to suffer, you, as my bestie, are going to have to suffer with me. Even though you're on the other side of the world. You'll do that for me, won't you? 'Cause I'd do it for you. I always get sympathy cramps for you, don't I?

DRU You do, and you know that I would do the same for you. Besties, dude. Can I put an avatar on here?

EM No.

DRU Why not?

EM This app is weird. It just does names. No pictures. No avatars. Nothing but text.

DRU Let me try. Er…how's this?

EM There're no avatars, Dru. I can't see any picture you post here.

DRU Maybe this one?

EM Still nothing. No. Avatars.

DRU OK, this is a cute pic. How about if I try this one?

EM You're doing this on purpose, aren't you?

DRU Trying to drive you insane?

EM Yes!

DRU No, but I'm so going to Google and see if there's a way to hack this app so that we can use pics. Text is just so…texty.

EM !!!

DRU What?

EM Sheesh, girl! I'm trying to unload to you! Bare my inner soul! Share my burdens.

DRU Soz, go ahead. I'm good now.

EM Honestly, it's like you aren't even interested. Where was I?

DRU Haunted room. Cramps. Underwear pervert.

EM That's right. Where should I start in the catalog of horror that is now my life? Well, first of all, as you can see by the fact that I'm texting you using a weirdo app, I didn't talk Brother (the most eccentric father in the world) into getting us a UK cell phone plan that included free international time, or which was able to use common, ordinary apps. So I'm stuck with only e-mail and YackApp, which evidently is part of the phone package. How on earth am I supposed to exist without Snapchat and WhatsApp and Instagram? Sheesh! But you know how my father is—if there's a buck to be saved, he's dibsed it.

And it's not even like I can use my phone a whole lot, since we have a limited family data plan that Brother watches like a hawk lest we dare use it like normal people.

"And if I hear any complaints," the Ancient One said when I told him he was being archaic as hell, "I will simply take back the phone, cancel the tuition at the very prestigious college into which I managed to get you admitted, solely by dint of pulling many strings, and inform your mother that you will be making your own way home, the latter being an act that I suspect you'll find difficult."

"Oh!" I said, outraged that he'd pull out my current state of insolvency in the War of the Generations (as I like to think of our conversations). "That is just going to make me point out yet again that I wouldn't be broke if I didn't have to pay for that stupid company car out of my own pocket."

"A company car which you totaled," Brother pointed out in that maddening way he has.

"That wasn't my fault!" I said, slapping my legs in frustration. Honestly, was any father ever so blind to reality? "I was trying to keep a latte from spilling on the carpet, which was a nice thing to do, especially considering that I wouldn't even have been in the car if the Weasel hadn't sent me out to get yet another latte because he's addicted to Starbucks."

"You ran into a parked police car, Emily," the father unit said.

I sniffed, and decided to adopt a dignified stance, rather than continue to argue with him (besides, I have yet to find a comeback to the parked-cop-car comment). "Regardless of the failure of my ex-employer to realize what a quality employee he had in me," I said, loftily waving away his argument, "not to mention the judge who garnished so much of my wages that I can't possibly live on my own any longer and had to move back with you—"

Brother grimaced.

I ignored him and continued, "As if that wasn't enough, I already agreed to the infinitesimally small data plan although it's utterly, utterly without reason."

"Hrmph," he said, and marched off to go unpack yet another box that Mom had shipped over here.

Great, now I've digressed to the point where I can't remember what I was going to … oh, yes. So here I am in England, horrified to be stuck only with some weirdo third-world-esque phone, with no future.

DRU Em, you're in England. For a year. Free! Lots of people would be thrilled to be there.

EM Lots of people are idiots, too.

DRU You have me there.

EM Let's just take a good look at why I'm miserable, shall we?

Why I Am Miserable: A List

- Lost lease on cute little studio apartment when owner sold out to new company who jacked rent up almost double
- Lost job due to slight accident with the Weasel boss's car
- Had no insurance because insurance peeps stopped autopay without telling me. (Isn't that illegal? It should be!)
- In debt for approximately two hundred years according to a (clearly dirty) judge who took the side of the Weasel's insurance company re liability, and thus ordered wages garnished
- Plan for student loan bailout canceled because student loan people say they won't give money while the judgment is active
- Likewise, free ride through local university was ground to dust when Brother said getting kicked out of college after two semesters was sign I wasn't serious. Then added something about education being a privilege, not a right. Fwah, say I.
- Daniel, formerly adored boyfriend and currently asshat heartbreaker, dumps me—cruelly, and maliciously—after almost two years because he is, and I quote, "tired of waiting for [expletive deleted]." The fact that we did everything but have actual sex seems to have escaped him.

In short, my dumpling, I have no job, no cute apartment with access to a pool, no money, no boyfriend, and no hope for my future at all.

DRU I admit, you've had a rough time of it lately.

EM Don't be surprised if you get a letter from Brother or my mom saying I died. My obituary will read: "Emily Williams, slightly fluffy twenty-year-old, died Tuesday night of broken spirits and lost convictions after being fired from her job, sued for reimbursement of damages that the car insurance wouldn't cover, and forced to move back home with her parents, an act so appalling that she willingly took up residence in Jolly Olde England simply to try to forget her woes." Or something like that.

DRU You're not slightly fluffy; you're curvy. That's super trendy now what with all the fat-shamers being roasted on Insta, and stuff.

EM And this is why I love you. Mwah. Although "fat" is very non-PC. Fluffy is in.

DRU Mwahback, and gotcha. Fluffy.

EM Dammit, I lost my place again. … Oh, yes, so here I am, but all is not lost, because holy hellballs, Dru, there are some seriously sexy-sounding men in this country, and I'm determined to spring back from Asshat Daniel. I learned my lesson there, yes sir! No longer will I be Emily the Introspective. Gone is Emily the Woman Who Wants a Meaningful Relationship Before Sex. Vanished into nothing is Hesitant Emily. I'm on the prowl now, babe. The first guy I see who I want to hook up with is going to be pounced on.

DRU You go, girl!

EM And there's a lot of such men around, let me tell you! Although all I've really seen so far are the guys who hang around historic sights, since that's all Brother has allowed us to see.

It's "Oh, look at that, Emily, that building is five hundred years old" this, and "That piece of Stonehenge has been standing in that spot for fifty gazillion years" that. Well, duh, it's a rock. It's not like it's going to sprout legs, buy a thong, and go to Tahiti for a windsurfing vacation, now, is it?

That was Brother who said the bit about the rock, BTW (the first bit, not the thong part). You know him—the man lives for old stuff like that. Pro tip from me to you: If you ever have to move back with your parents (something I do *not* recommend), and they take you to another country, do not, under any circumstances, agree to go sightseeing with them. Especially if your dad is a medieval scholar like Brother, 'cause I'm here to tell you that you'll end up looking at nothing but old buildings that should be plowed under to make room for more malls. Needless to say, he's in seventh heaven, and plans on writing some book about his historical studies during the year we're here.

Whatever, say I. If it'll keep him off the streets and out of my hair, I'm all for it.

DRU You have to admit, Brother is much more interesting than my dad. My dad is boring central.

EM There's interesting, and then there's downright eccentric.

DRU True dat.

EM "Can't we go see Windsor Castle?" I asked at one point, thinking that some minor European prince might be hanging around waiting to meet a groovin' American chick. A girl can dream, right?

"Maybe another day. Brother wants to see an old illuminated manuscript," Mom said. "It's very important to his research to see it in person."

"How about the dungeon museum? I heard there's one in London. That's not only cool—it's historical, too. Bet there's medieval stuff there."

"Another time, Em," Brother said, and went off about how wonderful the library was that we were going to. I tell you, Dru, I was going crazy being trapped in the car with them, traveling from library to library having to look at a bunch of moldy old books, with nary a pounce-worthy Englishman in sight.

Not that I'm here just to find one (well, OK, it's higher on my list of priorities than going to the college that Brother is teaching at for a year). It's just that The Situation is beginning to wear on me.

I mean, who else do you know who is still (technically, albeit not physically) a virgin?

DRU Well …,

EM No one, right? I must be the oldest living virgin in the world.

DRU Well …

EM Thank god for my purple hippopotamus.

DRU Yeah … but …

EM I'd go crazy without a battery-operated boyfriend.

DRU …

EM What???

DRU I don't see how you can be a virgin if you've … you know … enjoyed your purple hippo.

EM It's a state of mind. Sigh. Maybe Daniel had a point. I mean, we did everything else … but I just … every time I thought about having actual, real, parts-of-him-in-parts-of-me sex, it just got weird, and I ended up giving him a BJ so he'd let the idea go.

It's me, isn't it? Daniel is right and I'm the weird one. Well … to hell with all that! I'm an adult, I'm twenty, and I'm lookin' for a man! The new game plan is sex-or-bust, with no more hesitations, no more introspection, and no more delay!

DRU I love it when you go all badass.

EM Enough sex talk. So, I survived the sightseeing and Brother's driving on the wrong side of everything, and yesterday we arrived here at chez Williams aka the Haunted Mansion.

"What's wrong, Brother?" I asked when he pulled up before a creepy, old, creepy, dirty (and did I say creepy?) house that looked like it should have been condemned. "Are we lost? Out of gas? Did the engine fall out?"

"Nope," the man who spawned me answered in a cheerful *I can't wait to see this antiquity* sort of way that for the last two days had made the flesh on my back crawl. "This is our home away from home for the next year. Isn't it charming?"

Charming? The Amityville Horror looked more welcoming than the monstrosity that slouched at the end of the drive. Honest to Pete, Dru, it positively reeked of lecherous old men lurking in the garden trying to watch people undress at night!

DRU Ew!

EM "I am *so* not doing this," I said, taking a stand.

"It certainly is different than anything we have at home," Mom said, ignoring my stand-taking in that mom sort of way older women have. "When did Professor Carlson say it was built?"

"In 1588, by Dracula, no doubt," I answered, gripping my purse firmly. If anything weird even thought about grabbing me, I'd nail it upside the head with twenty-two pounds of makeup.

"Now, Emily, you know that Vlad the Impaler was born in 1431. It would have been impossible for him to build this house in 1588," Brother said. "Ten points if you can tell me during what empire Vlad ruled Walachia."

I am warning you right here and now, Dru—if your father gives you even the slightest reason to think he'll ever become a scholar, kill him. I know that seems harsh, but honestly, the historical pop quizzes alone are grounds for divorcing him as a parent.

DRU All my dad does is threaten to take me off his health insurance.

EM "Can we skip the crazy stuff and get right down to the exorcism?" I asked as the Parents hustled me toward the house. It's huge—I mean really huge—and old, and black and moldy-looking, with all sorts of windows that poke out and glare down on you. "Do either of you have any holy water?"

"It certainly does have atmosphere," Mom said.

"How about a spare crucifix or two?"

"Emily ... ," Brother said warningly. He did something to the front door and it squeaked open. Inside was a whole lot of black. I swear you could hear the bats rubbing their little batty paws together and cackling at the fresh dinner walking in.

"A Bible? A 'What Would Jesus Do?' sticker?"

"Not now, Em," Mom said, pulling me into the abyss. The door slammed shut behind us.

"Abandon hope, all ye who enter here," I said in my best hollow voice while striking a pose on the staircase.

That was a mistake. The tall, dark-paneled hallway made everything sound even more hollow than normal hollow. Kind of überhollow. Downright gothapalooza hollow. Boy, if you say the word *hollow* enough, it starts to sound weird. Hollow. Hoooollooow. Where was I? Oh, yeah, the House of Doom.

Brother eyed me when I blew dust off the banister. "She didn't get that smart mouth from my side of the family."

Mom smiled and patted him on the arm. "It's a defense mechanism, dear. Girls Emily's age feel it's a comedown in the world to have to return to the nest after flying from it prematurely."

"One, I'm not a girl. I'm an adult. And two, it was not my fault the cop parked right where I was driving!" I said stiffly.

DRU It totally was the cop's fault.

EM "They believe it's vital to appear flip on the outside even though they're riddled with insecurities on the inside," Mom finished, ignoring me.

"I am not insecure. I'm far from it, in fact." I rubbed my arms at the chill from the Gothic House of Horrors. "Although I would be happy to pretend I am if it got us out of here."

"Are you sure she's mine?" Brother asked Mom in what passes for Old-People humor. "Is it too late for a paternity test?"

I'll save you from the hellish nightmare that was the grand tour, as the Sperm Donor called it. Let me just say that the house is one big creep fest. If there aren't hockey-mask-wearing, homicidal, deranged ax-murdering child molesters living in the basement, you can paint my toenails and call me Sally.

DRU I gotta say, it sounds kind of fun.

EM You're insane, but we know that about you.

DRU I repeat: You're in England. For a year. For free, with nothing to do but go to school and meet dishy Englishmen.

EM If only it was that easy. Must go. Brother just bellowed upstairs that dinner is on, and it'll probably take me at least a week to find my way down to the ground floor (that's first floor to you and the rest of the world). I'll tell you about the underwear ghost later. Oh! I picked up a magazine at the airport that said Chris Hemsworth was in England filming a new movie—can you believe that Brother had no idea who he was?

DRU OK, your dad is deranged.

EM Preach it!

"He's only the star of the Thor and Avengers movies, some of the best man meat ever put on the screen for women to ogle," I told him, then made him look at the Chris Hemsworth fan site just so he could see who I was drooling … er … *talking* about. Brother pretended to stagger away after he sat through the candid pics, Avengers stills, and of course the video of that Dutch girl doing the interpretive dance with her homemade full-size Chris Hemsworth cardboard cutout (I really need to get me one of those).

"And this is how you spend your time online?" the Old One asked, appalled. "I am quite right in keeping you off the social media, if this is what sorts of things people do in their spare time."

I smiled my deep smile at him. "Turnabout is fair play, Brother."

"Eh?"

"You made me look at old books for two whole days, but man, do you squawk when all I ask you to do is listen to some blank verse poems written to Chris Hemsworth's fabulousness."

Oh, get this, you're going to die—the studio that the Hems will be working at is only ten miles away. I think we can guess what American female of legal age and plentiful bosomage is going to find herself in that area, can't we?

DRU Ya know, I thought it was going to be a horrible year with you in England and me here, but this is just like I was right there.

EM Right? Like I said, if I have to suffer, you have to suffer with me.

DRU Smooches.

EM Hugs and kisses.

EM Oh, how's the leg? Are you still playing Sims? What happened to your Sim Walking Dead family? Dammit. Missed you.

CHAPTER TWO

DRU I was thinking about your situation.

EM Ohai. What situation?

DRU The Daniel Situation.

EM What about it?

DRU I don't think you need a man. I mean, we don't these days, do we? Lots of the feminist sites say we don't.

EM You're just saying that because you have a boyfriend. I don't.

DRU I can't believe he said you had sexual hang-ups.

EM I know, right? I am so not an ice queen!

DRU Still, jumping the bones of the first guy you meet may not be smart.

EM Meh. I'm determined to make things different here. I'm not going to sit around wondering if he's the right man to jump into bed with. I'm just going to go for it. You know, once I find someone I want to go for it with. With whom I want to go for it. That sounds awkward. Gah. Grammar!

DRU You didn't finish telling me about the ghost in your room.

EM Didn't I? I thought I did.

DRU You're telling me stuff in your head again, aren't you?

EM It's the jet lag. OK, pull up a chair. Let me go voice-to-text again.

DRU And here I was worried the ghost had gotten you. Who would have sympathy cramps for me if you get taken by an underwear-fetish poltergeist?

EM Luckily, the ghost doesn't seem to be interested in anything but my undies. Which is creepy enough, let me tell you! The thought of spectral hands fondling my bras gives me the willies.

Here's what happened—we arrived two days ago. Since Bess is off to tour England for a week, I got the first dibs on the best bedroom. Brother and Mom took the Old People's room downstairs (so the Ancient One doesn't have to climb the stairs every night, and let me tell you, that's a blessing for those of us who like to sleep at night—Brother's knees sound like cannons going off when he climbs stairs).

So there I was with pick of the prime rooms, and of course I chose the tower room. Now, get this—the room is almost totally round. There's a turret overhead, but the room itself is round, with great curved window seats. Of course, the first thing I did was check the storage space under the window seats for dead bodies, severed limbs, pulsating hearts, etc., but they were empty.

DRU I really would not like to have your imagination.

EM Fine and dandy, say I, and I snag the room. I unpack my meager belongings right away into a hulking piece of furniture Brother says is a wardrobe (don't the English understand the necessity of a really big walk-in closet?) and tuck the undies and stuff away in a minuscule dresser. A side note: I can't believe Mom only let me bring two suitcases. How can I go out in public with only two suitcases full of clothes? I'd go shopping, but until I get a job, I'm sans funds.

Anyway, I went to do family stuff and when I came back, my underwear was all over the room.

All.

Over.

The room.

It was *so* creepy. I, of course, did the only thing I could do. I screamed.

Brother cracked and popped his way up the stairs (which was really kind of nice of him considering how old he is), and charged into the room looking like a sixty-two-year-old deranged rhinoceros—he had a hair thing going on that looked just like a horn. I really need to have a talk with him about the benefits of mousse.

"What's wrong? Are you hurt? What happened?" he asked in between gasps for air.

I stared pointedly at my undies lying all over the floor. "My underwear is all over the room!"

He looked around, the hair horn kind of quivering in an agitated sort of way. "Your underwear?"

There are times when I am positive that he doesn't speak the same language I do. "Underwear. As in, those things I wear under my clothes? Get it? *Underwear?*"

"I know what underwear is, Emily. And I can do without that smart tone."

"This from the man who springs Vlad the Impaler trivia quizzes at the drop of a hat."

"Those are different. They are educational," he said, trying to look noble 'n stuff.

I took a deep breath. "The fact remains that my undies are not where they should be."

He ruffled back the horn o' hair and looked around the room again. "Why have you strewn your clothes around the room? I thought you were excited about having the tower room?"

"I didn't strew anything around, Old One. I put my things—pitiful and in need of immediate replacement, not that you've offered to do so—in the drawer, but when I got back, they were all over the floor. I just knew this house was haunted, and now I've got proof." I shook an underwire bra at him. "We've got ghosts. I just hope you're happy! God only knows what the ghost is going to do with my—"

Oops! Almost let the cat out of the bag there. Don't need to explain to him about my boyfriend hippopotamus.

"With your what?" Brother asked.

"My … um …" I had to think fast. You know how suspicious my father can be. "Um … my personal things. You know, women's things."

"Oh." He didn't look like he believed me. "Regardless of that, there are no such things as ghosts, Emily. You probably simply forgot to put your things away."

"Even if I did forget—and I didn't, because unlike some members of this family who are so ancient they can recall what the Holy Grail looks like, I can remember things—but even if I *did* forget, I would not have thrown all my underwear around the room. Thus, either there's an ax-murdering maniac with an underwear fetish living in the basement who came up here while I was downstairs trying to make your laptop understand English wireless connections, or this room is haunted."

"Emily—"

"I'd prefer a ghost to an ax murderer, thank you."

"You can always use another room if you don't like this one."

"But I do like it," I said, grabbing the rest of my things and stuffing them back into the drawer. "It's the only nice room in this whole nightmare of a house. You always say I have to make the best of a bad situation, and in this case, that means I get the cool room. It's only fair."

"Fine," he said, running his hand through his hair again. It only made the horn stand up even more. "If you're done having this morning's histrionics, I have work to do. The dean of the college I'll be working for is coming by in a few minutes. I trust you'll be available to greet him?"

What is it with parents having you meet all their cronies? All they do is ask if you've met someone you want to marry, and why you ran into a parked cop car, and stuff like that. The last thing I wanted to do was to meet his dean, but never let it be said that I, Emily Williams, let an opportunity slip past me. "Let's make a deal," I said.

Brother groaned. "Not now, Emily—"

"The deal is this: I come down and be charming and pleasant to your dean, and you take me to the nearest mall and fund a shopping trip."

"I don't have time to drive you around, and we agreed that you would get a job while you're here if I got you a work permit.

Which I did. The rest is up to you. Besides, I need to be ready for the start of term next week—and speaking of that, so do you. Don't you want to bone up before you start university?"

I sighed. You know my feelings about that whole school thing—just when I think I've found a good degree that I'll really like, it turns boring after a couple of semesters, and I have to start all over with a different degree. I can only hope that something here will be different than what they have back home, because I'm running out of options of anything that interests me enough to stick with it. "About the mall—"

"Not today, sweetling," he said as he creaked and popped his way out of the room. I almost rolled my eyes at the "sweetling," but to be honest, I'm used to it by now. Brother thinks using medieval terms is cute. "Maybe you can worm some money out of your mother, although I wouldn't count on it. I'll expect you downstairs in fifteen minutes."

"I can't."

"Why?" he asked, pausing at the door.

I waved my hand at the wardrobe. "I don't have anything to wear. That's why I have to go to the mall."

"What you have on is fine. Downstairs in fifteen, madam, and none of your sulks, please."

I hate it when the parents pull that authority crap. Just because I was forced by fate and a lot of bad luck to have to move back home doesn't mean he can treat me like I'm twelve. Sulks! Did you ever? I have never sulked. I don't even know how to sulk!

DRU Wow, you say the word "sulk" enough and it really starts to sound weird.

EM ...

DRU What?

EM You interrupted my train of flow. Flow of thought. Train of thought. Whatever, you interrupted.

DRU Sorry. I got caught up in your drama and forgot we weren't talking on the phone.

EM Aww. You're forgiven. Where was I? Oh, the dean. I thought about ignoring Brother's demand altogether, but figured it might peeve off Mom if I did, which would lessen the chance of wheedling some pity money from her. Besides, it wasn't like this dean person was anyone important. It didn't matter what I wore. Right?

A few minutes later, there I was sitting in the room Brother calls the library, but which really looks (and smells) like a mouse's playroom—it's full of boring old books, not even the good kind like that Victorian erotica book I found (you remember, the one with all the "manly pillars of alabaster").

DRU And "grottoes of Venus."

EM Plump pigeons of breastitude.

DRU You made that one up.

EM Maybe, but it sounds like something the erotic Victorians would have said. Well, these books weren't like that. They were sermons and other deadly things like that—and Brother brought in this old geezer who's the head of the college. I started to stand up to shake his hand, when this totally fabulous guy came in behind the dean. Girl, I'm telling you, I must have swallowed back gallons of slobber! He wore skinny jeans that looked at least ten years old, a ratty old sweater over a "This is what a feminist looks like" tee, and he had dark gray eyes, a hipster goatee, and dark blond dreads. You know that I don't like blond men, but holy huevos rancheros, Dru, this man made me rethink my dark-haired-men-only stance.

DRU I've always thought that was weird of you.

EM I'm not weird. I'm fascinatingly odd.

DRU If that's what you want to call it …

EM Shush, you're distracting me again.

"Emily," Brother said, waving toward the hipster. "This is Aidan, the dean's son. He'll be working as my teaching assistant this year."

Aidan. Mama likes sexy names.

DRU Oooh, that is a good one. Almost as good as Raphael.

EM Crapbeans, I have to go. Mom insists I go with her to the grocery store, and since I'm hopeful of hitting her up for some much-needed funds, I shall toddle off to be the doting daughter. I'll text you as soon as I'm back. I haven't told you yet about what Aidan said, and why I almost committed Brother-acide, and Holly, and why I'm going back to high school. Kind of. Not really, but kind of. Oh, I'll tell you about it later.

DRU WHAT? You're going back to high school? What about Aidan? Emily! Don't you dare *Game of Thrones* cliff-hanger me like that!

EM Gotta run.

DRU You can't do this to me! Emily! COME BACK HERE!

EM Hugs and kisses.

YOU LOGGED ON

DRU EMILY MARIE WILLIAMS! You can't just tell me you met a hipster with a goatee and

dreads, and you're going back to the hellhole that is high school, and almost killed your father, and then leave me hanging! Tell me everything!

DRU Every.

DRU Single.

DRU Thing.

EM Hold on there, girlfriend, I said I'd text you as soon as I got back. Where was I?

DRU I flail my hands at you!

EM Hee hee hee. OK, I'll start with the best bit first: the professorial meet and greet at Oxwills University. Or rather, one of the colleges.

I know, it's confusing—I thought Oxwills was a college, but it's like a mega college, and there's all these little colleges within it. I think. I wasn't really paying attention when Brother was going on and on and on about it on the way to Oxwills. Aidan of the goatee wasn't at the party, which made me a bit sad.

DRU And why are you not telling me about him? What are you hiding?

EM I'll get to him. Be patient.

DRU Gah.

EM The meet and greet was a bit on the sad side as well, with no one under fifty except me and the daughter of a Latin teacher, who was about fifteen or sixteen. The daughter, not the Latin teacher.

"Hi," I said, parking myself next to the girl. She was vaguely Goth in a black top and leggings, and wore a really sad expression. No one was paying her any attention, and she had that look on her face that you get when you're not sure if your tampon has leaked or not, and you don't want anyone to look at you just in case it has.

She eyed me for a minute before saying, "Hullo."

"I'm Emily," I said, holding out my hand.

She stared at it like it was made up of bull testicles. "Holly Alton," she said, finally giving my hand a little shake.

"You have a parent here, too?" I asked, nodding at the herd of ancient ones who were milling around meeting and greeting and whatnot.

"Yes, my mother is a Latin professor, and my father teaches religious studies."

"Ugh. Oh, sorry if that came out rude, but neither of them sound like much fun. The subjects, not your parents. I'm sure they're a barrel-of-monkeys sort of fun."

Holly gave a little one-shouldered shrug, still eyeing me in a considering sort of manner. "They aren't. Are you a tutor?"

"Me? No, my dad is a visiting professor, and I came along to take a year of foreign college. I'm having trouble picking a major. So far, I've thought about psychology, English, art history, and justice, but none of them really are for me, although I was pretty good with the English composition classes. And the criminology classes I had at a community college were a blast. We got to go to the morgue and everything."

"Oooh." Her eyes widened, and she warmed up to me a bit. "Those all sound so interesting, except the morgue one."

"I'm thinking of archaeology next, or maybe something sciency. Do you go to school here?"

"No, I'm in the fifth form. It's too bad you're not a tutor—my parents are trying to find one for me, since ..." She stopped and, biting her lip, looked away.

I sensed a mystery and, Dru, you know how I love me a good mystery!

DRU You do. You love mysteries. Especially my old-time pre–politically correct Nancy Drew books that I used to get at garage sales. You know, the ones you stole from me.

EM I didn't steal them—I borrowed them. Reading is good for you. A mind is a sad thing to waste and all that.

DRU Dude.

EM ?

DRU You still have them. My books. The ones I spent my allowances on every month. The ones I loved and petted and which are hard to find, and now are worth a fortune on eBay.

EM You're delusional. What makes you think I have them?

DRU I saw them when I helped you pack, remember?

EM You must have hit the crack pipe particularly hard that day. Anyway ...

DRU I have never smoked crack!

EM *ANYWAY!* There I was at this party with a Goth girl going all emo.

"Since what?" I asked her, realizing that I was being a bit pushy, but what's the use in having everyone think you are pushy just because you're American, and not taking advantage of that bias?

Her gaze flickered away from me, and she gave another half shrug. "I don't do well at school."

"That's too bad. I didn't mind high school, myself, but I know that sometimes people can be dicks and make you hate it." I felt an odd sort of sympathy for Holly. She reminded me of that girl who was in our sophomore class for a couple of weeks before she left because she was bullied by the cheerleaders. Do you remember her?

DRU Marvella. Weird name, great hair. I think she was into corset training.

EM That's right. She passed out once in gym class and told Miss Miller it was because she had tightened her corset down another level, which I always thought sounded incredibly uncomfortable. The corset, that is. But boy, her boobs never moved during track.

DRU Better than a sports bra, that's for sure. Go on with telling me what happened with Goth Holly. Did she faint?

EM Nope.

"Those are my parents, there," I told her, nodding toward them. "My mom is in the yellow dress, and my father is next to her."

"The one with the—" She made a gesture indicating the hair horn.

"Yup, that's Brother."

She blinked at me.

"I know, it's confusing," I said, giving her an apologetic smile. "My father has always been called Brother. Evidently his sister started calling him that when he was born, and it stuck. Even my mom and my grandma call him Brother. It's a bit kinky, but what can you do?"

"That is ... different."

"Yup. Hey, what does tutoring involve? And ... uh ... I hate to be crass, but does it pay much? I need a part-time job while I'm going to college, and if all you need is some help with your classes, I could probably do that with one hand tied behind my back."

Holly brightened just a little. "I don't know what my parents are paying, but I can ask them. Would you really take the job?" For a second she looked horrified at what she said, and then her gaze dropped to her hands, and she muttered something about being presumptuous.

"Look, babe," I said, giving her a pat on the hand. "Any girl who can use the word 'presumptuous' in a sentence is a chick after my own heart. I'd be happy to be your tutor so long as we can come to an agreement about money. I don't need a ton, since Brother is paying for my classes and books and stuff, but I do need some clothes, and since my driver's license was taken away because I ran into a cop car, and the judge got all bent out of shape because the insurance company didn't tell me they turned the autopay off—anyway, because of all that, I have to take the driving test here in order to get a license. And that costs money."

"I'll go ask," Holly said, and, without waiting for me to tell her she didn't have to do it right that second, scooted off to find her parents.

DRU Aww. You made a new friend. A needy friend. That's awfully sweet, Em.

EM A job is a job. But I will admit, I liked Holly. She reminds me of a lost puppy.

DRU You always were a sucker for a lost puppy.

EM Long story short (I know, too late): I am now the official tutor of one Holly Alton, sixteen-year-old troubled girl. I almost backed out when her mom cornered me and asked me what experience I had with depression and self-harm, but after explaining to her that I was never into that because I was horse-crazy until I was fifteen, and didn't have time to be moody and depressed, she gave me a huge smile and said I was hired.

DRU That doesn't make any sense at all.

EM Right? But then, people really don't, do they?

DRU So is that why you're going back to high school? And why? You hated it when you had to go, so why would you repeat that now when you're in college?

EM Mum Alton said she really wanted me to be more of a friend to Holly than anything else.

"She has trouble at school interacting and communicating with the other children," Mum A. said, patting her perfectly coiffed hair. "Holly feels things so much, you know. The headmaster is willing to allow an advocate to attend some classes with Holly in an attempt to get her through this trying time."

"Attend classes?" I said, my voice all high and squeaky and probably able to cut glass at close quarters. "Whoa. I'm in college now! I graduated high school almost three years ago, and I'm not going back for anyone. I mean, Holly seems like a nice kid, but—"

"No, no, I phrased that poorly. You wouldn't be expected to attend the classes in that way—you'll simply be with her certain days of the week, anonymously sitting in the background and monitoring the situation so that Holly will be able to focus on her studies and not worry about any bullying, of which she has in the past been the target. The school is quite willing to work with us on this, and I'm certain will tell everyone that you are there in a nonstudent capacity. I'm sure it will be quite suitable for you to do your own studying during such times."

"Oh." I thought about that for a few minutes.

DRU The only way anyone could get me back into high school would be to pay me a metric butt-load of money. Metric. Butt. Load.

EM "Naturally, we would compensate you for your time and trouble above and beyond the standard tutoring rate," Mum A. said, which clinched the deal.

DRU Ha! Called it.

EM "Holly is rather withdrawn with others her age, so it will be a relief to know she is under the watchful eye of someone so mature."

"I'd be delighted," I said with my best trustworthy smile, and after haggling just a little over the salary, we settled it all, and I start tomorrow, before the college semester begins.

DRU You have balls of steel, girl.

EM Ovaries. We shouldn't base strength on male personal equipment. I have ovaries of steel. Wait, that sounds …

DRU Yeah. Uncomfy.

EM Balls it is.

On the way home, I noticed a sign on the side of the road that said PIDDLINGTON-ON-THE-WELD 1 MILE. I was just starting to snicker to myself about all the poor people that live in Piddling when Brother pulled off at the POTW exit.

"Hey," I said. You know me, never one to pull my punches.

DRU People with balls of steel never pull punches. Fact.

EM "What are you doing? Taking a shortcut to Ghoul Central? How come we've turned off here?"

"We live here, Emily."

Honest to Pete, I just about piddled on the weld (whatever that is). "What? You said we live in a town called Alling! No one ever said anything about a town that describes someone peeing on something!"

Brother glared at me in the rearview mirror. "Piddlington is a suburb of Alling. The town name has nothing to do with urine. Many British towns bear old and ancient names dating back …"

I groaned to myself and tried to stop listening. Whenever Brother gets going on anything ancient, he can talk until the end of time.

DRU So, you live in a town called …

EM Piddlington.

DRU Hoo. I'm really sorry.

EM As if things weren't horrible enough, now I am forever going to be cursed for being known as "Emily of Piddlesville."

DRU Could be worse.

EM I don't see how.

DRU My mom is from a place in Kentucky called Big Bone Lick.

EM I retract my objection.

Now on to the main subject. "Aidan," I hear you saying with those narrowed eyes that you get whenever I go off on a tangent.

DRU I never!

EM Look at yourself right now.

DRU I … it's … the sun is in my eyes!

EM Uh-huh. All righty, the tale of Mr. Hipster Aidan. Picture it: We're standing in Brother's library, and Brother and the dean are talking about something (probably ancient brass stuff or medieval tortures or those horribly dull books he insists on dragging us to see), and in walks Aidan. Now, I'm being very dignified. I didn't drool on him, or throw myself on him, or remotely look like I wanted to ask him if he'd like to go up to my room and take care of that pesky virginity problem I have.

DRU You are the epitome of class, babe.

EM "So you're going to Gob-botty?" Aidan asked with an insouciant smile.

"Gob-botty? I thought it was Oxwills."

He grinned. My knees melted. I had to hold on to the chair to keep up the pretense that I was standing.

"Gobbottle is the name of the liberal arts college at Oxwills. We who tread its hallowed halls call it Gob-botty. Botty, get it?"

"Oh, gotcha." I laughed with him. "Botty. Ha."

DRU What the heck is a botty?

EM I had to do a Google search, because I didn't know, either. It's slang for butt.

DRU Butt? You're going to Butt College?

EM Oh, it gets better than that, because "gob" means mouth.

DRU So ...

EM Yup. I'm going to mouth-butt college. In Piddle City. Can I die of embarrassment now, please?

DRU I don't know how you get yourself into these predicaments, I really don't.

EM !!!

EM There's more, so I'm not going to take time to point out the obvious right now.

"What degree are you taking?" Aidan asked.

"Well, I was thinking of archaeology. I'm not super into history like my father, but I spent a summer volunteering at a dig site back home, and I think studying that might be fun."

"Excellent, then I should see you around the college. I'm in Gob-botty with Dr. Williams, of course."

"Of course!" I said brightly, and not at all like I didn't know what college my own father was working at. "So you're into history, then?"

"Law, actually, but my dad is a Gobbottle man, and I agreed to spend a little time on the historical aspects of civil law before I go for my doctorate."

"Awesomesauce."

"Awesome ... *sauce?*" He tipped his adorable head to the side and scrunched up his gray eyes in a way that had me pushing him to the top of the Deflower Emily list.

DRU Girl.

EM Hey, it needs to be a list. And Aidan is on it.

I felt I needed to explain Americanisms to him, though. "Awesome is good, but really awesome is awesomesauce. Do you not speak Interwebs?"

He grinned. "Not nearly as well as you. I try to stay away from social media like that, to be honest. I much prefer connecting with people on a personal level, one that eschews the trivial, and really drills down to the bare bones. I like the way you talk, though. You're very ... free, aren't you?"

"You have no idea just how free I am," I said, going to flip my hair over my shoulder, but it was balled up in a messy bun. I decided I'd better play down my Facebook addiction (which is going to make my life a living hell since our data plan sucks) and be cool. "I'm from Seattle, you know, so we're very hip to all things technology. So, if we're going to be around the same buildings, we should see each other around campus, yes?"

He batted his lashes over his big gray eyes and smiled at me. It was a knowing smile, a smile that said he didn't find me trivial, and instead wanted to connect with my bare bones on a personal level. It was a smile that hinted he'd be more than able to take care of The Situation, and then some. It was a smile I felt in my lady parts, and you know what that means—either I need to be drinking more water and take some cranberry pills, or he might be *the one*. Do you think it's too early to sign up at the bridal registry?

DRU I think you'd do better to take a UTI test.

EM "I'll make sure of that," he said with a little waggle of his eyebrows. "Assuming Dr. Williams isn't too much of a taskmaster, that is."

"Brother?" I made a face. "I've heard people say a lot of things about him, but taskmaster isn't one of them."

"Brother?"

"My father. Everyone calls him Brother. He hates his real name. We humor him."

He nodded. "An eccentric, eh? He'll fit right in at Gob-botty. Perhaps I could show you around before the term begins."

Are you insanely jealous with my femme-fatale-ness yet?

DRU Uh ...

EM You should be. Minutes after I meet a hipster hunk, he's making butt jokes, and offering to show me around. OK, so he probably weighs less than me, and he kept sliding glances at my boobs when he thought I wouldn't notice (you know how sensitive I am about them being so enormous), but even with that, he was pretty fabulous.

"I'm sure Emily would love to be shown around town," Brother said, nosing into my conversation as if he had a right to. He had his boring old dean to talk to; who told him he could snag my hipster, too? "She's been a bit nervous about starting school in a country well-known for its academic excellence."

I stared at him. Who was this stranger, and why was he talking such utter bullshit about me to these people?

DRU Fathers, man. Amiright?

EM "I'm sure she'll have no difficulties whatsoever," the dean said, giving me a smile where his dry old lips peeled back to expose dentures. "Getting a doctorate in medieval history like your esteemed father, are you, young lady?"

I opened my mouth to say hell no, I'd rather have a Brazilian than step foot in a medieval history class, but Brother slapped a big old hammy hand down on my shoulder and hauled me up to his side. Honest to Pete, Dru, I just about died of embarrassment … until he totally and completely ruined my life with what he said next.

DRU *clutches hands and holds breath*

EM "Emily is our little changeling, actually. She can't settle down to a degree, and was fired from her last job for destroying her employer's BMW, dean old bean." Or something like that. Brother is taking this living-in-England thing way too seriously. "Her mother and I are hoping this trip will help her to mature."

Mature? *Me?*

DRU Well …

EM WHAT???

DRU Nothing.

EM I gawked at Brother in sheer and utter horror, unable to speak, so gobsmacked was I.

"Ah," the dean said with a knowing look. He tilted his head toward Aidan. "My boy will be delighted to take her under his wing. He's a wonder with the wallflowers, you know."

Wallflower! I slid a glance at Brother that warned him of his imminent death.

"That's very kind of you, Aidan," Brother said, squawking a little when I dug my elbow into his side so he'd let go of me. "Perhaps you can give Emily the help she needs picking just one area to focus on. Naturally, she'll have some time, since there will be general education classes to take first."

"Brother," I said through my teeth, grabbing his arm and pulling him with me. "Might I speak to you a moment?"

"I'm talking with the dean—"

"I'm so sorry, Mr. Dean," I apologized, still dragging my father over to a corner that was devoid of people, and thus would not make me die of shame on the spot. "I'll bring him right back, I promise."

"That man is one of my colleagues," Brother protested when I released him into the safety of the unoccupied corner. He rubbed his arm as he spoke. "Just what was so important that I had to leave a quite enjoyable conversation?"

"It might have been enjoyable for you, but certainly wasn't for me. Brother! I am so not a wallflower, and I don't need to mature. And you know the only reason I haven't graduated is because I'm simply trying out a number of degree options before I settle on one."

"This is why you dragged me away?" Brother shook his head and tried to leave, but I blocked his way.

DRU I love how you talk to your dad. I couldn't do that with mine, but Brother is kinda cool that way.

EM I have another word for it.

DRU You have to live with him, so that's understandable.

EM So, so understandable.

"What was that business with general education classes?" I asked Brother. "I told you I was thinking of archaeology."

"The admissions department made it quite clear that you'll be starting with all the other new students this year," the father entity said, nodding and waving over my shoulder at the dean. "I'm sure you'll get along just fine with general classes while you decide on which path you will pursue."

I gawked at his words. "But … if I go in as a freshman, I'll have to do all sorts of silly general education requirements that I shouldn't have to take because I've already done them back home."

"Unfortunately, this college doesn't recognize the transfer credits—" "Well, they can just change that!" I said, feeling all the blood drain out of me at the thought of the diversity, and awareness, and cultural-sensitivity general education classes I'd have to take again.

You remember how boring those classes were.

DRU Cheese on toast, do I! I hated every minute of enforced diversement.

EM Diversity?

DRU I like diversement better. I mean, I get that it's important for people who don't understand that sort of thing, but we're not like that. My dad is black! My mom is white! I *am* diversity!

EM Diversement.

DRU Hush. I'm being dramatic.

EM Roll with it, sister.

DRU No, I'm done.

EM Exactly. And I refused to be penalized because I was switching schools for a year. Not to mention the fact that they'd take up one out of the two semesters I'd be in England. "How hard is it for them to matriculate my existing classes?" I asked.

"We are guests in this country," my parent said soothingly, casting worried glances at the dean.

"That doesn't mean I have to be punished," I interrupted. "Dammit, Brother, I don't want to have to take those ridiculous classes again. If I get any more culturally aware of biodiversity and ethics in the workplace, and any other of those horrible sorts of classes that are needed today just to graduate, I'll start pooping protest signs."

"Emily—"

"You promised me a whole year of fabulous English college courses, ones I couldn't get back home. You said it would be enriching and mind opening, and all those other fabulous things. You said I could dabble in whatever I wanted for the entire year, and now you're saying that for one of the terms I'll be repeating bullshit classes."

DRU You said that to him?

EM I did.

DRU You are my new hero.

EM Smooches.

I took a deep breath, during which time Brother patted me on the arm. "I realize you're upset, Emily, but this is a situation out of both our control. I suggest you look on the bright side."

"Then I simply won't go," I said, taking a stand. Firm Emily is firm, right?

DRU Right.

EM "I believe," Brother said, flashing a perfectly horrible smile over my shoulder at the dean, "that our agreement was that I would pay for you to come with us if you attended Oxwills. If you no longer wish to do that, then you may return home."

"But … you rented our house for the year to the professor you swapped with," I pointed out. "I wouldn't have anywhere to stay."

Brother raised his eyebrows. "Indeed."

DRU Tricksy Brother!

EM Mom came over at that point, which is probably a good thing, because you know, I really didn't want Aidan and everyone there to see me murder my father—or, worse, burst into tears. Either way he'd probably get the wrong idea about me. Anyway, Mom came in and asked with that *ignore Emily making a scene* face how things were going.

"The man you married has just pointed out that I have no choice but to take general education diversity classes. *Again.*"

Aidan, possible hunk of my dreams, smiled and sauntered over to join us. Could he be any more adorable? I think not. "Did I hear a mention of diversity classes? It's not that bad,

Emily. If you take all of the boring classes in the first semester, you can indulge yourself for the rest of the year in as many archaeology classes as you can handle."

I sighed, knowing full well I was doomed, so I gritted my loins and girded my teeth and all that. "I suppose so, although I would very much like to get the person responsible for evaluating transfer credits into a small, soundproofed room for about five minutes."

Then Mom said

DRU ???

DRU Em?

DRU Emily?

DRU Crapballs, I forgot to get a duress word for you.

DRU EMILY!!!

EM Sorry, had to answer the phone. I have to leave; Mum A. called to ask if I'd go with Holly to do her school uniform shopping before the stores close. Evidently she (Mum A.) can't miss some important Latin meeting, and it's the last day for Holly to get her stuff.

Remember when our grade school wanted to go to baby-poop-yellow-and-green uniforms, and I wrote to Amnesty International, and they wrote back to say that they didn't think that being forced to wear a school uniform qualified as a torture?

DRU Oh, I remember that. Uck. Mom made me model the test version for the school board.

EM Yup. I took a picture of you wearing the horrible thing, and sent it to the Amnesty people, after which they responded that, yeah, it actually was pretty awful after all, and they'd open a case for me if the uniform was put into place. I'll let you know how poor Holly's uniform compares with the one we almost got stuck with.

DRU I shudder for you.

EM More later. I'm not through telling you about Aidan yet, and there's tomorrow … must go. Let me know if you've left the house yet.

Hs and Ks.

DRU Later, tater.

CHAPTER THREE

EM I'm never going to live through this year.

DRU Maybe it won't be as bad as you think, maybe … oh, what am I saying? No one should have to be Culturally Ethical via Diverse Logic more than once in their lifetime.

EM I love that you knew exactly what I was going to say.

DRU You're my sister from another mister. Of course I know. Now tell Mama all.

EM OK, that just sounds weird with the mister thing in there.

DRU Yeah, I regretted it the second I sent it. Pretend it never happened.

EM Done. The class thing really bothers me, but I'm striving to let it go.

DRU Smart. Nothing you can do about it.

EM I reserve the right to bitch about it periodically, though.

DRU Of course.

EM So, I survived, although just barely, the trip to Valentine's, a scabby old store in glorious downtown Piddlesville that caters to the Indentured School Slaves. The woman who runs the teen area had big poufy pink hair that looked just like cotton candy, and she kept calling Holly and me "dearie." It was beyond weird.

Before I describe the horrors that poor Holly has to wear, let me tell you about POTW. First off, it's very small, which is no surprise, because I can't imagine anyone who wants to live in a city with that name. There's a High Street with a couple of cool shops, and a handful of grotty shops ("grotty" is a local word; it means grotesque—IMHO, there's a lot about POTW that's on the grotty side), a Second Street with gas stations and a McDonald's, and that's about it. Valentine's is the local department store, although how anyone can even think of buying anything there is one of those mysteries that will never be solved.

The clothes in the window were so nineties I almost heard the theme to *X-Files* playing. (The old *X-Files*, not the new one. Wait, it has the same theme song, doesn't it? Never mind. Moving on.) Inside was even worse—it was dim and dusty and the wooden floor creaked, and the whole place smelled like old cabbage and mothballs.

"If this is what your civilization has come to," I said, stopping and gawking when I saw the school-uniforms section, "then I think we should wipe the slate clean and start over. I thought you guys were supposed to be so sophisticated?"

Holly eyed the uniform under a sign for her local school, and blanched. She actually blanched, Dru. Have you ever seen a Goth blanch? It's not pretty. "Kill me now. Please. It'll be a merciful ending, so no one will blame you."

"Tempting as it is to put you out of your misery, I think your parents would have a thing or two to say about it. Ugh. Really? You need all this?" I consulted the list that Holly had given me. "Seriously, dude, I'm going to give you the e-mail of an Amnesty International guy who might be able to help. Although at least your uniform isn't baby-poop yellow. You have that to be thankful for."

Holly stared at the rack of maroon clothes, and blanched again. It was downright creepy how pale that girl could get just by staring at something.

Since I think you'd like Holly if you met her, allow me to provide you with the list of what the poor kid has to wear five days a week (remind me to google excuses to get out of school, so I can help her out if things get too tough):

DRU Emily!

EM What?

DRU Reminder: get the poor kid out of school now and again.

EM Moving on, Miss Taking Everything Literally.

Item: blazer

Description: maroon, with school emblem

What I think: The school emblem looks like one of one of those testicley aliens from *Doctor Who*.

DRU Tentacley?

EM No, testicley.

DRU Not a word, bro.

EM Should be! I have no idea what the emblem is supposed to be, but it's blob-like. Maybe their school mascot is an alien blob? Or an alien testicle. At this point, I'd say either is an option.

Item: school tie

Description: maroon and teal diagonal stripes

What I think: It's crap!

"A tie?" I asked Holly when she picked it up with the very tips of two fingers. "Wow, they really make girls wear a tie here? I guess that's good in that they're not discriminating due to your gender, but who looks good in a tie other than Diane Keaton twenty years ago?"

"Maybe I can use it to strangle myself," she said morosely, and I had to give her a sharp look because her mom told me in an e-mail that I'm supposed to let her know if Holly starts hurting herself or talking about suicide. However, in this case, I think she was fully justified in her comment. Seriously, maroon and teal.

DRU That's a color combo that could strike a small animal dead from half a mile away.

EM That school has a lot to answer for.

Item: blouse

Description: white.

What I think: Honestly, Dru, it's terrible. The material is thirty percent polyester, and you know what that can do to your pores.

"You wouldn't think a white blouse would be a problem, would you?" I said to Holly.

She sighed and looked even sadder than before. I decided to buck her up a bit.

"I bet you could pick a different white top to wear in its place. Something that breathes, and maybe has a little style to it. Something tolerable."

At which point Pink Hair strolled by and said, "The school is ever so particular what the girls wear. If you don't want a demerit, dearie, you just stay with the standard blouse."

Holly's shoulders slumped. I had to punch her lightly in the arm just to let her know I cared.

DRU You are the bestest tutor ever.

EM Well, I mean, you have to feel for the kid.

DRU Yeah, but if anyone can make her life bearable with maroon-and-teal hell surrounding her, you can.

EM Love ya bunches, babe.

DRU Love ya back.

EM Item: skirt

Description: teal, pleated all around, knee-length, with maroon band at hemline

What I think: It looks like something my grandmother wears to church.

"Knee-length?" I said, looking at Holly. She was wearing a midthigh-length black leather skirt, with black-and-white striped tights.

She shuddered.

"I didn't think so," I said, stuffing the horrible thing into the basket. "Thank heavens I took sewing in high school and learned how to hem. The hemline on this puppy is going up several inches."

She actually smiled. I felt like the champion of the world.

DRU There you go! *Project Runway* ain't got nothin' on you.

EM There were also optional teal "trousers" (these people have a different word for everything, I swear), but Holly agreed that they were worse than the skirt.

"Besides," I said as we hauled the basket of stuff up to where Pink Hair was chatting behind a counter, "with a skirt raised to a proper height, you can show off your legs."

"I'm supposed to wear black tights with the skirt," she said, pointing at a pile of black hairy objects.

I smiled. "There're black tights, and then there're black tights. Don't worry, I'll take you shopping for something that doesn't look like it can use a shave."

We gathered up the rest of her things (PE stuff that we couldn't do anything about) and toddled off to get some much needed refreshment at a local burger joint.

Oh, poop, BRB.

DRU *Waits.*

EM Back. I had to answer the phone, since the Oldsters were too busy examining something in the basement (blocking up the portal to hell that's no doubt down there). Bess is in Liverpool. She says she's met a "bloke" who's evidently really hot, and he's taking her to see some Beatles museum or something.

And just when I got back to my room, what did I see? That's right, my underwear was all over the floor again.

DRU What?!?

EM Honestly Dru, it's starting to creep me out. I just stood there in the room and felt invaded. And violated. And invalidated as a person. Whoever (or whatever) is doing this totally needs to go to some diversity and cultural-sensitivity classes and stop nullifying my right to underwear privacy.

DRU That is just so freaking weird. OK, we've got to think of some way to beat this pervy ghost.

EM You're a Pisces; you're good at all that mystical stuff. Work me up a spell or something, would you?

DRU Consider it done!

EM I meant to tell you about shopping here. Cast your mind back the day the dean and Aidan visited here. Mom came into the room, and started talking about the university and local sights until she turned to Aidan and said, "Emily is dying to visit the nearest mall, Aidan. Can you tell me where it is? She won't be happy until she checks out all of the stores."

"Mall?" he asked, his adorable eyebrows pulling together in an adorable frown that was just so ... well, adorable. "There's

Valentine's if you like to buy traditional, but most of the students go to the army and navy stores, or any of the other secondhand shops. We're very much into upcycling, you know."

"Upcycling is good," I said slowly, a horrible cold, clammy feeling twisting my stomach into a ball. "But some things you don't want used. I mean, I like to save the planet as much as the next girl, but I draw the line at wearing someone else's old undies!"

DRU Ugh. Double ugh. Not happening.

EM "I think you'll find that the shops here thoroughly clean the clothes before they resell them," Aidan said.

I stared at him, not sure if he was joking or not.

DRU He had to be joking.

EM You'd think so, wouldn't you? But he wasn't joking. He actually meant that people buy used undies.

DRU Nope. Nope. Nope.

EM "There are shops in town," he repeated, evidently seeing the horrified expression on my face. He took a step back.

It was an effort, but I managed to get a grip on myself. Yeah, yeah, I know, malls aren't as important as something like world peace, but there is a line to be drawn, and I draw it at used undies.

DRU Noping right on out of there.

EM "There is a big mall up north, but it's a bit of a drive," Aidan finally admitted. "But I wouldn't advise going there. It's nothing but conglomerates and empires built on the backs of poor indigenous people. If you like, I can show you around a few of the shops here. The ethical shops."

"Ah," I said, toying with a moldy book sitting on an end table, deciding that a tour around local shops would be better than no shops whatsoever (other than the grotty Valentine's). "That would be lovely, thank you."

"Thursday?" he asked, the mustache part of his hipster goatee smiling at me.

"Sure," I answered, trying hard not to grab him and kiss him in front of the Ancients.

Mom said thank you and gushed over him for a little bit. It was disgusting. I think she's having a midlife crisis or something; I'm going to have to have a talk with her. Then the dean gave me another denture grin, and Aidan said he'd pick me up at two, and they left.

So that's my introduction to British men, and your first look at a Potential Deflowerer. Of course, the immediate dilemma is what I should wear—should I go for slouchy and comfy, so he doesn't lecture me about sweatshops and children forced into factory work, or assuming that's what everyone around here wears, should I go for coolly sophisticated? I could wear my WonderBra, but I'm not sure if I should hit him with fabulous breastages right off the bat. It might be too much too soon, especially if he's used to women wearing used bras.

I believe I *will* allow him to kiss me if he tries. Purely in the interests of seeing what the men here are like, you understand. Think of it as kind of a social experiment (hey, I wonder if I can use that for credit in one of those horrible General Ed classes they're going to make me take—it's worth a shot), one that will further the peace between our two nations.

And since I know you're thinking about it, no, I did not ogle his manly bits, despite the fact that he had on skinny jeans. For one, I've never really gotten the hang of ogling without making everyone aware that's what I'm doing, and for another, his dad was standing right there. I couldn't ogle him without doing a comparison, and that's just too creepy to even consider.

How on earth did we get on the subject of old-man dangly parts?

Dru? You still there?

Hello?

Druuuuuu???

DRU Sorry, had to pee and it takes forever to do that, and I didn't want to take my phone because I almost dropped it in the toilet last night what with the crutches and trying to get my pants down and everything. Reading back.

EM How long until you get a walking cast and can ditch the crutches?

DRU Another two weeks, hopefully. Never, ever break your leg in four places.

EM I'll try not to. So, what's up with you? Tell me all, sister.

DRU Nothing. No can drive. No can walk. No can do anything but sit and binge Netflix. That's why your messages are so good.

EM Poor you. I feel kind of guilty telling you all about what's happening here, but not hearing about your day.

DRU My day is utterly boring and filled with an itch I can't get to because it's on a spot where they put the screws and metal plate in, and other tedious, meh stuff. I don't want to talk about my life. I want to hear about yours.

EM OK, but I'm here if you need to vent about the itch and what you're watching that's good.

DRU I appreciate that. Think I'm going to bed now. It's almost midnight. Smooches.

EM Sorry, forgot about the time difference. Hugs and kisses.

CHAPTER FOUR

EM Morning, sleepyhead!

DRU It's two in the afternoon. You really need to get a grip with the time differences. Oh, and it's raining here. *Again.* Mom is at work, my leg itches, and I've watched all the episodes of some weird British detective series in honor of you. I'm bored. Fill me in on all the fun things you've been doing.

EM Sleeping, mostly. Oh, you mean going out shopping with Aidan?

DRU Sure. First off, what did you wear?

EM That was a bit of an issue.

DRU Leggings?

EM Yeah, I didn't really want him to see me in them.

DRU They're so comfy, though.

EM Right? But I had an impression to make, so I went with the batik halter-top dress I got at the craft fair we hit last year.

DRU Oh, good choice. That should say just what you want: that you're cute, but not insensitive to others in distant cultures. And that you love the planet.

EM And it makes me look fabulous.

DRU Tell me everything about the date.

EM It wasn't really a date. But it was fabulous!

DRU What did he say?

EM He was fabulous!

DRU Did you decide he was the Lord of Virginity Removal?

EM Well, he wasn't *that* fabulous.

He picked me up in his dad's car (which explained the scent of Old that permeated everything) and lectured me for about ten minutes on why I ought to get a bike so I can ride everywhere, and reduce my global footprint, and all sorts of stuff like that. Then he drove to greater downtown POTW, which, as I mentioned, basically consists of two streets. He parked near a bank, and we trotted down the street, stopping at a couple of the shops. There aren't very many to pick from, and they were all of the thrift shop variety, so I browsed through stuff that wouldn't be creepy to wear, although to be honest, it all looked pretty well picked over.

Once we had done the shops and looked at the sights (an old church, a graveyard, and a post that some king put up a long time ago), Aidan asked me if I'd like to stop by the local for a butty.

"Local what?" I asked, wondering if a butty was like a botty. Yes, Dru, only in England will you find that even the smallest town has a local butt shop.

"Pub," he said.

"Groovy," I said. I had a lager and lime (yummy!) and Aidan also bought us each a sandwich, which for some reason is called a butty (and here I was thinking I'd gotten the hang of British English). He told me about his historical law classes that he'll be studying this year, and just when he got around to asking me what I did back home, a couple of his friends rolled up.

DRU This is so much better than anything Netflix has.

EM "Those are my mates," he said, waving his sandwich/ butty at two guys. I gave them the eye (you know the old saying: one potential deflowerer is good, but three are better).

DRU !!????!!

EM Not at the same time.

DRU I was gonna say!

EM One of the friends was very tall, with dark brown hair and brown puppy-dog eyes, and the other was blue-eyed and had really short black hair with blond tips on the ends.

"That's Fang," Aidan said, pointing at the tall puppy-dog guy, "and Devon. This is Emily. She's going to Gob-botty this year. Her dad's the visiting scholar I'll be slogging for."

"Poor lass," Devon said, twirling a chair around and sitting down with the back to his front. Normally, I'm not one for guys who make obvious moves like that, but I have to admit that Devon did it with style and panache, and I gave him a seven out of ten for overall impression. "You don't look like a Gob-botty girl to me."

"I didn't realize there was a look to a liberal arts college, but yes, I'll be doing something in Gobbottle."

Devon grimaced and stole a potato chip from my plate (oh, wait, they're called crisps here), giving me a completely heart-stopping grin as he did. "Don't mind, do you? I'm a bit fagged. Here, Fang, get us a pint."

Whoa! I stared for a couple of seconds before I realized that either I misheard, or once again, Odd British Meanings for Common Words had struck.

Fang, who had just sat down, got up again and went to the bar.

"What's up, Aid?" Devon asked, stealing another chip. I pushed my plate toward him and told him to knock himself out.

"Not much, just been showing Emily the shops. Devon's in his last year at Carolyn," Aidan told me, adding for my information, "College of Engineering."

"That's right," Devon said, taking a huge glass of beer from Fang. "Industrial engineering. Good money to be made there."

"If you're with the right company, sure. But you can make more through R and D with some of the big conglomerates than you can in practical engineering," I pointed out.

"Ho-ho, will you look at the little lady talk," Devon laughed, setting down his pint. He leaned forward and grabbed my hand. "Now, what would a fair thing like yourself know about research and development?"

Why is it that men think they are the only ones who have an interest in science?

"I can't imagine that even in a country where women didn't get the vote until 1928 is such a condescending and sexist comment tolerable," I said stiffly, and immediately struck him off the Potential Sexy Time Participants list. "As it happens, I have an interest in many things, science being one of them. I have been thinking of trying either an archaeology or physics degree, so less of the 'little lady' business would be welcome."

Aidan crowed with laughter.

DRU OMIGOD, I'm laughing so hard! Go, you, Em!

EM "Brainy bird, are you?" Devon said, pulling my hand up to his mouth. I thought for one horrible moment he was going to bite me, but all he did was kiss my knuckles. Which I had to admit was kind of cool, but was it cool enough to make me forgive that sort of sexist attitude?

DRU So much no.

EM Definitely not. But then he apologized immediately thereafter, and I decided to forgive him.

DRU Mmm. Not sure you should have, but I'll wait to see how this episode of Emily Does England turns out before I make a final decision.

EM The guys talked about their jobs for a bit, and it turned out that Devon was the only one who just went to university without working—I gathered from the hints that Aidan dropped that Devon's family was pretty loaded—and then they chatted about mutual friends who I didn't know.

Fang was pretty quiet, speaking only when the other guys asked him a question, but he smiled and laughed with them. He had a really nice voice, kind of deep, but the sort of deep that you feel vibrating through you, and a delicious accent that I could have eaten up with a spoon.

DRU Ooooooh!

EM It turned out that he was older than Aidan and Devon; he'd already been through his undergraduate work, and was in vet school in the next town over.

I put him on the Has the Voice and Eyes of a Possible Mate list, not just because I think him being a vet is nice, but also because every now and again he'd give me a look where his eyes were smiling at me, like we were sharing a secret.

DRU Omigod, that is the meltiest thing ever! Tell me you hooked up with him!

EM Dru! I'm not a sleep-with-a-guy-the-first-time-I-meet-him sort of girl.

DRU You're not a sleep-with-a-guy sort of girl, period. At least, not yet.

EM And thank you for pointing out again just how weird I am. Anyhoodles, everything was lovely—me at a table with three very attractive men who hung on my every word—until *she* came in.

DRU I knew it! I was waiting for the icky ex to show up!

EM How on earth did you know there was an ex?

DRU Dude, there's always an ex somewhere. Go on. I'm going to get some popcorn, because this is so much better than Netflix, but keep texting, and I'll scroll up when I get back.

EM Now I want popcorn, thank you very much.

"There you are, love," this tall blonde said as she glared at me for a moment, then leaned over and planted her lips on Aidan. Quite obviously deliberately, too. "I've been looking for you. I thought you were taking me to the club tonight?"

Aidan shot me a quick look but didn't say anything when she plopped herself down in his lap. "Erm ... that's not until later, Tash."

"No harm in getting started early, is there? Who's your little friend?"

Now, let me describe this woman so you can understand why I instantly disliked her (and no, it had nothing to do with her sucking Aidan's face when I was considering him for the Ritual Deflowering).

First of all, she wasn't so much taller than me, so she really didn't have any right to call me little. Then there was her clothing—if Aidan was a hipster, she was a Dumpster diver. I swear, she looked like she was wearing clothes that other people had thrown away, and yet if you looked closely, you could see the distressing was done by hand.

Yup. She was a faux hipsterette. The worst kind.

DRU Ugh.

EM She sat snuggling up to my potential sexual partner, cooing at him and touching him and blowing in his ear until

Aidan looked uncomfortable. Obviously he was too much of a gentleman to push her off his lap, which says a lot about him. Unless he liked her there … you don't think that was it, do you? Naw, it couldn't be. She was clearly not at all his type. He was just being polite.

DRU I dunno. Some guys like to make you think they are all that and a lava lamp.

EM Lava lamp?

DRU He's a hipster, right? They love lava lamps. Everyone knows that.

EM Huh. I had no idea. Regardless, I decided to give him the benefit of the doubt, despite his hipsterism.

"Emily, this is Tash. She's Devon's cousin."

DRU And the judges take fifty points away from Devon.

EM "Emily's from the States."

"And she's going to be a physicist or an archaeologist," Fang said, surprising me a little by the way he seemed to be coming to my defense.

I gave him my best smile in return, the one where I let my eyes twinkle. He grinned back. I decided right then and there that although he wasn't as drop-dead handsome as Devon and Aidan, his personality and character did more than make up for that, and he moved up to the top of the Virginity Removal Service list.

DRU Hooboy on Fang suddenly pulling into the lead.

EM "Isn't she sweet, though," Tash drawled.

DRU Ha! She doesn't know you very well.

EM I gave her a look that should have singed her. … Hey!

DRU What?

EM I'm not sweet?

DRU Uh …

EM !!!

DRU I'm not saying you're not nice. But sweet … eh …

EM I snort at you. SNORT AT YOU. Where was I? Oh, yeah, the hipsterette.

"Tash works at the beauty salon next to Garfinkles," Aidan said.

Garfinkles was the consignment shop in Piddle-me-sil-ly-ton. It had a lot of really crappy clothing, which explained Tash's obvious lack of fashion sense.

"Yes, do come round sometime," she positively purred, turning her shoulder so her left boob rubbed up against poor Aidan. "I'm sure we can do something with your hair."

Now, you know my hair is one of my weak points, but for her to say that in front of everyone … it hurt. I don't like to admit that, but it did.

DRU Awww. You know I love your hair.

EM Smooches. All is forgiven.

DRU What is forgiven?

EM Your non-sweet jab.

DRU That wasn't so much a jab as it was an observation.

EM MOVING ON … despite being hurt by the rude hair comment, I simply smiled as nicely as I could, and was extremely pleasant.

Kill with kindness, that was my new policy with regards to Tash the Face Sucker.

Tash stuck to Aidan like a tick on a hairy dog, and even Devon winking at me twice didn't take away the bad taste that Tash had left on the day.

"I'll take you home if you need a lift," Devon said a bit later, when I said I really needed to be getting home so I could call Holly's mom for instructions. "Since Aid is busy."

"I'm not busy," Aidan said, standing up.

Tash gave first him, then me, the most god-awful look I'd ever seen.

"Aidan," she said in a drawn-out, irritated sort of way. "We're going out."

"Not till later. Come on, Emily, I'll run you home now."

Fang was quiet until I left, his gaze moving between Aidan and Devon, with brief little stops at me.

I made a face at him when Tash started bitching at Aidan (who ignored her, much to her frustration).

Fang smiled, and I added a gold star next to his name on Shag List. He had a really nice smile.

DRU I like him. I like him a lot.

EM You haven't even met him.

DRU I feel like I have, and I like him. You have my blessing to pick him for the sexy-time extravaganza.

EM Thank you. In the end, Tash refused to leave Aidan, so we had to suffer her riding along with us. She beat me to the front seat, too, which just goes to show you how insecure she is. Still, she works during the day, and he'll be at Gobstoppers with me, so the prospects for a potential boyfriend don't look completely hopeless.

DRU You're the only girl I know who can show up in a country and instantly have three men topping her de-virgining list.

EM I am rather pleased with the herd of men up for selection. But enough about me. Have you talked to Vance lately? Is he back from Chicago? Has he tried to get jiggy with you while your leg is in a cast? Inquiring minds need to know!

DRU ...

EM What?

DRU "Get jiggy with you"? What are you, the 1990s?

EM I heard it on a weird TV channel.

DRU Give it back before the time lords come to take you away. No, since you asked, no sexy times with Vance the Man. He's been helping his father at the cabin.

EM Bah.

DRU You said it, sister. It's just one more reason why I'm so enthralled with your sudden abundance of men. I can get my jollies through you.

DRU Em?

DRU You still there?

DRU Well, damn.

YOU LOGGED ON

EM Sorry, phone died, and the battery didn't tell me it was low. I tell you, Brother finds the cheapest phones available.

DRU I wondered if you'd gone away since we talked yesterday.

EM I did. Or rather, I am. I'm in the Lake District with the parentals. And hello.

DRU Howdies. How is it? Lake-ish?

EM Pretty, but that's about it. Nothing too thrilling. Lots of scenery and people standing around gazing into water while thinking deep thoughts. I guess a lot of poetry was written here, so I thought I'd better try it, myself. You know, just in case I had poetry inside me aching and yearning to come out.

DRU Do you?

EM Nope. I introspected as much as I could, but staring at the water and thinking deep thoughts is boring as hell. All I could think about was the sort of lake parasites that crawl up your hoohaw and lay eggs, and how embarrassing it would be to go to a doctor and have to explain you have weird lake parasite eggs in your girl bits, and then of course, the doctor would have to take them out, and you know how doctors are these days—everything ends up on Snapchat and YouTube—and the last thing that's going to attract men to my lady garden is lake-parasite-removal videos and memes plastered all over the Interwebs.

DRU You have the weirdest mind ever. How you can look at a pretty lake and imagine your pink parts going viral online is beyond me. Also, ew.

EM So instead, I sat in the hotel room, binged on UK Netflix, and made annotations to the Men I Wish to Engage in Nondeviant Sexual Acts With list.

DRU As opposed to the Men You Wish to Engage in Deviant Sexual Acts list?

EM But of course. Those are a completely different group of men.

DRU And to think you don't even read erotica.

EM Meh. What's up with you?

DRU I'm here to officially tell you that I was wrong, and you were right.

EM Of course I am.

EM ER ...

EM About what, in particular?

DRU My nips.

EM Oh, lordisa, you weren't still thinking about getting them pierced, were you?

DRU Yeah.

EM I shudder at you.

DRU Now you're overreacting. You remember Amber from that sorority we thought about getting in before you got kicked out of college?

EM I left it because I wanted to get a full-time job. I wasn't kicked out.

DRU Uh-huh. Anyway, she's been sending me little vids about her new piercing (not gonna say where, but just think about a female version of a Prince Albert), and I asked her about the nips, and she said they were really hot when her BF plays with them.

DRU Em?

DRU You still there?

EM Sorry, was googling Prince Albert. Big mistake. But how did I not know about this? Men actually do that?

DRU You are so naive.

EM I'm not so naive that I think sticking bits of metal through my nipples is fun. Or worse, the Lady Garden.

DRU You have the weirdest names for your vag.

EM Comes from having a medieval father.

DRU Well, anyway, I decided after much thought and a little poking around on my boobs that I would pass on the piercing. Nipples should be pinched, but not pierced. That's my new life motto.

EM *clutches boobies* Not even pinched!

DRU I meant gentle pinches. You know, sexy pinches. Oh, wait, you don't know.

EM Hey, just because I haven't had actual sex with an actual man's actual penis doesn't mean I have lived in a cave my entire life. I've been groped! I've kissed guys! I've even done a few things I'm not going to mention here, because hip though I am, I'm not the sort to go into specific smutty details.

DRU Since when?

EM Shush, you. Regardless of all that, you don't need to flaunt the fact that you thought ahead and lost your virginity years ago, so that you don't have to make up lists of men who you think you might like to do the job. Besides, it makes me want to run right out and throw myself on Hipster Aidan.

DRU So you haven't done it yet?

EM *sigh*

DRU There, there, little punkin. Someone out there has got to want to have sex with you. Don't give up hope.

EM Gee, thanks for the pep talk.

DRU Gotta run. Lovies!

EM Sad, sexless smooches back.

CHAPTER FIVE

EM Dru? You there? WAKE UP!

EM I have important stuffs to tell you!

EM Dammit, girl, don't be telling me you aren't awake at … uh … calculating … 5:43 a.m.!

EM Dru?

EM sigh

PERSONAL AND PRIVATE JOURNAL OF EMILY WILLIAMS

Note to self: come up with a really smart title if this ever gets turned into a smutty book and/or movie franchise.

Note to self: also change my name so people don't know this is my sex life they're watching or reading about.

Note to self: also change other people's names. Just in case they sue me for using their names and take away all the money I make from the movies and books.

OK, where to start. First of all, I'm doing this because there are just some things that I don't think Dru needs to see. I mean, she tells me about some of the things she and her (many) boyfriends get up to, but not down and dirty details. Because no one needs to hear about that.

Note to self: was the (many) catty? Think about removing that, even though Dru does seem to attract men like flies. Not that men attract flies. Oh hell, this whole literary thing is more complicated than I thought. Dru attracts flies like men attract … wait … never mind. Moving on.

So, last night, which would be Sunday night, I was walking home from one of the shops in Piddlesville, where I bought Holly a little "you can do this!" starting-school present of a nice leather journal to write all her emo poetry in (*note to self: check to make sure she writes emo poetry before including that in the book/ movie*), as well as buying myself a "you sure shouldn't have to be doing this, but you're going to have to because the system is screwed" gigantic box of milk chocolates in many flavors, when halfway home a beat-up old VW Bug pulled up and shook a couple of times at me.

I had to set down the bag with Holly's journal and my chocolates (opened, because if I have to walk a mile and a half home, there is going to be some hard-core chocolate eating going down) in order to find the pepper spray that Bess gave me, just in case there were white slavers in the car.

Or the deranged ax murderer who lives in my basement.

Or, hell, even the underwear ghost. I had no idea who or what was in that car; all I knew is that it pulled up next to me with steamed-up windows that you couldn't see through, and it shook in an agitated and possibly malevolent manner at me.

"Emily?"

"Eek!" I may have shrieked a little when a hollow voice emerged from the car. It knew my name! The hell-beast car knew who I was! I clutched the pepper spray, prepared to attack whatever ghoulish thing leaped out at me. "Whatever you are, go away!"

The window nearest me rolled down, and Fang peered out of the car, accompanied by two dog heads that clunked painfully with his.

"Fang!" I said, clutching my chest. "What the hell, dude! You scared the living crap out of me. I thought you were some sort of depraved sex ghost who wanted to lure me into his clutches to have his wicked and yet ghostly ways with me."

Fang, wincing and rubbing his head, shoved one of the dogs back and reached through the window to the outside to open the car door. "Sorry. Saw you on the road and thought you might do with a lift."

"Give me a sec," I said, still clutching my chest, as he got out. "Gotta make sure I'm not going to have an actual heart attack. What are those?"

He smiled wryly when I pointed at the two giant dog heads poking through the window. "That would be Voltaire and Spotted Dick."

I pursed my lips and eyed him to see if he was having me on. But no, his face was perfectly innocent of shenanigans. "Spotted Dick the dog?"

"Yes." He gave a little sigh, then another wry smile. "They're not much to look at, but they're friendly."

"Uh-huh. You didn't happen to be making out in the car on the way here, did you?" I asked, nodding toward the fogged-up windows. "Air blower doesn't work in the car, and the dogs get hot and pant a lot. If I roll the windows down, then they stick their heads out and get bugs in their eyes," he said, and ran his hand through his hair like he was self-conscious.

It was an odd move to make me feel all squidgy inside, but that's what it did. I realized at that moment that I was standing on the side of an isolated road, with no one around but a dishy Englishman with a dishy English voice, and he was on my Jump His Bones list.

"Gotcha. As it happens, I'd love a ride home. This journal I got for Holly is heavier than I thought, and I'm making myself sick by eating too many chocolates." I patted the nearest dog head (Voltaire's, I think), which just made the other dog bay mournfully until he got some window time, too. "They're nice. If a bit slobbery."

"That they are. Who's Holly?" he asked, fighting with the passenger door for a few minutes before he got it opened.

"She's the girl I'm tutoring/advocating. Um?"

"Dick!" Fang said loudly, and I thought for a moment he was swearing, but then he snapped his fingers and the giant bloodhound named Spotted Dick scrambled off the seat and into the back with his buddy. Fang used his sleeve to wipe off the (none-too-pristine) seat of the car and said, "Here you go. Mind the package on the floor. It's some vaccines I'm using in the morning on a herd of cattle."

I minded the package, and got myself into the car, thinking to myself how very nice he was, and that although he didn't have the panache of Devon, or the sexiness of Aidan, he could quite probably turn my crank.

And that, of course, got me thinking. Here was a man, a nice man, one who I knew did not have a girlfriend. Why shouldn't he be the Deflowerer?

He got into the car, and asked me about Holly as we drove through the gathering darkness. I answered somewhat absently, because I was adding up the pros and cons of sex with Fang.

I liked him. He was nice. We both liked the same Doctor Who (David Tennant), we both liked to watch old black-and-white ghost movies, and he was going to be a vet. I loved animals! And most important of all, I thought he liked me. But was he pounce-worthy?

Old Emily would have probably waffled over that point for at least a few weeks. But New Emily was different. New Emily wasn't going to take weeks or months or even years to decide if a man was pounceable. No, I had to take charge of my sexuality. I had to make sure that I didn't turn a nice friendship with Fang into a Daniel situation.

"Sounds like you've taken on quite a job," he said when he pulled up outside Casa du Creepy. I noticed he gave it an odd look, like he couldn't quite believe such a house existed.

"It should be interesting, that's for sure," I agreed, coming to a decision. If I could think of a way to ask Fang to have sex without sounding like a ho, then I was going to go for it. "I haven't been a mentor before, but I looked up a bunch of motivational stuff online, and printed out little sayings that I can lay on her at appropriate moments of self-doubt and depression. Which, if your high school was anything like mine, was pretty much the entire school year."

"Ah." We sat staring at the house for a minute, the only sound being that of the dogs panting down my neck and periodically snuffling my hair.

Just say it, Inner Emily urged me. *Just tell him you like him, and would he care to have sex.*

I can't do it like that! I told Inner Emily. *I need ... I don't know, a sign that he's interested in me sexually. Then I can pounce.*

"I don't suppose ..." Fang cleared his throat. "Since you're interested in science and physics, I don't suppose you like stargazing, do you?"

"I used to love it when I was a kid, but we don't get much of a chance to do that sort of thing in Seattle."

"Ah. Well, I'm supposed to be on badger watch tonight for a local conservancy, and I thought if you didn't have anything better to do, the stars are bright out in the woods. Where the badgers are. That I'm supposed to watch."

He sounded five different shades of embarrassed, which melted my heart. "Where do you do that?"

He named a local wood a few miles outside Piddlesville. "The conservancy has a hide there. We try to man it every night, and it gets a bit lonely out there." He made a little face. "No one comes around because it's a protected area, so I usually just read for six hours."

Bingo! Inner Emily said. *There's your sign. You, him, an isolated area ... the ideal spot for sexual congress.*

"Do you have a blanket or something to sit on?" I asked before agreeing with Inner Emily.

"Several. It gets cold in the autumn."

Inner Emily raised her eyebrow at me, and I had to agree with her that he was pretty clearly sending me the Sex Is On for Tonight signal. And that's why I said, "That sounds like fun."

"We can go now, if you like. I was going to head up there in a bit anyway."

Score! Inner Em cheered. *We're gonna have sexy times, we're gonna have sexy times.*

"Sure. Just let me dump off this stuff and tell the Old Ones that I'll be back later."

I ran in the house, dumping the bags and alerting Mom that I had a date to stare at badgers. I did not mention sex, even though Inner Em was yammering away about all the things she wanted us to do.

"Badgers? The animal sort?" she asked, looking up from where she was perusing a catalog of local community arts classes.

"Yup. Be back later."

"Have fun. Don't get bitten by anything," she warned, returning to her catalog.

"But what if I want to be bitten?" I said to Inner Emily as I ran down the front stairs.

"By what?"

Fang was outside his car, wiping off the windows, which somehow had managed to steam up outside as well as inside.

"Um. You?" I said, shocked the second the words came out of my mouth. Inner Emily began to do a celebratory dance at New Emily's forwardness and take-charge attitude. No more sitting around and wondering for me!

Fang stopped wiping the front windscreen and gave me an unreadable look. "You want me to bite you?"

"You know," I said after a moment's horrified thought, "that's really hard to answer for a couple of reasons. For one, I can't believe my mouth said that without first asking me if it was OK. For another, if I say no, maybe I will change my mind later and then you wouldn't feel it was appropriate, because you understand that when a woman says no, it means no, and not yes, or maybe, or possibly I'll change my mind later. But if I say yes, then you'll think I have some weird biting fetish, which I don't have."

By now it was almost fully dark outside, and I could see his face only via the light coming from the windows.

His lips twitched.

"Would you rather I forgot I heard you say that?" he finally asked, and finished wiping off the window, throwing the rag he'd used on the backseat, whereupon both dogs pounced on it, and snarled their intent for possession.

"Would you mind doing so? I can let you know if you need to unforget it, but until that time, let's just pretend I didn't just put my foot in my mouth."

He laughed, and helped me open up the car door. "I will be happy to, but I don't think your foot is anywhere near your mouth."

The area where Fang was supposed to stare at badgers ("Doing what?" I asked at one point. He just shrugged. "Being badgers.") was right on the edge of a forest that is evidently part of some nature reserve. There were two badger-watching people just leaving when we pulled off the road, and Fang let his dogs out to go potty and stretch their legs.

"Go to sleep," he told the dogs, stuffing them back in the car after they'd run around for a few minutes.

"Can't they come with us?" I asked, feeling bad for them.

"They'll be happier sleeping, trust me. They're pretty lazy, and more importantly, I don't want them to go after a badger."

"Oh, yeah, that'd probably be bad news, huh?"

Fang handed me a flashlight and a couple of small plaid blankets, then collected a thermos and mug, a notebook, a second flashlight, and his cell phone and, after making sure the one window that functioned was rolled down, told the dogs to go to sleep.

"Will they be OK with the window down like that?" I asked, glancing over my shoulder as we crossed a fallow field toward the dark line of woods that jutted out into the field like an accusatory finger. "Anyone could steal them. Or your car."

"Really?" he asked, cocking an eyebrow.

I thought for a minute. "Yeah, I see what you mean. The car … yeah. But the dogs are another matter."

"If a stranger tried to approach them, they'd let me know," was all he said, and we trekked onward into the outer edges of the forest. I tried to think of how I was going to put the moves on Fang, but decided that this was a situation where too much planning was going to make things more difficult than they needed to be.

I'd just wing it, I told myself. I'd let the spirit of the moment move me … and then I'd pounce.

Fang told me what the local badger-watch group was doing, how they monitored the badgers to ensure their well-being, and other various altruistic badger-related motives. We settled down on the blanket at something he called the hide (which was really just a forest-green ratty tarp draped in a rough approximation of an open-faced tent) and sat for a while in silence just watching night fall, and listening to all the little noises of animals and birds settling in for the night.

After about half an hour, I stopped looking at the sky, stopped listening to the birdies go to sleep, stopped wondering if the snuffling noise was a wild boar about to attack, and instead noticed how nice Fang smelled.

And how warm his leg was where it was almost touching mine.

And how nice his eyes were, even though I couldn't see them because it was so dark, and he'd turned off the flashlights.

Was this the moment? I wasn't sure, and I didn't want to do something that would freak him out. But I'd been down that hesitation path before, and all it had gotten me was some nasty comments from an asshat and a crushed heart.

The longer I sat next to Fang, the more right I felt about my decision. For one, images started going through my mind, erotic images, thoughts of Fang stark naked and lying on the blanket with a come-hither look. Thoughts of us riding off together into the sunset in his battered car, his dogs drooling out of the windows, and us living happily ever after.

Thoughts, of pure, unadulterated sex. Not near sex, not just hands and mouths, but the whole enchilada.

Fang felt right in a way that Daniel never did. It was now or never, I thought to myself, trying to work my nerve up to doing something. Should I just jump him, or casually mention the fact that I'd be open to a little romping of the sexual sort?

It was at that moment that he softly cleared his throat and said, "Would you like—"

"Yes!" I said, not letting him finish the question, and jumped him, knocking him onto his back so that I could kiss him all over his face.

He let me do that for a few minutes; then his hands got into the action, and he started kissing me back. By the time he had his hands under my shirt, cupping my boobs, and was sending his tongue on a foray into my mouth, I'd decided that Inner Emily and I had made the right choice. It was time to finally become the Woman Formerly Known as a Virgin.

"I have some rules," I said when I sucked my tongue back into my own mouth. Somehow, I'd managed to maneuver myself so I was sitting on his groin, my hands quickly working down the line of buttons on his shirt. I was a bit breathless, but I wasn't sure if that's because he was awesome at kissing, or if I was super nervous at being so proactive and stuff.

"All right," he said, his hands just as busy as mine.

"First, you have to use a condom. I have no diseases, and don't want to get pregnant—not that I will, because I get a shot that takes care of that—but diseases are totally out. Second, I don't like jealous men, so if you're the kind of guy who can't stand his girlfriend talking to other men, then this whole thing is a bust. And third, I'm a virgin. Well, not technically, because I have toys, very effective toys, and I had a boyfriend for two years, although we didn't have actual sex. We had other sex, you know, hands and mouths and stuff, not that you care, but I just want you to know that it's not like I haven't been with a man. I just haven't let Mr. Happy visit Emily Land. Do you agree to the rules?"

"Yes," he said, sliding my shirt off over my head so he could better molest my breasts. "Although I don't have any condoms with me."

"No problem, I have some," I said, lunging to the side for my purse. "Always be prepared, that's my motto. Now, as the senior partner in this experience—wait, you have had sex before, right?"

"I have," he said gravely, although I swear I heard laughter in his voice.

"OK, so you're the boss, then. At least so far as this goes. What position would you recommend using for someone who technically isn't a virgin, but still hasn't had a man's dangly bits go visiting her nicely tucked-up lady garden?"

"Whatever makes you comfortable," he said.

"That's far from helpful," I said, squirming out of my jeans. I thought for a moment, then peeled off my undies and thanked my stars that it was too dark out for him to see that I needed to prune the aforementioned lady garden. While I was doing so, he plucked off his shoes and socks, and shucked his jeans.

"Would you like me to put the condom on for you?" I hesitated, even though I told myself that I wasn't going to hesitate—I was just going to go full steam ahead. "I understand that can be a lot of fun."

"Not tonight," he said in his proper English voice. I could see him working the thing on what appeared to be a blob of flesh.

There was enough light from the moon, which had come up, to see shapes, but not enough for me to distinguish too much. I squinted at his groin. "Should I … um … did you want a blow job first?"

"I think," he said, wrapping an arm around me and pulling me down into his side, "that as this is your official first time, we'll just focus on making sure you have a good experience, all right?"

And he did. Oh, holy cow, did he. He headed straight for ground zero, and let his fingers go wild. And then his mouth got into the act, and I came unglued. I mean, Daniel had done the same thing, but man alive, was there a difference in technique. With Daniel, it was pleasant … but Fang was like a superhero of oral sex. He made me scream with delight.

"Shh," he said, looking up from where he was molesting my hootenanny. "You don't want to scare the badgers."

I looked down my body to where I could see the shape of his head against my flesh, and couldn't help myself. I giggled. *Softly.*

"Are you laughing at what I'm doing?" he asked, a hurt note to his voice.

I tugged him upward so that he was lying the length of me, then kissed him. "Hmm," I said, feeling all sorts of wanton and shameless. I'd never done *that* with Daniel! "Different. I think I like it better when it's just you."

"I don't," he said, then reached down to adjust my legs.

"No, I wasn't laughing at you. I was laughing at the idea of badgers running away because you're incredibly good at oral sex. Should I reciprocate?"

"Another time," he said, and positioned himself at the Temple of Tingles. (*Note to self: come up with a better euphemism for the movie.*)

"This is really a vulnerable position," I said nervously, not quite liking how it felt to have my legs spread in such a way that he had access to everything down there. "I feel like I should apologize for the fact that I don't wax, but I would like to point out that normally I do trim, although I do that for my own happiness, and not because men think women's privates look better without any hair. I'm so not into men body-shaming women."

"Emily," he said, the tip of him nudging me.

"Yes?" My voice seemed unnaturally high to me.

"Relax. If I do something you don't like, just tell me, all right?"

"All right," I said, taking hold of his arms and bracing myself.

And then he slid into me. Every single muscle I possessed in my nether bits stood up in shock before suddenly deciding that they liked this new plaything much better than my toys. Much, much better.

"Oooh," I said, my hips flexing when he stroked into me. "Oh, that is really nice. I mean, really, really nice. If I'd known how nice this was, I'd have jumped you that first day we met. Holy moly. Can you … does it help if I do this?" My crotch bucked upward toward his.

"Yes, but you have to time it so I'm entering, not exiting," he instructed, and after a few misses, I finally got the rhythm down, and after that … well, to be honest, I just let go and had the orgasm to end all orgasms. The kind where my legs went stiff, and I stopped breathing, and I swear fireworks went off over our heads. And then he gave a couple of extra-hard push-es, which just felt even more marvelous than before, and every muscle I had tightened around him in happy little hugs.

He jerked a few more times, muttering something under his breath as he collapsed on me, his breath as rough and jerky as my own.

"Well," I said a few minutes later, when he rolled off me with a squishy noise. I lay there still panting, my heart slowing down after its big race. "I'd certainly call that a successful deflowering."

"Was it everything you expected it to be?" he asked breathlessly.

"Oh yes. That and more. Wow. Seriously, wow. I really enjoyed that."

"I'm glad. I enjoyed it as well."

"This must be the postprandial glow. I like it. I want to snuggle with you and stroke your chest, and maybe just listen to your heart beating." I rolled over onto my side and suited action to word. "I'm so glad you wanted to do this. The ground isn't the most comfy place for it, but the blanket definitely helps."

He draped an arm over my naked back, not saying anything for a few minutes.

"Emily?" he said at last.

"Hmm?" I was drowsy, which was a bit odd since I thought men always went to sleep after sex.

"Would you be upset if I told you that although I'm honored you picked me to be your first, I was actually going to ask you if you wanted some tea?"

It took a minute or two before that sank in. I sat up and stared down at the oval that was his face. "Oh my god. OH MY GOD!"

"Shh," he warned, sitting up and wrapping his arms around me. "Remember the badgers."

"Are you saying," I asked in a furious whisper, "that you weren't going to ask me to have sex?"

"Yes, but I'm glad you wanted to. I figured I'd have to take you out several times before we'd get to that point."

"Ack!" I said in an almost silent yell. "I just threw myself at you! I'm a shameless hussy! WHAT MUST YOU THINK OF ME?"

He chuckled, and pulled me up against his chest (nice soft hair, not too much, but not so little he looked like a naked chicken). "Sweetheart, I think you're a smart woman who knows what she wants, and doesn't play games. Which puts you at the top in my books."

"I shall now die of mortification," I said to his left nipple. "I will never be able to face you again, let alone do this with you again, which is a shame, because I already want to do it again."

"Ah," he said, and at the weird note in his voice, I pulled back. "About that. As a matter of fact, I'm going to be away for a few weeks. I have to go help a vet up north with some sheep. And I have to be honest with you, Emily—I haven't been looking for a partner right now, because I'm doing a lot of work out of the area for whatever vet needs help. I need practical experience, and I have to take what's available, so right now, a girlfriend just isn't uppermost in my mind."

"Oh my god, are you trying to break up with me? We just hooked up!" I said, aghast. "Is it because I jumped your bones before we established a lengthy nonsexual relationship? Because if it is, you should know that I like you for more than just your really awesome body. And sexy parts. I like your mind, too, Fang."

His voice sounded choked when he said, "I'm glad to hear that you'll respect me in the morning."

"Good, because I will. Honestly, I'm not at all the type of woman to value sex over a good relationship. I have lots of friends that I've never had sex with. Which I guess is really obvious since you were the first, but I don't want you thinking I'm a *wham, bam, thank you, mister* sort of woman."

"I don't think anything of the kind." His hand was warm on my back as he rubbed it gently. "I just want to be fair to you. I don't think a long-distance relationship would work for me, and I'm loaded down with work and classes, and don't have a lot of time to spend with anyone, let alone a woman who I want to be with."

"Oh." I thought about that for a bit. I really didn't want to give him up, but at the same time, I could see what it was he was saying. "How about … what if we do a friends-with-benefits thing?"

"A what, now?"

"Friends with benefits. We are friends, and when you're around, we have benefits. That's this part. When you're not around … well … I think we'll just leave that up to each person to decide."

He was silent for a moment, then said, "That sounds like a logical solution. Will you be happy with it?"

"Yes," I said, feeling better about the whole jumping-his-bones thing. I would have died if I thought he'd just had sex with me to keep from hurting my feelings. Trust the English to go to the extremes to be polite. "I think it's an ideal solution, actually. That way there's no hurt feelings, no expectations other than when it works out that we can… not scare the badgers … then we'll do that."

"Then that's what we'll do," he said.

"When do you have to leave?"

"Tomorrow afternoon. You know, I'm scheduled to be here until midnight, and if you give me a half hour to recover, I'm willing to give the benefits another go."

"Oooh," I cooed, and resumed postprandial position.

Whew. I'm exhausted just writing all that up, not to mention hot and bothered remembering how awesome Fang was, and now he's not here for me to jump again.

Sigh.

YOU HAVE SENT A FILE ATTACHMENT TO DRU

EM I know you're not there, Dru, but when you are, read the attached.

EM It's a text file.

EM An *edited* text file. I took out all the smutty bits. You'll have to wait for them to be made into a movie to find out everything that happened, but until then, I thought you'd like to see the before and after parts. Also, that way I don't have to type it all up again.

EM Hoo baby is my summation, in case you are wondering. Hoo baby!

CHAPTER SIX

DRU What's this?

DRU Reading.

DRU OMG!

DRU You're no longer a virgin?

DRU Let fly the doves and sing hallelujah!

EM I know, right? If I'd known just how much fun it was with a guy before … well, no, I shouldn't say that, because it was seriously awesome with Fang. And now I have a friend with benefits, and how great is that? I can still entertain the idea of other men if Fang is off doing his own thing, and there won't be any horrible scenes or feelings or trouble. It's the best of all possible worlds!

DRU Um … yeah.

EM What?

DRU Nothing. Fang sounds … mmrowr.

EM No comment other than, oh, hell yes!

EM BTW, I meant to tell you about Holly, but got distracted with Mr. Mmrowr. Let me give you the deets, and I'll warn you, they're seriously drama queen fodder. Not only did some chick try to humiliate me (me! the most reasonable of all people ever!), but I almost got expelled, except of course for the fact that I'm not going to high school.

DRU Only you could get expelled from a school you aren't even going to.

EM I know, right? I'll start at the beginning so you can see what sort of a situation I'm in now.

Holly's mom, Mum A., called me early in the morning to give me the schedule for the week, and to tell me that she cleared me with the school, so they wouldn't freak out that I was trying to abduct Holly or anything like that.

EM ...

DRU What?

EM You aren't going to point out that I don't at all look like the sort of person who would abduct a kid from school?

DRU Well ...

EM MOVING ON!

"In fact," Mum A. said in her rushed way, "Dr. Alton and I agree that it would be better for Holly if you appeared to be just another student rather than a tutor specially brought in for her. That is so much less attention on her, and won't allow the other girls to think she's receiving special treatment. So while you won't be doing any schoolwork there, you will *appear* to be attending the school."

"Wait, now, what?" I asked. "You do know how old I am, right? That I'm over twenty?"

"But you have a very young face, and I'm sure there will be no problem with the other students wondering about you attending one or two classes where Holly is at risk if we tell them you are American and picking up a few extra classes."

"But—"

"You did agree to mentor her in a few classes when we agreed to your substantial salary arrangement," she reminded me, and I damned my need for money.

"I did, and I will, but I am sure as shooting *not* wearing that hideous uniform."

"Simple maroon trousers—" she started to say.

"Absolutely not."

She made an annoyed click of her tongue, then said, "But it would be much simpler—"

"No," I said firmly. "If it makes you happy, I will agree to pretend I'm a teacher monitor or something like that while secretly watching out for Holly, but that's it."

"Very well, I will do what I can," she said tightly, and after giving me the time of Holly's most troublesome classes, she hung up.

DRU Helicopter mom!

EM You don't know the half of it! I met Holly a few blocks from school, where her housekeeper let her off.

"How you doing?" I asked her as we started walking toward the school. "I'm not going to ask you if you're excited about a new year at school, because I know full well what a horrible nightmare the first day can be, but I hope it's going to make things less hideous knowing I'm around for a while."

"Oh, it is," she said, her face absolutely dead white. Even her lips were ghostly. "I'm so glad you agreed to be my tutor. You don't know how ... how ..." She stopped and seemed to choke up.

I punched her lightly on the arm. "I know. Hey, I got you a Hellish Nightmare Begins present." I gave her the journal, and she got all verklempt on me.

"Have you ever thought of ... you know ... a little make-up?" I asked as we approached the gates of the school. "Not that I think there's anything wrong with the Goth look, but sometimes, a little confidence in the form of lipstick, eyeliner, and a really light dusting of bronzing powder can really make a difference."

DRU You were wearing all that, weren't you?

EM Maaaaybe. In a tasteful and subdued way.

DRU Highly doubtful, but go on.

EM Are you by any chance denigrating my makeup abilities?

DRU No, I'm saying all that in daytime is hard to imagine as subdued.

EM Hrmph. Now you made me lose my place. Oh, yes. Holly was duly impressed with my suggestion.

"Wow," she said, staring at me. "That's really specific."

DRU Girl has a good eye.

EM "'Use what you know' is what an old English professor used to say. All right, so your mom says I'm going undercover as some sort of teacher spy. Should we split up before we get inside, and then I'll sit in the back of your first class and make sure no one makes your life any more hellish than it has to be?"

"Oh," she said, and stopped, looking really worried. "Oh."

"Oh?"

"Didn't Mum …" She bit her lip. "Didn't she tell you that she talked to my uncle—he's the headmaster—and they worked out that you're going to pretend to be a student?"

"Yeah, she mentioned something about that, but I told your mom it wasn't going to fly. Not only am I five years older than you—there's the uniform to think about."

She looked crestfallen, Dru, absolutely gobsmacked crestfallen.

DRU Oh, poor Holly. How could you be so mean to her?

EM I would point out that I was being anything but mean, but there's more.

DRU Goody. Although if you made Holly cry, I'm going to cry, too. You know how I am.

EM Sympathetic cryer.

DRU I get it from my mom. Go on.

EM Well, as if that wasn't enough that Holly was standing there looking like her favorite hamster had just died, the second we got into the main entrance, some chick came up to me.

"Are you Williams?" The girl, dark haired and with a smug-as-hell attitude, wore a little hat and had the end of her tie tucked into her shirt.

DRU Maybe she was a victim of the school uniform, and wasn't as bad as she looked.

EM Dru, she had a clipboard with her.

DRU Never mind. She was clearly pure evil.

EM Exactly. However, mindful that I'm an adult, and have wages to earn, I slapped on my nicest smile, and said, "Yep."

"Thought so." She eyed me from my toes to my hair, and wrinkled up her nose like she smelled something bad. "You *look* like an American."

"Really?" I glanced down at myself. I wasn't wearing anything with stars and stripes, just had on a pair of chinos and my navy blue Indian-embroidery shirt.

"Yes, really. Could you have on any more makeup?"

DRU What a bitch!

EM I knew you'd have my back, girl.

DRU I mean, even if you did have on enough makeup to scare a clown, that's no call to jump all over you the second she sees you.

EM A clown? Seriously?

DRU Sorry. Forgot that you're swearing the makeup was tasteful and subdued.

EM Apology accepted. I tell you, Dru, before that moment, I'd thought that Holly's parents were a bit, you know, over-protective. I mean, who hires someone to watch their kid in school? But all of a sudden, I started to think that if this was the sort of people she had to hang with, maybe there was a reason Holly needed help.

"What's the matter?" Mistress Snotmaster said with a sneer.

DRU Ha! Em: 1; Snotgirl: 0

EM "Cat got your tongue? It's probably better if you don't talk. Follow me. I'm the prefect for the fifth form. You have to go to the headmaster before your form room." Her gaze shifted to Holly, who was clearly trying to sink into the earth. "Alton. I see you're still with us. Didn't slash your wrists deep enough?"

"Right, that's enough out of you," I said, wanting to slap the smug look right off the mean chick's face.

DRU Go, Emily!

EM "Demerit!" Snotty said, pointing at me, and made a note on her clipboard. "Keep it up and you'll find yourself out on your fat American ass."

DRU Oh! She didn't! You are so not fat!

EM Thank you. Love you.

DRU Love you, too. What did you say? Man, this is better than all the soaps put together!

EM I can tell you what I wanted to say, but it would be seriously potty mouth. Instead, I just said, "You little—"

"This school doesn't allow students to wear cosmetics, so you'd best wipe that off before the head of form sees you. She doesn't tolerate sluts in her class. Girls' lavatory is at the end of the hall." She turned on her heel and marched off to blight someone else.

Holly looked like she wanted to cry.

DRU Oh! I am just so pissed off! Poor Hols.

EM "Well, that chick is seriously unpleasant," I said to Holly, trying to buck her up. "I'm going to have to put my mind to what we can do with the Little Hitler there. And I'm going to be sure to report her to the principal. So where is this guy? You said he's your uncle?"

"Yes," she said, almost a whisper, and pointed down a hall.

I took a look at her as we worked our way salmon-like through the hordes of kids. She looked devastated, and I made a mental note to tell her parents that I thought they should put her in another school. One without dictators from hell roaming the halls waiting to prey on the weak and vulnerable.

DRU I second that suggestion.

EM I marched into the headmaster's office, fire in my eye, and vengeance in my heart. We had to wait a few minutes before a fake-blond secretary told us we could go in.

"Miss Williams?" A man stood up and came around his desk to shake my hand. He looked a lot like Russell Crowe, which earned him some bonus points. "I'm Mr. Krigon. I understand you're here to give Holly the help she needs to succeed. Won't you sit down?" He smiled a really nice smile that made me feel a little better.

"Absolutely," I said, frowning when he didn't tell Holly to wait outside. I didn't like the way he just nodded to her, like she was a piece of furniture or something. Dehumanizing, that's what it was. "And can I say right off the bat that there's a real pain-in-the-ass student who jumped all over me when we got here."

"Ah, no doubt that was one of our vigilant proctors," he said, sitting down and making a vague gesture toward me. "You're not wearing the proper uniform."

"That would be because I'm not a student," I pointed out, getting a bit irate. Didn't he care about the Little Hitler?

"Of course you aren't, but given Holly's … special circumstances … her mother and I thought it would be best for her self-confidence if you were to blend in with the other students. Obviously, you won't be expected to do the schoolwork—I'll discuss the situation with Holly's teachers—but if you could give the appearance of being a member of the school, I'm sure it will go a long way to keep Holly from falling into the dark place again. Eh, Holly? No more cutting yourself?"

Holly squirmed and mumbled something about not wanting to hurt herself.

DRU What a jackass!

EM I wanted to punch him despite the Russell Croweness.

DRU Me too, and I wasn't even there.

EM It was all very awkward. Then he made it worse by adding, "Holly's been having some intensive counseling over the summer, and she's in a much better place mentally. She's promised her mother that there won't be any more trips to hospital to have her stomach pumped."

I slid a glance toward Holly. She looked about as miserable as a person could be without actually dying of mortification.

And that's what did it, Dru. That's what made me throw away my common sense. Because I remember what it was like to feel like everyone was against you, even your own parents, except of course, Brother and Mom were actually pretty cool and didn't dump a lot of emotional crap on me like Holly's parents are clearly doing to her.

DRU I one hundred percent back you up on this.

EM "Right," I said, standing up, which made Holly get to her feet, too, a startled look on her face. "You want me to pretend to be a student? Fine, I'll pretend to be a student. I'll even wear the uniform, although you seriously need to get someone who isn't color-blind to pick the next one. But I am taking my own classes at Oxwills, and I'm not dumping them to repeat high school."

"Of course not, of course not." He shuffled some papers around. "I have your university schedule here—Patricia gave it to me yesterday—ah, I see you have classes only two days a week, on Tuesday and Thursday. We will naturally excuse you from the classes Holly takes at that time. If you attend two classes a day with her on the other three days of the week, I believe that will be sufficient. Eh, Holly? That will be sufficient?"

She mumbled something about it being wonderful.

I seriously wanted to yell at him. How could anyone be so insensitive to the poor kid?

DRU He's a monster.

EM "I'll put it around the school that you are a transfer student who only needs a few classes to graduate your American school system. That way no one will question your sporadic attendance," he said, guiding us to the door. "I'm sure we're all grateful to have you keep our little Holly from any more of those attempts to take her from her loving family."

I gave him a look to let him know I thought he was a jackass, but said nothing other than, "Sounds good."

Holly was silent as we left the office, but as soon as we got away from the secretary, she stopped me and said, "Thank you, Emily. I promise I won't—I know it's horrible for you, but it really means so much to me—and my mother is so ..." Her hands flailed as she came to a verbal halt.

I gave her a friendly poke in the arm. "I know, kid, I know. Let's not worry about thanking me, OK?"

"I feel so bad about making you be here when you probably want to be at university—" She stopped, giving me a look like she expected to be smacked.

"Don't feel guilty," I said cheerfully, a thought having occurred to me. "I'm going to hit your mom up for extra battle pay because of the uniform, so you're actually doing me a favor. I'll be able to save for a driver's license as well as send home the monthly payment the judge insists I make."

She looked interested in that, and I promised to tell her about it another time. She took me to her first class, a literature class. In it, ten girls were standing around chitchatting. Not a single one said hi to Holly, who went to a seat in the back of the class. I took the one next to her and plopped down, making a mental bill out to her mom.

In walked a tall, horsey woman—I mean, she had a long face like a horse, and her hair kind of looked like a mane—and the first thing she did was point a long, horsey finger at me and said, "You! What's your name?"

"Emily Williams," said I, kind of startled into a response. Honest to Pete, I thought the British were known for being so polite!

She sniffed, kind of like she smelled cooked cabbage or something, and gave me the eye. "You're the Yank. Well, Williams, there are a few rules you will learn immediately. First, we do not sit until the teacher has given you permission to sit. We do not appear on school grounds without the proper uniform. We do not wear necklaces, rings, or other jewelry. We do not wear cosmetics."

Everyone in the class laughed at me. Honestly, Dru, it was so enraging that I didn't know whether I wanted to cry at the horse lady or deck her. A quick glance at Holly reminded me why I was there, though, so in the end, I decided on a course of Gandhi-like passive resistance. So I pretended to yawn.

"Alton, you will show Williams the girls' loo so she can wash off her face. You will remove all jewelry except your watch." She peered closely at me, her beady little eyes getting even beadier. "And that includes all of those earrings that are studding your ear. Do your parents know you have them?"

Everyone looked at me like I was some sort of a freak. I did the only thing I could do. I said, "Well, duh!"

She pulled herself up and snorted (just like a horse). "We do not address our superiors in any tone but that of respect."

I decided the time had come to make a stand, and hoped Holly would take note of the proper method of dealing with bullies.

"*We?*" I said, giving a light, mocking laugh. "What, you have a pocket full of worms?"

DRU Sorry, had phone call from doctor's office. Reading back.

DRU Ha! I love it!

EM Horse woman looked stunned, which made me think no one had ever answered her back.

I pressed on. "For your information, I don't take my earrings out for anyone. If I did, the holes would close, and it took me eight months to get all five holes pierced. And as for respect, I give it to people who've earned it."

So, OK, in hindsight that might not have been the best thing to say, but Brother always said I should never let anyone trample my rights, and to stand up for what was important to me, a lesson that I thought Holly could benefit from seeing in action.

DRU I love it when you're all badassy.

EM Everyone in the classroom gasped. Miss Horseface gave a snort that rattled the windows; then she grabbed me in one horsey claw and dragged me out of the room and down the stairs to the office.

"Unhand me!" I demanded en route, but she just muttered under her breath and kept frog-marching me, more or less tossing me into a chair next to Russell Crowe's secretary.

I had to sit there for fifteen minutes while she talked to the headmaster. She said nothing when she came out, just gave me a rude stare and marched off to spread evil and cruelty in her wake.

Krigon and I had a little chat about expectations (his and mine, which, let me tell you, never the twain shall meet) and he promised to explain the situation to the teachers later that day. Then he sent me off with a warning of how vulnerable Holly was. I borrowed a piece of paper from the secretary and wrote out a scathing letter to the Altons while waiting for Holly's class to end.

I met up with her about forty minutes later outside a class, where a line of girls were standing and talking ... and ignoring Holly.

DRU I hate them. Every single one of them.

EM "Heya," I said, pulling up behind Holly.

Her eyes were huge. "Did you get in trouble?" she whispered.

"Me? Are you kidding? They can't do anything to me except fire me, and actually, they can't even do that—only your parents can." I gave a shrug. "Honestly, kid, you're going to have to deal with asshats like the people here once you get sprung out in the world. I've found the best way to do so is not to let them get you down. Just remind yourself that karma is a bitch, and they'll get theirs someday."

She looked thoughtful, but just at that moment, the teacher, a short, round butterball of a woman, rolled up and herded everyone into the room. I followed Holly to the back, and stood like a nice little drone next to a desk until La Femme Butterball told us we could sit.

Is it any wonder our four-score-and-seven-years-ago forefathers decided they'd had enough of this sort of totalitarian behavior?

DRU Wow. Just wow.

EM I was just planning a second scathing letter (this time to the editor of the local paper) about the sorts of bullying that went on in the local schools when all of a sudden the Butterball opens up her mouth and starts bellowing at the top of her lungs. "GOOD MORNING, CLASS. IT'S NICE TO SEE SO MANY FAMILIAR FACES BACK HERE THIS YEAR."

I stared at her for a moment, then glanced around the room. Other than the slightly dazed look on the faces of the kids in the first row, no one seemed to think anything of the fact that the teacher was yelling her brains out.

"BEFORE WE BEGIN THE CLASS, MARIAH WILL HAND OUT THE HOMEWORK TIMETABLE AND DIARY. YOU ARE RESPONSIBLE FOR UNDERTAKING YOUR COURSE WORK ON A REGULAR AND SYSTEMATIC BASIS. DO NOT POSTPONE IT UNTIL YOU ARE NEAR THE DEADLINE. YOU WILL ALSO BE GIVEN YOUR GSCE PLANNING AND REVISION DIARY. THESE DIARIES ARE A VERY HELPFUL AID TO YOUR STUDY, SO DO NOT LOSE THEM."

There was a low-pitched humming noise in my ears. Either it was a brain aneurysm, or I was going deaf.

"NOW WE WILL COMMENCE. THIS TERM WE WILL STUDY TWO OF SHAKESPEARE'S GREATEST WORKS—*ROMEO AND JULIET*, AND *HAMLET*. WE WILL BEGIN WITH *ROMEO AND* ... YOU, GEL, YOU IN THE BACK WITH THE FRIZZY HAIR. WHAT IS THAT YOU HAVE?"

I looked around to see which of the frizzy-haired students she was bellowing at; then I realized it was me.

DRU Is it wrong of me to say I kinda knew something like this would happen?

EM Yes.

Everyone in the class turned around to look at me (I really should be used to it by now), and remind me to text the pope, because I am most definitely next in line for sainthood. They all—with the exception of Holly, who looked like she was going to barf—smiled smug little smiles at me. I couldn't help wondering why *everyone* was picking on my appearance. I looked just the same as I've always looked, and no one at home ever said anything nasty about my earrings, or the fact that I have curly hair that refuses to give proper respect to the flat iron.

I was feeling like enough was just about enough. I looked at the Butterball and cocked the Eyebrow of Questioning, and said, "Who, me?"

"YES, YOU, GEL. WHAT IS THAT IN YOUR HAND?"

I held up my hand. "Fingers?" Ten out of ten for style, huh?

DRU High five, sister!

EM "NO, NO, THE BLUE OBJECT."

I held up my phone. "It's a phone."

"A WHAT?"

I sighed and stood up. Evidently, in this country, if you stand, it makes people understand you. "A cell phone, although my father refused to spring for a good one. But don't get me started about budget data plans. I assume you people *do* have phones in this country?"

"THEY ARE NOT ALLOWED IN SCHOOL DURING CLASS HOURS. PUT IT AWAY."

The Bellowing Butterball turned toward the blackboard and started to write stuff, yelling at the top of her lungs all the while. The smarty-pants girls snickered at me a bit longer before turning back to the BB-ball.

"I'm so sorry," Holly said, her face paler than pale. You know that song "A Whiter Shade of Pale"? Yeah, that could have been written about Holly's complexion. "And please don't mind Ann and Bertrice. They always act like that around anyone who's different."

I went home after that class, since I had to meet with my so-called adviser at Gobbottle (and complained most vocally about my own academic woes). After that, I gave Holly's mom an earful, got an advance on my salary to buy a stupid uniform, and got out my little tablet that I play games on and set it up to take notes on all the crap Holly has to get through. I figure I'll document it all, then let her parents see that she's not the one who has issues.

DRU Geesh! Can you please tell Netflix about your life, so they make a series out of it?

EM It's a lot more fun to read about than to live through, let me tell you.

DRU I feel bad for Holly.

EM Me too. She's a nice kid, and she isn't getting treated nicely at school.

EM You feel bad for me, too, right?

DRU You're getting paid.

EM I have to pretend I'm back in high school.

DRU You're still getting paid.

EM I have to put up with little shits like the girls who pick on Holly.

DRU But you're protecting Holly by doing so.

EM I have to wear a maroon and teal uniform.

DRU True dat. OK, you can have sympathy, too. But don't waste it all on one big blowout.

EM It's like you don't even know me.

EM Joy of joys, the stuff we shipped out before we left Seattle was here when we returned to Mansion du Ghastly. Mom is happy because now she has her own towels (I'll never understand her), Brother has his books, Bess—back from jaunting around England on her unemployment money, the brat—has her laptop, and me? I got nothin'. Other than a lot of grief from Brother when I downloaded the latest Sims game to his laptop.

"I had to sell everything I had before I left just so I could make that first payment that the evil and clearly corrupt judge made against me," I pointed out when he was complaining that my game hogged all the hard drive space. "You said I could use your laptop if I needed to."

He snorted. "I simply asked you if you would leave me a little space so I can save my work. Your silly games aren't necessary to our health and happiness, but my notes and assignments are."

I straightened up to my full height and glared up at him. Mom had made him brush out his hair horn, but he still looked goofy. "The Sims is not silly, Sir Unibrow. It's a simulation of people and their families and friends and dates and neighbors. You can build a house, decorate it, and then make Sim people to live in it. It's all about interaction and relationships and family units and all that stuff that you Oldsters are always going on about, and has pertinence and relatability to those horrible classes I have to take YET AGAIN, thereby wasting one of my two semesters at Oxwills. So in conclusion, it is important to my health, happiness, and general educational welfare."

Despite my shooing him away, he stood there with a really confused look on his face. "Unibrow?"

I sniffed and loaded up the SimWilliams family. It was time to let the Grim Reaper have his way with SimBrother.

"Did you just call me Unibrow?"

"Maybe," I told the computer.

He shook his head and left the library, muttering things about blood tests and paternity lawsuits.

DRU Ohai.

EM There you are. I felt like I was talking to myself.

DRU Had to shower. I tried to hurry so I'd be back for the latest episode of How the Emily Turns.

EM The what, now?

DRU Soap opera.

EM Have you suddenly turned into my grandma?

DRU Hey, when you can't go anywhere for six whole weeks, you watch whatever weird stuff shows up on the retro TV channels. Do you want the synopsis of the latest *Gunsmoke* ep I watched?

EM You really are my grandmother. How's the leg?

DRU It alternates between being hurty and itchy. Walking cast is next week. My life is boring.

EM Bah. It isn't.

DRU Trust me, it is. Mom goes to work. I sit here watching TV and looking for a job that isn't beyond horrible. Mom comes home and asks me if I've found a job yet. Then we watch more TV until it's time to go to bed. Rinse and repeat.

EM OK, that would make me a bit bonkers.

DRU Amen, sister. You are the only thing keeping me sane. Tell me what's going on with you other than Brother not getting it about the Sims.

EM Well, as I told you, Bess has arrived. She made a big deal about it, too, zooming up to the House of Horrors on the back of a motorbike. The guy she was with looked like he was a hippie or Jesus or something—long brown beard, scraggly hair, no fashion sense, etc. Bess introduced him to Brother as some sort of a monk, but you know Bess—she's as radical as they come. Anyhoodles, after Monk left, and Bess had her hissy fit about me getting the tower room—which I told her came with an underwear-obsessed ghost—she came stomping into the bathroom later and demanded to talk to me.

"Excuse me, do you notice that I'm (a) naked and (b) taking a bath?" I asked. She just sat on the toilet and started poking through my trays of makeup.

"I remember you in diapers, squirt, so don't get uppity with me." She picked up one of my concealers and squinted at it. "Don't you know this stuff is nothing but a waste of money?"

I gasped. Concealer? A waste of money? Well, yeah, maybe for her with her perfect skin and her perfect face, it was a waste of money, but the rest of us had dark circles under our eyes to hide from public knowledge.

DRU Dude. A good concealer is worth its weight in gold. Your sister is cray-cray.

EM A fact I've pointed out to my parents more than once.

"I hope this is not tested on animals," Bess added as she shook the container, then set it down to open up the case containing my one hundred and ten different shades of eye shadow.

"Of course it isn't. I wouldn't use anything that was."

DRU It's like she doesn't know you at all!

EM "Good. I don't know why you have to wear so much makeup, Em. It's not like you're ugly. I guess it's just a phase you're going through. When you get older like me, you'll realize that you don't really need it."

I ground my teeth as I fluffed up my diminishing bath bubbles. I hate it when she gets all worldly older sister on me. She's only two years older than me, and I, at least, had moved out of the house.

DRU Um …

EM OK, OK, I had to come back, but still! I was the first one to leave.

DRU True.

EM "This stuff will clog your pores if you wear it all the time," Bess said. "You're much better off allowing your skin to breathe. If you keep slapping on the makeup the way you do, you'll look like you're eighty before you're thirty."

I turned on the hot water with my toes. "Thank you so much for the advice, but my skin breathes just fine. Did you want something in particular, or are you just trying to see me naked, you perv?"

She rolled her eyes and set down my blush. "I've seen you naked, stupid. It's nothing to get excited about. I wanted to know if you'd like to come with me next weekend. I'm going to Suffolk with a bunch of others to protest the nuclear plant there."

"No, thank you." My sister, the radical political activist.

DRU She always has been weird that way. Do you remember the Greenpeace protests she made us go to?

EM The ones where she made me stand in front of her as a meat shield because she said I was, and I quote, "the approximate size of a Buick"? Oh yes, I very much remember those protests.

DRU She was exaggerating. You were the size of a nice little Kia, not a great big Buick.

EM !!!

DRU *giggles*

EM Anyway (firm glare at you, missy), since Bess has caught me in that trap before, I wasn't about to let her do it again. Good causes are all well and fine, but the people she hangs out with are always so … intense. Besides, I had enough to cope with. I soaped up my fwoofy soap thing and prepared to shave my right leg.

"The government wants to build a new generation of nuclear power plant, rather than using renewable resources like solar and wind power."

"Uh-huh." I resoaped, then shaved my left leg. "Poop, the razor's going dull. Would you hand me a new one?"

She tapped her finger on my flat iron. "A recent poll showed that more than seventy percent of the people responding said they preferred renewable energies rather than new nuclear power stations."

"Yes, well, that's all very interesting, but right now I'm in full crisis mode, and if I have to go to my new college with hairy legs, I'm going to fall right over and die. Razor, please?"

She handed me a new razor. I recommenced shaveage.

"In addition, a recent study found that forty wind farms off the eastern coast of England could produce as much energy as all of the nuclear power plants in Britain put together; plus the creation of such wind farms would generate sixty thousand new jobs."

I sighed. Once Bess gets going about something, she never lets up. "You're forgetting one important thing." I raised my arm for pit shaving.

She frowned. "What's that?"

"You're not British. Why should you be telling them what to do with their country?"

DRU Oooh, burn!

DRU Em: 1; Bess: 0

EM She *tch*ed and rolled her eyes and made that annoyed face that she always seems to make around me and no one else. "Emily, the day will come when you're going to have to learn that—"

I stopped shaving my armpit and finished the sentence with her. "—that we're all living in a global village, and that means we have to care for each other, no matter what our nationality."

She stuck out her tongue at me, which was a really juvenile thing to do. I threw my fwoofy soapy thing at her.

DRU Which, of course, *isn't* a juvenile thing to do.

EM Of course not.

DRU !

EM ?

DRU Sarcasm, Emily.

EM I know what you were doing. I just decided to ignore it.

DRU Fair enough. Go on.

EM Where was ... oh, that's right. Bess. As if it's not bad enough I have a father who thinks everything medieval is the most fascinating thing on earth, I get stuck with a perfect sister who spends a couple of days in England and she's already made a ton of friends, has a (assumedly more than friends-with-benefits) sexual partner, and doesn't need to wear makeup to hide her Uncle Fester–level dark eye circles.

I swear to you, Dru, Mom and I are the only normal ones in the family, and sometimes I have my doubts about her.

DRU Yeah, but your definition of normal isn't really that of everyone else, is it?

EM I can't help it if my family has warped me. Hey, speaking of warped, no news on Vancey-pants?

DRU If you are referring to my delicious and adorable BF, Vance, by that horrible nickname, yes, of course I've heard from him. He's coming to Seattle as soon as fall semester is over.

EM Not before? That's like months away, isn't it?

DRU Yes, but he sexted with me the other night.

EM DRUSILLA KAYE ANDERSON!

DRU What?

EM You sexted? You, who wouldn't give me your credit card number when I wanted to sign us up to that online porn place?

DRU It was my mom's credit card.

DRU And we were fifteen at the time. Plus, you couldn't even look at the website without blushing bright red and falling off my bed.

EM Doesn't matter. Do I want to know what you sexted? No, wait, that sounds wrong. I don't want to know specifics, just … you know … did you enjoy it?

DRU *sigh* Actually, no. I'd just taken the last of my pain meds, and was a bit sleepy, but Vance wanted to go for it, so I just kind of let him do his thing and dozed. Also, I may have … um …

EM WHAT???

DRU Sent him some things I found online because I was too sleepy to think them up. I'm going to hell, aren't I?

EM For copying and pasting sexts to your boyfriend? Yeah, that's hell-in-a-handbasket material right there.

DRU Oh well.

DRU At least I'll have you there with me.

EM Sistahs for life!

CHAPTER SEVEN

DRU You there?

EM Yup. Sleepy. Thinking of a nap, but I have to read a chapter of utter and complete crap.

DRU Diversity stuff, eh?

EM You got it. What's up?

DRU I think I created a monster. Vance called last night and wants to sext again. He said he really liked what we did the other night.

EM When you plagiarized your sexts?

DRU It wasn't plagiarism! I just … uh …

EM Copied someone else's sexts that she put online. Plagiarism, babe.

DRU Ugh. I don't want to think about it anymore. Entertain me.

EM I don't know how I can top plagiarized sexy texts.

DRU Try. Bored. How are the classes (yours, not Holly's)?

EM Bearable, although I almost fell asleep in Integrated Social Theories and Disciplinary Articulation, and the second one—Statistical Methodology in Post-Enlightenment Diverse Cultures—is even more dull than Bioethical Cognition, Communication, and Creativity Underwater Basket Weaving, or whatever that horrible class is we took together.

Now you see why I've been making such a big fuss about wasting one of my semesters on this crap.

DRU Basket weaving would have made it interesting, at least. What news of the sexy-pants Fang? Aidan? The dishy guy with the blond-tipped hair whose name I can't remember?

EM Blond-tips is Devon. Fang is off somewhere up north doing things to sheep and cows that I probably don't want to know about. I wish he'd call me, or at least text, but so far, he hasn't done either. I think that's a sign that although the Great Deflowering of Emily was pretty darn impactful for me, it was more or less just a nice interlude for him.

DRU Awww. Are you sad?

EM Kind of. No, not really. Well, maybe. I just wish he was here.

DRU Maybe you could go see him on the weekend?

EM I think he's pretty much busy seven days a week. You're pitying me, aren't you?

DRU Of course not.

EM ...

DRU OK, but just a little.

EM The thing is, we agreed to be friends with bennies, and I don't have a problem with that. I just ... wish he was here to have bennies with.

DRU I understand. Now that the itch has been scratched, you want more scratches.

EM The visual imagery in that could be better put.

DRU Yeah, sorry, I realized that after I hit Send. Isn't there anyone else whose bones you want to jump?

EM Well, there's Aidan. He's cleaned up a bit now that the semester has started, and he has to be Brother's official helper monkey in class and such, although he's still definitely Head Hipster of Hipsterville. I even saw him using an old manual typewriter when I went to complain to Brother that the Post-Enlightenment Diverse Cultures class won't let me use my e-mails to you as the basis for the research project due at the end of the class.

DRU *settles back for the latest ep of How the Emily Turns*

EM "Hiya," I said when Aidan looked up from his old-timey typewriter.

"Good morning. How do you like Gob-botty?"

I shrugged. "I'm sure it has better classes than the two I'm taking, but other than that, it's fine. I like the old buildings."

He grinned. "You wouldn't be Dr. Williams's daughter if you didn't." He stood up and stretched, and pulled down his "Give Peace a Chance" tee, and said, "I was just about to get some lunch. Do you have time?"

"For food? Oh yes."

DRU This sounds promising. Lunching together could lead to itch scratching!

DRU Ew. Forget I just typed that.

EM Thank you, I was going to say. Now, you know there is nothing worse than that feeling of going into a dining hall when you don't have anyone to sit with, and you don't know what spots are off-limits because the professors sit there (god forbid anyone without tenure should sit amongst their august personages), and where the garbage cans are, etc. So when Aidan rescued me from certain lunchtime hell, I could have kissed him. OK, maybe the kissing was just uppermost on my mind, but I did really think about it when he showed me where to sit (near the windows), what food to avoid (anything fried, processed, or which used to have a face), and where the booze was (yes, they have alcohol at lunch here).

He introduced me to two of his law buddies: Peg and a redhead named Lalla. Ditzy, but nice. Peg is a lesbian who talks really fast and laughs very loud, and is wickedly funny. I bet she'll make a hell of a lawyer.

DRU I like the sound of her. I give you my permission to make her your In the UK Bestie. So long as I retain Worldwide Bestie Above All Others status.

EM Thank you for such generosity. I went home to crash, and maybe give myself a much needed mani-pedi, but Holly called me all breathless and strangle-voiced (you know, how you get when you're trying super hard not to cry).

"I know you're not supposed to come to school with me today," she said, doing an odd little pant into the phone. "And I hate to bother you when you're at your own classes, but it's French this afternoon, and I … it's the same girls as were in the classes you saw yesterday … and this morning, they were saying I should go back to my shrink and things like that. I know Dr.

Benson said I should remember that they are hurting inside, and that's why they're lashing out at me, but, oh, Emily ..."

Her voice trailed off into a sob.

DRU Dr. Benson?

EM Her therapist. She sees him once a week.

DRU Gotcha. Poor kid.

EM I got up off my bed and was already digging out the Maroon Skirt of Fashion Death. "What time does the class start?"

"In forty minutes. I hate to ask you—"

"Don't worry about it, Holly. I'll be there with bells on. What room is it?"

Which is why half an hour later I strolled down the hallway wearing the stupid skirt, a lovely off-white lace camisole with matching shrug, and a backpack with my Integrated Social Theories book that I figured I'd read while the other kids learned French.

I assumed that by now Russell Crowe had told the teachers who I was, and to leave me alone when I was in their classes, but the second I stepped foot in Holly's French class, I was hit with a wall of French.

"Beaucoup merci frog legs, escargot?" the teacher asked me, pointing to a chair. The two evil Snickerers from the day before plopped down in the front row and immediately started snickering as I stood there trying to decide how best to deal with them in such a way that it wouldn't kick back anything bad on Holly.

I decided to deflect their attention. There's nothing bullies love more than someone new to pick on. Well, they wanted a target? Fine, I'd give them a target. So I smirked at them and said, "Sorry, I had two years of Russian, but didn't even once look at French. It's *merci*, isn't it? *Merci*, then," and took the seat the teacher was pointing to. Snickerer Ann leaned over and rattled off a mouthful of French at me, then laughed when I didn't respond.

I mouthed a couple of things to her that I'd learned from Sasha, the office manager at my old job, and smiled to myself when the instructor gave an annoyed sniff.

And as for French … well, I figured the teacher must know I was not a speaker, and wouldn't call on me to do anything, so I was pretty safe there. So I settled back and prepared to pick up a little French (how hard can it be to do that when you've learned Russian?).

The answer: bloody hard.

Get this—there was not one single word of English spoken during the whole class. I thought England hated France? Every time the teacher came around to talk to me, I had to pretend I had something in my throat, and hacked and coughed and wheezed until she (I have no idea of her name—I think it's Madame Garçon or something) moved on to the next person. So I spent the whole of the class pretending that I understood, nodding, and saying, *"Oui, oui!"* a lot.

Holly told me later that French is compulsory here, which just thrills me to death. I told the teacher afterward that I wasn't really there to learn French, and was Holly's helper monkey, but she just babbled at me in that language, and shoved a textbook into my hands.

DRU Wow. So now you're going to have to really learn French? #ouch

EM "OK," I said to Holly when the teacher ran off to eat some cheese, or whatever it is French teachers do when they're not inflicting verbs on people. "Do not panic. This is not a desperate situation."

"I'm so sorry," she said for the umpteenth time in the last five minutes. Honestly, this girl seemed to feel bad about every single thing that happened to me. "I thought you spoke French. Everyone does."

"Not back home. Spanish is the preferred language *du jour,* so of course, I went for Russian, which was the cool language. But like I said, don't panic. I've always had a bit of a knack for languages, if I do say so myself, so I'm going to view this as an opportunity to learn something new. So buck up, little camper. We can do French together."

That seemed to cheer her up, and when I left her at her last class, she swore she'd help me with whatever I needed in French, which was a nice change.

DRU Lookit you, making her feel all needed and nurturing! #goyou

EM I know, right? I thought it would be good for her, and it seemed to work.

DRU You can add her to your UK Bestie list, too. So long as you mention that I'm stuck at home with no job and a banged-up leg and a boyfriend who goes to college two states away, and thus I reign supreme over all the sub-besties. #Iamthequeen

EM You are all graciousness.

DRU #mwah #smooches #lovesyababe

EM DUDE!

DRU #wha'?

EM What is with this sudden hashtagging everything?

DRU Everyone hashtags, Em!

DRU You need to get with the IG, girl.

EM I so do not! And you need to cut back on the hashtag addiction, babers. If you don't, the next thing you know, you'll be sending me pictures of yourself with a puppy snout and ears and little popping pink hearts over your head.

DRU SENT YOU A PICTURE

EM *shakes fist* I'll get you! And your little dog, too! Wait, you probably won't get that reference since you hate *Wizard of Oz*. Gah!

YOU LOGGED ON

EM Hey, got a text from Tabitha. When did Vance grow a goatee? Is he going hipster, like Aidan? I thought he wanted to go into the military next year? Do they let you be a hipster there? Looks like they had a fun time at the state fair, regardless of the goatee question.

YOU LOGGED ON

DRU EMILY MARIE WILLIAMS!

EM Ohai.

DRU Don't you ohai me, missy-pants. Just what do you mean, Vance was at the fair with Tab?

EM Tabs sent me piccies.

DRU !!!

DRU *steams*

DRU #boyfriendbedead

EM Woops. I thought this must have been a sanctioned outing.

DRU #Iwillfreakingcastratehim

DRU #withadullbutterknife

DRU #slowly

EM Dru …

DRU One more.

DRU #sooverhim

EM Better now?

DRU Not in the least. Dammit, Em! He told me he was going to his mom's cabin for the weekend.

EM Maybe he went there after?

DRU To his mom's cabin? The one where you can sunbathe nude and no one will see you?

EM Honestly, how would I know what they did? I'm halfway around the world, and have problems of my own, like a pervy ghost.

DRU That rat! That rat bastard! I bet he took her there and they got naked!

EM Wow. That escalated quickly.

DRU Do you think they had sex? I bet they had sex. I bet Vance dumped me because my leg is being a pain in the bitch, and now he's out having sex with every girl who'll shag his sorry ass.

EM Um …

DRU Not literally.

EM Thanks for the clarification. Also, hee hee hee on the "pain in the bitch." I think you meant pain in the ass, or son of a bitch.

DRU GAH! You're changing the subject! That means you think he was having sex with Tab! Double gah! Triple!

EM OK, first of all, no one said anything about sex at a cabin. No one said anything about sex, period. Tab just sent pics from the fair. And second—

DRU So help me, if you tell me to get a gr—

EM Get a grip, girlfriend! Maybe you should talk to him to ask what's up.

DRU Gah! Hold, please. Texting the rat.

DRU LOGGED ON

DRU You still awake?

EM Barely. I was watching a Bollywood movie with a hunky dude in it, but I need to get to sleep soon. Did you talk to the cheater … er … boyfriend?

DRU No. He didn't answer my message or my texts. He's probably too busy out boinking. #ratbastard

EM I'm going to allow you that one because you're upset. Is there anything I can do? Do you want to tell me how evil he is? What you'd like to do to him with your crutches? Potential new BFs you should swipe left or right on?

DRU No. I'm going to take my last pain med and take a nap until Mom comes home, and then I'm going to get the walking cast put on early, and then get a job and move out and never talk to that asshat again.

EM …

EM OK, then. Hugses.

DRU What happened to you today?

EM Meh.

DRU Go on, tell me.

EM I'm being supportive and letting you vent all over me. I can't be supportive at the same time I'm telling you the weird shit that keeps happening to me.

DRU Consider this taking my mind off my troubles. What weird shit happened?

EM Not much is new and exciting in today's episode of British High School Drama, although our stalwart heroine was sent to see the Horseface Teacher for so-called disciplinary action (Russell Crowe was off at some seminar or something).

DRU What did you do this time?

EM I would be offended that you even ASSUMED I did something wrong, but I know you are emotional and hurty and not thinking straight.

DRU !!!

EM The snotty girl with the hat (her name is actually Karen Duff) turned me in for telling Holly that the games skirt they make the girls wear for sportsing was obviously the creation of a deeply perverted mind.

DRU Are they that short?

EM Yup. And pleated, so you see everything when you spin.

DRU Which, of course, you have to when you wear a pleated skirt.

EM Of course. It fwoofs out. That's always entertaining. I can't believe the little snot ratted on me.

DRU Did you get revenge?

EM Not yet. I had planned on using Holly's free period to work on the paper I have due next week, but instead, I spent the entire time sweeping up the girls' locker room.

EM And then I found out that the Duff is Tash's little sister. No wonder she's an asshat! She clearly has it in for me.

DRU That chick is toast.

EM Which one? Duff or Tash?

DRU The first. No, both.

EM I love it when you get bloodthirsty.

DRU *sigh*

EM More hugs. Wish I was there so we could binge-watch Netflix and eat way too much pizza.

DRU Miss you.

EM Likewise, sistah. You OK now? I'm falling asleep, but I'm here for you if you want to vent more.

DRU No, I'm fine.

DRU Bitter, sad smooches.

EM Smoochback.

CHAPTER EIGHT

EM I'm going to pre-entertain you, so that when you get up and are all sad and angry and hurt and wanting to kill someone, you can read this instead.

EM "So," I said to Brother when he strolled in the door this afternoon. (The man hardly works. It's amazing the way he gets paid for doing nothing but writing a few papers and teaching a couple of classes. Why can't I find a job like that?) "Would you like to explain this?"

He raised his Unibrow. (Still no signs of plucking, but I'm not giving up hope. I put Mom's extra pair of tweezers on his pillow. Maybe they'll get kinky and she'll pluck his Unibrow for him.) "You seem to misunderstand the basic principles behind the parent-child relationship. Traditionally, it is the parent who asks for an explanation of the child."

"Let's keep our mind in this century, shall we?" I said, and held out the newspaper that Mom had given me.

He took it and read. "Ah. How nice. Very flattering. Hmmm. *Dr. Williams, noted medieval scholar, distinguished lecturer*, mmmm. Yes. Very nice. I had no idea the university would notify the local papers of our arrival here in their fair land."

"You are missing the important part." I pointed to the sentences in question.

"*Professor and Mrs. Williams are accompanied by their two daughters, Bess and Emily. The former will be apprenticing at the studio of renowned local potter Alvin Guildston, while the latter will be attending Piddlington-on-the Weld's own prestigious Dalmark School.* Ah. I see what you are complaining about."

"You bet your booty I'm complaining. I am so not a high school student!"

He just looked at me. I happened to have just come home from helping Holly deal with a *Romeo and Juliet* spot quiz, and was still wearing the blasted skirt and blazer. "You look like you are."

"Come on, Brother, you know full well that I'm only doing that because I feel sorry for Holly."

"And therein lies the source of your trouble—your own folly in agreeing to pretend you are something you are not."

I whomped him with the newspaper. "You're the one who's always yammering on about helping out your fellow man. I'm simply trying to help Holly the best way I know how."

"A commendable goal, but perhaps you need to reevaluate your methodology of achieving said goal."

"Oh, you and your historical doublespeak. Aidan says you layer that on him thick enough that you shouldn't have any left for your nearest and dearest." I was a bit disgruntled by his "You made your bed, now you have to lie on it" attitude, mostly because I knew he was right.

"Aidan?" Brother lowered the newspaper and gave me that *Have you been in the proximity of a male of the species?* look. You know, the one he always gives any man who I'm seeing.

DRU LOGGED ON

EM "Aidan Spencer, the dean's son. Your indentured servant at the college, remember?"

Bess walked by, a hideous plant in her arms, and a SAVE THE BOTTLENOSE DOLPHIN sign tucked into the back of her jeans. "Emily's got a boyfriend, Emily's got a boyfriend."

"You can stuff your plant where the dolphin don't shine," I told her. She grinned and went out to the kitchen.

"Oh, him," Brother said. "Nice boy. Polite. Going to be a lawyer, though. Bad choice there. What about him?"

Honest to Pete, Dru, my father would get on a saint's nerves! How I'm going to live down having it blared to everyone in POTW that I'm in high school again, I'll never know.

I need chocolate. Or a tiara. No, chocolate *and* a tiara. I deserve it for all the crap I have to suffer in the name of helping Holly get her feet under her.

DRU I wouldn't count on getting a tiara.

EM Ohai. How are you feeling?

DRU #don'twanttotalkaboutit

EM OK. I'm here if you do.

DRU I meant to ask you yesterday and forgot. ... Is Holly getting better now that you're keeping the bullies away?

EM I think so. Some days are better than others. Some days she kind of withdraws into herself and looks emo and pale and anguished. But there are more good days now than bad days. Did you get some sleep?

DRU No. Maybe. I don't know. I don't want to talk about my messed-up life. Tell me what you did today.

EM I hate it when you are blue, but I totally understand. Um. Today ... well, I had to pretend I was practicing to be a mime in Holly's French class. I even wrote up a little note for Madame Grayson saying that she really needed to talk to Russell Crowe about who I was, and that I'd just pretend I wasn't allowed to speak in order to give her an excuse not to call on me in class. She gave me an odd look, but so far so good.

DRU Hold on, text.

EM From the rat?

DRU Yeah.

EM *waits*

EM Dashing to kitchen for sandwich. This waiting is making me hungry, and I missed lunch.

EM Back.

EM You haven't been arrested and your phone taken away because you made threats to V over the phone, have you? It's been almost half an hour.

DRU Sorry, I'm here. I feel much, much better.

EM Oh, good. Tell all. Well, all that you feel comfy telling.

DRU He apologized for not answering my call and text, but he slept sixteen hours. He thinks he had a stomach bug or food poisoning because he had the trots after the visit to the fair.

DRU He also apologized for not telling me he was taking Tabs out. It was totally platonic.

DRU He said he felt sorry for her because she'd been dumped by the barista she'd been seeing (the one with the hunchback, not the one with the Mohawk).

DRU He said he thought he'd told me, but must have forgotten, and that he would never, ever dream of seeing someone else romantically, but he knew I would want him to be a good friend to Tab.

DRU And of course I do.

DRU She must feel horrible being dumped by a hunchback barista. I think Vance was being awfully sweet to try to cheer her up.

DRU Why aren't you saying anything?

EM I was waiting for you to finish. You done?

DRU Yup.

EM OK. First of all, dear god, woman, did you not sit through the exact same diversity classes that I did? You don't call someone with a hunchback "the hunchback!" You refer to them in compassionate yet empowering terms, like "the differently backed," or "the guy with one shoulder interestingly higher and thicker than the other." Sheesh. I can't take you anywhere! Besides, I know that guy—his name is Gio—and he's an awesome artist, and is very cool.

DRU Oh, man, is that who she was dating? I love Gio! He used to draw penises on my latte when I'd go there all last summer. He isn't a hunchback at all. He just has one shoulder that's a bit scrunched.

EM Seriously, you did not just say the h-word again.

DRU Sorry. Will purge from vocab.

EM Thank you. As for Vance ... if you're happy with his explanation, and don't think it's the least little bit coincidental, then you go, girl. I'm here for you if you need me.

DRU That sounds like you don't believe him!

EM It really doesn't matter what I believe, does it?

DRU Well … no.

EM Right. I have to toddle off. Aidan asked me to go to the local club with him and his buddies tonight. Peg and Lalla said they might be there, and of course, Devon will probably be there as well, along with all of their respective girlfriends/boy-friends/gender-nonspecific-friends. I have to see what items in my pitiful and totally unacceptable array of garments I can wear. Stay strong, my dumpling.

DRU Enjoy the club. Snog the ever-livin' pants off him.

EM You really miss Vance right now, don't you?

DRU Girl, I'm putting fresh batteries in the pink bunny o' pleasure right this minute. I plan on wearing them out. And then putting more batteries in. And wearing those out, too.

EM And on that unsavory mental image, I exit.

YOU LOGGED ON

EM DRU! Something horrible has happened. SOME-THING HORRIBLE!

EM Are you there?

EM It says you're online.

EM Wait, are you … er … pink bunnying? Because if so, never mind.

DRU What? No, I was getting soup. What's your crisis now?

EM It's not just a crisis, it's A Crisis. With capital letters.

DRU Uh-huh. Can't find your nail polish?

EM I snort at you.

DRU Brother say you can't date until you're thirty?

EM Trust me, he's said that so many times Mom and I just laugh at it.

DRU Homework for high school getting you down?

EM I ha at you. No, my dear little comedian, my problem is this.

EM I really want to wear my slinky red dress tonight, to amaze and delight Aidan.

DRU Slinky red dress?

EM The one that looks like it was painted on.

DRU Oh, the one that's too small for you. Go on.

EM It's not too small! It's supposed to look like that!

DRU Mmmhmm.

EM It's a style, you boob. A formfitting, curve-enhancing style.

DRU It's also two sizes too small, but go on.

EM *deep, steadying breath*

DRU I love it when you go drama queen.

EM When I tried the dress on this afternoon, I found out a horrible thing has happened.

DRU Your butt expanded?

EM My butt has expan—hey!

DRU Hee hee hee. Totes called it.

EM I hate it when you do that.

DRU It's all those chocolates you were stuffing yourself with to make you forget Fang.

EM I don't need or want to forget him. He'll be back by the end of the month, and then we can get jiggy again.

DRU I might seriously have to question our continuing relationship if you use the phrase "get jiggy" again.

EM Sayeth the woman in denial about her cheatin' man.

DRU He did not cheat!

EM Anyway, I think the butt/dress situation has to do with the change in hemispheres or being too close to the Greenwich time thingie, or maybe it's the ghost.

EM Oh, update on undie ghost—the duct tape worked beautifully, thank you!

DRU I dare any ghost to fondle your bras while a web of duct tape is holding the drawer closed.

EM You do sometimes have good ideas.

DRU *Chica*, I am *made* of good ideas.

EM Now I have to work my butt like mad until this evening.

EM Do you still have that issue of *Vogue* that has the butt exercises? If so, will you take a picture of the article and text it to me? I'm doing cheek clenches every chance I get, but it's kind of hard to walk and clench at the same time.

EM I tried doing them when I came downstairs, and Mom asked me if I had to go to the bathroom.

DRU I'm disturbed that you think V is cheating.

DRU You have no proof of that.

DRU I know him better than you. He'd never two-time me like that, especially with Tabitha the Hun.

DRU Not that he would two-time me with anyone.

DRU So what did you end up wearing other than the red dress?

DRU Tell me when you get back.

EM I just don't want you to get hurt, babes. And you're right, I don't know him as well as you, so I'll just leave a little warning to be careful, and move on.

I'm sorry to say that those butt exercises don't seem to be helping much. I clench and do the pelvic thrusts whenever no one is looking, but I think people are starting to notice.

"UTI?" Bess asked as I was clenching and thrusting my way out to get the mail.

"Not even!" I said, and then did a couple of thrusts at her as she marched off to meet with her boy toy Monk.

"I have told myself I don't want to know, and so I don't," Brother said, walking past me with a hand blocking his eyes. I gave him a couple of pelvic thrusts, too.

Ew. Wait. That sounds just all sorts of wrong. Forget I said that.

Oh! You mentioned *High School Musical* (or rather, the drama without the singing and dancing) and I actually have some news for you there. The English lit teacher (who yells everything—her name is Mrs. Spreadborough, and no, I'm not kidding) is the head of the fifth form, and she came up to me yesterday while I was working on a collaborative project ("Diversity in the Workplace and You!") for college, and I figured that once again, that snotty Karen Duff had turned me in for something. I swear Tash is behind all of this. The last thing her sister, Karen, tattled on was two days ago when Holly and I used the tennis court during her study period.

That got us sent to see Russell Crowe, where I told him, "My father always says that half of studying is mentally digesting the work, and we were digesting while we were having a quick game. Exercise promotes brain stuff, you know."

He didn't buy that. Holly and I both swept out the girls' locker room.

Anyway, Mrs. Spread pulled me aside after class. And before you ask, yes, R. Crowe says he told all the teachers that I wasn't really a student and to not expect work from me, but I'm not sure how many of them actually listened to him, because they all give me assignments. I just never do any of them. Anyway, the Spreading One pulled me aside, and said she had a project for me. Actually, she bellowed it at me, and I made a mental note to leave some hearing aid pamphlets in her mailbox.

"I HAVE A LITTLE PROJECT I THINK YOU MIGHT LIKE, WILLIAMS," she screamed. "I KNOW HOW YOU YANKS LIKE HALLOWEEN, SO I'M PUTTING YOU IN CHARGE OF THIS YEAR'S HALLOWEEN PARTY."

Now, my first thought was, no way, José, but then I started thinking about it. Who puts on the best parties in all of Seattle? Well, OK, it's you, but I'm the one who helps you. What the Spreadable said next really clinched it for me.

"SEE MISS DARLING IN THE OFFICE FOR INFORMATION ON THE BUDGET. YOU MAY ORGANIZE A TEAM OF VOLUNTEERS FROM THE FIFTH FORM."

You see where my evil thoughts are going, don't you? Heh heh heh. Oh, yes, I'll organize a team of volunteers, and I know one Miss Karen Duff who'll be given the worst, the most grungy, filthily repulsive job I can find. Then we'll see who goes tattling to Russell Crowe every friggin' day!

I could get used to this revenge stuff.

Oh, the underwear ghost has struck again. When I clenched and thrust my way into my room to see how my butt was doing vis-à-vis the dress, my undies were all over the floor. There was a bra on top of the wardrobe, but—and this is so weird—the duct tape was still x-ed tight across the front of the drawer! Isn't that creepy? I'm starting to think it's either Mom or Brother doing it, and if it is, I really hope it's Mom, 'cause if it's Brother fondling my things, I'm really going to disown him, and spend years in therapy.

Update on butt vs. dress forthcoming, just as soon as I wrap it in Saran Wrap for a bit to see if I can sweat off some of the excess.

EM Hugs and kisses.

CHAPTER NINE

DRU So? What's the decision on the dress?

DRU Inquiring minds want to know.

DRU And by inquiring, I mean people who are still forbidden to drive while their leg is in a cast.

EM Oh, hellos. Well, since all the clenching and thrusting doesn't seem to have made much of a difference to my butt, I've decided to wear my tiger dress.

EM You have a tiger dress?

EM Of course I do. I just said I did, didn't I?

DRU What's it look like?

EM ...

EM Like a tiger!

DRU Like an actual tiger, or just tiger stripes?

EM It's like you're a stranger who doesn't have all of my clothing memorized. It has diagonal stripes that do an excellent job of hiding the problem with my butt.

DRU Your butt has a problem now? Other than expanding?

EM Ha ha, you so funny. Fishnets or lacy nylons, do you think?

DRU IMHO, fishnets always say questionable morals.

DRU But men like them.

DRU They think they're sexy (which is stupid, because if they ever wore them, they'd know that all they do is rub your thighs raw).

DRU What are you doing?

EM Trying on the fishnets. Guess my ass isn't the only thing that expanded. I'm going with lacy nylons.

DRU Sound choice.

EM I forgot to tell you the other day—I'm reading the hints and tips section of the Sexy Womyn website for when I want to do a hoedown with Aidan, or when Fang comes back.

DRU ???

DRU *Do a hoedown?*

EM Stop picking on my euphemisms. Sexy Womyn has a section on arousing men. Bess came in while I was reading it, and told me I should practice on a carrot, which is beyond embarrassing!

EM I mean, I was with the Asshat for two years. It's not like I don't know how to do a hand job.

DRU Then why were you reading some porn website?

EM It's not a porn website—it's all about empowering women to take charge of their own sexuality, while providing their partners with fabu sexy times. I'm just making sure that I'm not missing something. You know, because I came late to the game.

DRU What game? I'm confused.

EM Sex! Sex is the game! I'm late to it!

DRU I thought Fang was out of town?

EM Gah! I was simply saying that because I just did hand jobs and blow jobs before Fang, I wanted to make sure there wasn't something more I should be doing now that I've moved beyond sexual training wheels.

DRU You have the weirdest problems of anyone I know.

EM Speaking of problems, SimEmily is ralphing all over the place, and slapping anyone who comes to her house.

EM She even yelled at her husband, SimLiamHemsworth, and you know that SimEmily never yells at SimLiam. Ever. Not even when he was gettin' it on with SimSinthia, the woman who lives next door and likes to sit in her hot tub naked during the middle of the day.

EM I wonder if there's a Sim virus going around. Are your Sims OK?

DRU Again, you have the weirdest problems. My Sims are all fine.

EM Gotta run.

EM Message me later.

DRU About what?

EM Your feels re Vance.

EM I promise I won't give you advice on how to set his hair on fire.

EM Or give you the number of a guy who would tattoo "LOSER" on Vance's forehead.

EM I'll just keep those thoughts to myself.

DRU Winner of the Best Friend of the Year Award.

DRU *NOT!*

YOU LOGGED ON

EM Visualize the glory that is womanhood: pink-and-black dress in alternating diagonal stripes. Black faux stilettos. (I refuse to ruin my feet wearing actual stilettos. Give me the ability to not deform my toes over fashion any day.) Lacy stockings. Pink ribbon dripping down my back like … um … something really pink. Hair up in messy bun that took a good hour to get right. Glitter on the upper boobs.

I am a goddess! Wish me luck for more fabulous sex!

YOU LOGGED ON

EM Crapballs! Mister Monthly Visitor is here! No wonder my butt is huge. Why now? Why tonight? I can't possibly romp in a sexual manner if I'm going to be all blechy. *muffled sob*

YOU LOGGED ON

DRU Sorry about the MMV. Hope you weren't too crampy. Going to bed now, but I'll leave my thingie on so I can hear you when you come back and tell me how the club went.

EM I'm here, I'm here. Oy.

EM You awake?

EM No?

EM Hokay. This is going to be really long, so I'll get as much of it done as I can before you wake up. As you know, last night was clubbing with Aidan. It started out well, with him coming by to pick me up, and for once, he wasn't dressed like Hipster of the Year. He wore black jeans and a black shirt that set off his blondness, and I was thinking pretty smutty thoughts about how the evening was going to end despite the hellish nightmare going on in my girlie bits.

"Emily has to be back by ten," Brother said, passing through the hall where I was getting my coat.

"Like hell I do," I yelled after him.

Aidan looked at me like I was an alien. "Your father has you on a curfew?"

"No, that's his idea of what passes for a joke. Just ignore him."

Brother stuck his head out of the study at that point and added, "I don't want her drinking, either."

"Brother, you are so embarrassing me!" I hissed, and tugged on Aidan's sleeve to get him away from the horrible man who spawned me.

"It's not legal for her to drink back home. I know it is here, but I'm sure you respect our traditions, as we do yours. Also, if you plan on drinking, you are not to drive Emily home."

"GAH!"

"Don't worry about Emily, sir. I'll take good care of her."

Poor Aidan, driven to say "sir" by the ramblings of a deranged, tyrannical father.

Brother narrowed his eyes at Aidan, the Unibrow and hair horn making him look even more than normal like a rhinoceros. "And no sex! I absolutely forbid any sort of sex! She's too young."

"Brother!" I bellowed, marching over to the door and slamming the flat of my hand against it. "I am twenty! I know you have to do the fatherly-concern thing, but sheesh! There is such a thing as *too* fatherly!"

Aidan gave Brother a kind of strained smile. "Mr. Williams, I—"

"Nothing. No inappropriate touching, nothing. You understand me?"

I thought lovingly of the roll of duct tape up in my room, and how much I'd like to see it across my father's face at that moment.

"I respect Emily, sir," Aidan said, all righteous and gentlemanly. Whereas I was contemplating patricide. "I would never dishonor her."

"It's a good thing you mentioned honor," Brother said, and went into a ten-minute spiel of how ye olde knights of yore honored women, and what was wrong with society today that couldn't be fixed by a wallop upside the head with a sword or two. I think that's what he was going on about—I really wasn't paying too much attention. Instead I was wondering exactly how you draw and quarter someone, and whether it would be enough to SHUT BROTHER UP.

Honestly, I could easily have killed him right then and there, but Aidan would probably think the worst of me, so I didn't.

We finally escaped. I apologized all the way to the club, but Aidan just laughed and said, "My father is just as bad with my two sisters, and the oldest one has two sets of twins. Just last week he told my younger sister that he wished he had an actual working chastity belt, because he was tired of them getting pregnant and moving back home with all their kids."

"No wonder your dad gets along so well with Brother," I said.

The club was on the other side of POTW, and was located in the basement of a warehouse. It was decorated with big steel girders decked out with Christmas lights, and exposed pipes, and peeling hazardous-material posters. The whole place smelled like rusty pond water.

It was really packed, lots of people, music from a pretty good DJ, and everyone was dancing, dancing, dancing. Aidan grabbed my hand and dragged me to the rear, where a bunch of round tables and those little white plastic chairs people have on their patios were set up.

"There's the lad," he said, and hauled me over to where Devon was. Devon had two girls with him: a redhead with her hair spiked out, standing behind him rubbing his shoulders, and a blonde with long poufy 1980s hair (it must take a whole bottle of hair spray to get it looking like that), who was rubbing her hand up and down his leg. Even so, he grinned at me and winked, and did a little wolf whistle when he looked over the tiger dress. I thought about giving him the Slit-Eyed Look of Pure Scorn for flirting with me when there were two other women slobbering on him, but decided against it. He was very sexy in leather pants and a kind of see-through red shirt that showed off not only a bona fide six-pack, but also an elaborate tattoo of a dragon coiled around his left arm.

You know how I love me some tats!

DRU Nrng.

EM Oh, there you are. What time is it?

DRU Two a.m. Sleeping. Keep going.

EM Sorry for waking you.

DRU Frrn.

EM Poor widdle sweepy Dwoo.

Back to club adventures.

"How goes your classes?" Devon asked over the noise of the people and pulsing music.

"Fine. Boring as hell."

He laughed. "That's Gob-botty for you."

Aidan disappeared for a few minutes, and when he came back, he had two big pints of beer, one of which he plopped down in front of me. Now, you know me, Dru—I'm not averse to imbibing beverages of an alcoholic nature, but it did kind of take me by surprise.

I mean, he'd just promised Brother that he wasn't going to drink and drive, and yet here he was chugging back a big old pint of beer. I know I'm going to sound terribly lame, but it made me kind of uncomfortable. I mean, I trusted Aidan, I really did, but it still made me … worried.

"What're you looking so glum about, ducks?" Aidan asked, shoving the pint he bought me up against my hand.

"Nothing. It's just that the music is giving me a bit of a headache." See? Lame.

"Get that in you, and you'll feel worlds better," he said, giving the beer another nudge.

"You know, I think I'm going to pass on that. Beer tends to make me sleepy, and I want to enjoy the evening without being tired."

"Well, if you don't want it …" He snagged the glass, and downed it.

He snuggled up next to me after that, putting his arm around me and stroking my leg with his other hand. Devon, who had been snogging the poufy blonde, got up and went off with both girls to the dance floor.

Aidan laughed when he saw the surprise on my face. "Our Dev's quite the lad with the ladies."

"I guess," I said, watching the three of them dance together. "I've heard of a ménage à trois, but I've never seen one before."

Aidan choked and shot beer out of his nose. Poor guy, I have to admit I felt a bit sorry for him then.

"Holy crapballs, I'm so sorry." I helped him wipe up the beer that splashed on his pants, not saying anything when he wrapped his arm around me again, and started licking my ear.

I think something's wrong with me, Dru, I really do. Here was a very handsome man, who was no doubt going to be a super-successful lawyer, making moves on me that I'd been anticipating ever since I met him, and when he trailed his tongue around the edges of my ear, all I could do was think about slugs sliming their way down a flowerpot.

Inner Emily pointed out that Fang didn't do that. Inner Emily pointed out that although we had a very healthy regard for Fang's excellence in the bedroom department, we had other interests in him that went beyond the physical.

Fang isn't Aidan, I told her.

Exactly, she said, just like that made sense.

And it didn't make sense, not really, Dru. I mean, Aidan was gorgeous (out of his hipster clothes), really gorgeous, and he was evidently as interested in me as I was in him … and yet, something felt off. Not quite … *right*, if you know what I mean.

That's stupid, I told myself. *You were perfectly fine pouncing on Fang, and yet you're acting weird just because Aidan is being flirty. Just kiss the man and forget about the whole ear thing. Remember that you're a new woman with a new plan.*

So I turned my head to lay my lips on him, but before I could, he took my hand and started rubbing it on his crotch.

I know, I know. I'm no stranger to touching men's dangly bits. Lord knows I've done enough hand jobs in my time with Daniel to understand just how everything works, but nonetheless, Aidan slapping my hand on his noogies shocked me. And not in a good way.

That was the moment he chose to swoop in for a snog. Well, as you can imagine, I was a bit on edge what with my soggy ear and the fact that I had a handful of man crotch, and all of a sudden there was his tongue smooshing itself between my lips.

"Ack!" I screeched, taken by surprise, and jumped straight up at least a foot. My chin hit his nose. Hard. What was worse, my hand jerked as well, and my ring (you remember, my grandma's ruby ring) got caught on some weird tab thing he had on his zipper, which meant my hand was stuck there, flailing wildly.

"Bloody hell," Aidan snarled as he jerked back, holding his nose and glaring at me. "What the hell is the matter with you?"

"I am so sorry," I said, snatching up a napkin and handing it to him. "I just wasn't expecting you to do that. And I think my ring … ack … what sort of zipper do you have? My ring is stuck on something."

I gave it a yank, causing him to yelp and grab my caught hand. "What the fuck! Are you trying to rip off my balls?"

"No, I told you, my ring is stuck on your zipper tab thing … ung." I wiggled my finger free of the ring, and rubbed the deep marks on it caused by the struggle. "Can you please … thank you."

He twisted the ring off and handed it to me with a snarl. "Next time you want to give me a hand job, take your bloody rings off."

"Who said anything about giving you a hand job?" I said with dignity, putting the ring onto a different finger, one not bruised.

"You've been giving me signals all week that you fancy me." He used the napkin I gave him to mop up his nose, which was bleeding a little. I could swear he said something more, something involving the words "stupid" and "twat," but I couldn't be certain over the pulse of the music.

Devon and Poufy Blonde came back just then.

"Nosebleed?" was all he said, raising an eyebrow at Aidan before handing him some napkins.

Poufy B. tittered, and Devon gave me a long look when Aidan snapped that he was going off to get another drink.

Devon's other girl materialized right about then, and the three of them went back to whispering whatever it was they were whispering to one another, and pretty much making out. All three of them.

I tried to maintain my natural dignity (stop laughing—I do too have some), but it wasn't easy. Honestly, Dru, have you ever known anyone so cursed as me? Ever since I met Aidan, I've had him on my list of men whom I badly wanted to know better, and when things finally started moving in that direction, I break the man's nose, and come close to gelding him.

I would have cried except that would have made my nose run, and I just didn't think I could cope with looking even more ridiculous.

Do you think sexy time with Fang has ruined me for other men? It doesn't feel like that's it, but at this point, I don't know what is going on with my sexual self. Maybe I'm just weird.

"You all right?" Devon asked when the two girls stopped nibbling on his face and started nibbling on each other's faces.

I nodded, but couldn't look at him, because then he'd see that I was fighting back tears.

"I know I'm not who you fancy, but would you like to dance?"

I almost burst into tears at that point, but we Williamses are made of pretty heavy-duty stuff, so instead I swallowed back the tears and nodded again. Devon took my hand and led me out to the dance floor. By then the two girls were snogging like crazy, which made me feel a little less guilty for taking Devon away from them.

"You look like you're going to a baby-roasting competition," Devon said while we were jammed together by the crowd, not so much dancing as more kind of bouncing up and down while rubbing on each other. It should have been a highly sensualized thing, but all I could do was worry about what sort of a fool I'd made of myself with Aidan.

"That is a singularly horrible analogy," I answered, summoning up a smile, which, if I'm honest, felt like it was pretty awful.

Judging by the way he flinched, I guess it was as bad as I thought. "I thought it suited the situation. Is there anything you want to tell me?"

Like what? I thought to myself. That I was an idiot? That I was sexually cursed, that I had thrown myself at a man and failed miserably—no, not just miserably, but in Typical Emily Fashion?

I shook my head.

"All right, then. Let me know if you need a shoulder to cry on." He winked at me and waggled his eyebrows, but all I did was tuck away a mental note that perhaps I should move him up a couple of positions on the Shag This Man Right Now list.

When we got back to the table, Aidan was there with Devon's two girls (who were now feeding each other bits of pineapple from a fruity drink) ... and Tash. She was leaning into Aidan, whispering to him. His eyes were on me, but he was whispering right back at her, and then she laughed.

Great. Just what I needed. He was telling her how the Curse of Emily had struck, and they were no doubt laughing at the gawkish American who was freaked out by a little ear-slugging and crotch-holding.

The sad thing is, Dru, that was the high point of the evening. The rest of it went downhill fast.

Aidan made it clear he wasn't thrilled with me, and to be honest, the wad of tissue he had stuffed up one nostril just reminded me of what a boob I was.

After some desultory conversation, Aidan sucked back yet another beer, belched, and said, "Last pint for me, mate," when

Devon came back with another round of drinks. "I promised Emily's dad I'd have her back safe and sound by ten."

"That was a joke," I said, horrified. "I am an adult. I can do whatever I want. Until I trashed my boss's car and went into debt for the next twenty-six years, I lived in a cute little apartment on my own. I had a boyfriend. I stayed out all night if I liked. And I had no trouble giving men hand jobs!"

Yes, all right, that was my wounded pride talking. And it was just my luck when I hit that last sentence that the music stopped, and everyone in the surrounding five miles heard me.

I banged my head on the table a couple of times as everyone broke into laughter. See? Curse of Emily.

"Isn't that cute? She's pissed," Tash said with her barracuda smile. ("Pissed," by the way, means drunk in England. I know! Sometimes they are so … British!)

I thought about telling Tash that she had a bit of green stuck in her teeth, then decided not to. It would serve her right to go around with food in her teeth and not know it.

"You know, I think perhaps you're right, and I have had enough of tonight." I stood up and looked around for my purse.

"When was the last time you had a curfew, Linda?" Tash asked. Linda was the poufy-haired blonde. She stopped necking with the redhead and looked over at us.

"My hubby doesn't care when I'm home, as long as I don't wake him when I come in."

"Hubby?" I asked, confused by what she was doing out with Devon and the redhead if she had a husband.

"We're polyam." She went back to snogging.

DRU Polyam?

EM Polyamorous. Multiple partners.

DRU Gotcha.

EM I didn't know you were awake.

DRU I'm not. Go on.

EM Tash smiled again, another really mean smile.

DRU They ought to put her out in cornfields—I bet the crows would take one look at her smile and drop down dead.

EM "I guess it's nice when a dad watches out for his special-needs daughter," Tash said with a knowing smirk. "But I couldn't stand being controlled like that."

"Wow, way to trash-talk people who are differently abled," I said, then realized I had made it sound like I was one of them. And then I thought—so what? Let her think what she wanted. I will admit that I hoped Aidan would say something in my defense, but all he did was finger the bridge of his nose and smile at Tash.

"I think it's a nice change," Devon suddenly said. He'd been watching some other woman a few tables away, evidently not bothered at all that his two dates were now clearly more into each other than him.

"What is?" Tash asked.

"A father who cares enough about his daughter that he wants her home before anything can happen to her."

"She's an adult!" Tash said, pointing at me.

Devon gave a half shrug. "Which just reinforces my point. Her father cares. My parents never worried about what I was doing. Hell, they were hardly around when I was growing up, and now they're far too busy enjoying themselves to do more than ring me on my birthday and Christmas."

I was thinking of the best way to respond to that (without being maudlin or trotting out platitudes) when Aidan interrupted my train of thought.

"Come along, then," he said after he drained his pint. He stood up and kind of swayed, which made me even more worried. You remember a few years ago when I told you that one of my cousins was killed when the guy she was riding with plowed into the side of the freeway overpass? Vicki was a few years older than us, and after that, I promised Mom and Brother that I'd never ride with anyone who was drunk.

And yet here I was about to ride home with Aidan. I'm not saying he was ripped to the tits, but he weaved a bit as we said good-bye to everyone.

I was sure Tash was going to make a stink, or offer to come with us, but she didn't. She just smiled and looked like the cat who'd eaten all the cream. "Come back as soon as you're done taking Cinderella home, love."

Aidan inclined his head in what could be a nod, or he could have been giving her a look that told her he'd rather be eaten alive by fire ants than hang out with her. I couldn't see—his back was to me—but after the kiss/nose episode, I was willing to bet it was the first.

It was at that point that I realized my dating had hit a new low.

"Godda bleed the sausage," Aidan said as we headed for the exit. There were bathrooms down inside the club, of course, but they had lines out the doors. Aidan muttered something about using the bathrooms for the other businesses in the building, and we toddled up a couple of flights of stairs to a long, cold hallway. "Stay here. Be out inna tick."

He went into the men's room. I rehearsed how I was going to gently yet firmly take the car keys away from him, and drive myself home (and then call him a ride so he'd get home safely), damning the laws prohibiting me from driving in England. A draft blew bits of paper, crumpled sticky notes, and a few other forms of debris around the floor, and although I could still hear the sound of the music from the club downstairs, the upper floor was quiet. Eerily quiet. The kind of quiet where you start imagining that a building is a living entity, and you are an invader in its guts.

Aidan came out of the bathroom. He didn't look annoyed, which was good, but he wasn't walking quite right, which was bad. I didn't want to get killed if he drove us home, so I trotted out my best excuse. "I was thinking that perhaps you'd let me drive home, since I'm going to need the practice of driving on the wrong side—"

Aidan pushed me up against the cold cement brick wall, his breath hot on my face. He smelled like beer and breath mints (not a thrilling combination, I can tell you). I gasped in surprise when his hands skimmed my body as he leaned into me.

"Oh, baby," he said. The way he said "baby" was just … well, creepy. I mean, part of me was relieved that he had changed his mind and wanted to kiss me again, but I wasn't sure if it was all the beer he'd drunk, or if he really did want me.

"Um … Aidan …" One hand was groping my breast, while the other was yanking up my skirt, and heading for Ground Zero. And suddenly, rather than enjoying a little wickedly public naughty time as I expected, I just wanted to get out of there. I felt trapped, and sick to my stomach. "You know, I don't think this is such a good idea."

"What's wrong, duck? You want this, I know you do. I can tell by the way you've been looking at me." He kissed me then, and I have to say that although I liked Aidan, I truly did—when he hadn't been drinking—at that moment, I really didn't want to be kissing him.

"Right, that's about enough of that," I said, shoving him back hard when his fingers tried to dip into me. "I'm sorry if I gave you the wrong impression—actually, I was more than willing to get a little busy with you, but that was before you started drinking. I have since changed my mind, so if you don't mind, I'm going to take your car keys, and will drive your car to my house so you don't try to drive it home. Then I'll call you an Uber and you can go wherever you want. Sound good? Excellent." I marched off before he could reply.

But not before he could grab me. He snagged my arm and jerked me back, not hard, but enough that it got my blood pumping, and not in a good way. "Little tease. The least you can do is take care of me."

"Take care of you?"

"You know what I mean. Open wide." He tried to shove me down onto my knees in front of him, but you know me—no means no, and if he didn't understand that, then he was going to suffer the Wrath of Emily.

"Dude, you have no idea just how stupid you are being," I said, and, making a fist, punched him in the noogies.

When he doubled over, swearing up a blue streak, I ran down the corridor to the stairs that led outside.

I know what you're thinking—what happened to wanting to jump Aidan's bones? All I can say is that there can be a huge difference between what you think is going to happen and what really does happen.

Part of me—Peacemaker Emily—wanted to make excuses for him, putting the blame on the beer he'd drunk, since he hadn't behaved like that to me other times. But then Honest and Insightful Emily pointed out that no one poured those drinks into Aidan but himself, and if he was going to get like that, then I didn't want to have anything to do with him.

At the same time, though, he really turned my crankshaft. I know, life is weird, and our emotions are the weirdest of all.

I ran downstairs, and just as I reached the door to go outside, it swung back. Devon stood in the doorway.

"Oh, hi," I said, feeling like an idiot for having jumped when the door opened.

"There you are. I was looking for you."

"For me? Why?"

He grinned. "Had an idea that Aidan was totally legless."

Oh, great, the worst night of my life, and I have to try to decipher more Englishisms. "Legless?"

"Pissed. Drunk."

"Oh. Yeah, he was a bit, so I ... uh ... I decided to make my own way home."

Devon held the door open for me. "I'll take you home if you like."

I stopped and gave him a long look. "What about your girlfriends?"

"I think you saw the answer to that," he said with a wry twist of his lips. "They wanted to bring me into the act, but obviously changed their minds."

"Oh. Sorry about that." I bit my lower lip as I considered him. "This is going to sound stupid, especially after that whole thing with my father, but how much have you had to drink?"

"Too much to drive," he said, handing me his keys. "I'll let you do the honors."

"That's awfully sweet of you. Are you sure you don't mind?"

He took my hand in his (it was nice and warm) and started off down the street to the car park. "Don't need to have my license taken away from me, now, do I? You can drive, yes?"

"Sure," I said, ignoring the spike of guilt that I didn't have a license anymore. And just so you know, yes, we made it to my house perfectly fine, but not because I drove. Just as we made it to the car, Linda and her redheaded girlfriend came trotting out, calling to Devon that they wanted a ride home, too. So I sat in the back with Devon while Linda dropped me off at home.

Devon got out of the car to walk me to the door, but he stopped after a few steps and whistled. "That's some house."

"It's haunted," I said, and considered informing him that my underwear drawer was possessed.

"Is it? I wouldn't doubt it. Lots of ghosts in these parts."

"That's heartening to know." We stopped at the door, and he gave me an odd look.

"Thanks, Devon. I appreciate you...and Linda and ... er ..."

"Patsy."

"Right, Patsy. I appreciate you guys bringing me home."

He grinned. "I enjoyed it. Been a while since I had the chance to be a gallant knight."

"Good night, Devon."

"Night, brainy bird." He put a hand on either arm and leaned forward until his lips just brushed mine. It was wonderful—until I realized exactly what it was: a pity kiss.

And so you have it—just when I thought I'd hit the all-time low in my dating life, I start getting pity kisses. Clearly, my romantic life has come to a premature end.

EM You're asleep again, aren't you?

EM Yell when you're awake. I need you to tell me that my life isn't as bleak as it seems right now.

CHAPTER TEN

EM You're still sleeping? Gah.

EM I'll go work on that stupid paper while I wait for you.

DRU LOGGED ON

DRU Soz, took one of Mom's sleeping pills and it knocked me on my ass. Let me read back.

DRU You wrote a whole book, didn't you?

EM It was a horrible evening. What do you think?

DRU Hang on, still reading.

DRU Wow. OK. Done.

EM My romantic life? Yeah, I agree.

DRU Aidan totally needs to apologize to you.

EM Agreed.

DRU You didn't lead him on, right?

EM I don't think so. I didn't touch him or flirt with him.

DRU Then he owes you an apology. Which you should accept gracefully, at which point you've got him by the short and curlies.

EM Who says I want Aidan by the short and curlies (and ew for the imagery)? I don't want to have a hold over the man—I want a relationship based on mutual attraction and respect, and all that other crap we women want, and seldom end up getting.

At least I sure don't.

DRU I can't blame you there.

EM Not to dis your advice, but I ended up talking to Bess about the situation.

DRU She is your sister. You're allowed.

EM I know, but you're my bestie, and you always have good advice. It's just that you were sleeping, and I was going crazy in my head.

DRU I know that feeling well. What'd sis say?

EM. Oy. You know how she's always yammering on about women empowering ourselves and not allowing men to objectify us, and all that business? Well, she came in this morning to borrow my red shawl, and she found me lying on my bed amidst the tattered remains of my romantic life.

"What's the matter, pip-squeak?" she asked as she dug around in my wardrobe for my shawl. "Got dumped by your date last night?"

I looked up from where I was hugging a Liam Hemsworth pillow (yes, I brought the set of all three brothers). "How did you know? Who told you? Does it show that I almost broke Aidan's nose and got my ring stuck on his fly, and he got his fingers into No-Man's-Land, at which point I punched him in the balls, and then Devon and his lesbian lovers had to drive me home, at which time any last hope for a romance in my life died a sad and miserable death upon the altar of the Pity Kiss I received? You can tell all that just by looking at me, can't you?"

She blinked a couple of times, turned around really slowly, then closed the door to the hall and dragged a chair over to the bed. "Whoa, there. I was just teasing you, Em. No one told me anything, although if all that happened to you, I don't blame you for rolling around on your bed with the Hemsworth brothers. You want to start at the top? You broke Aidan's nose? He stuck his hand in your hoohaw?"

DRU What is it with you Williams girls and your euphemisms?

EM One word: Brother.

DRU Point taken. Go on.

EM "Not quite to the first, and damned close to the second." I sniffled back a few tears of self-pity, and wiped my nose on Luke Hemsworth (I'll wash him later). "I think I'm cursed, Bess, I really do. First Fang goes away, evidently never to return, and then Aidan turns out to be an asshat when drunk."

She raised both her eyebrows. *If she doesn't watch out, she's going to have a Unibrow, too.* "Sounds like you did the right thing in taking him down."

"Oh, I know I did the right thing." The memory rose in my mind of him rolling around on the cold hallway floor, slurring various swear words. I started to snicker. "I shouldn't make light of it, because it definitely was not funny at the time, but … damn. Who walks up to a woman and grabs her by the crotch like she's a six-pack?"

"Men who get their balls bashed, that's who."

We looked at each other and started laughing. I laughed so hard I fell off the bed, which made Bess laugh even harder.

"See, you're feeling better already. OK, so what happened then?"

I told her the rest of the sad tale, ending with Devon clearly feeling sorry for me. "You don't think I was wrong for bashing Aidan in the dangly bits, do you? I mean, technically, that could be considered assault, although he sexually assaulted me first. But he has to work with Brother, and I expect I'll see him around and stuff, and I hate to make things … weird."

"No, I think you did the right thing. First of all, to hell with his feelings. He certainly wasn't thinking about you at all—he clearly just wanted to get his rocks off. And second, who cares if Brother has to work with him. It's not like he's going to bitch that you wouldn't go down on him after fingering you in a hallway."

"Jeez, Bess, make it sound as tawdry as you can," I protested.

She shrugged, stood up, and went back to the wardrobe to pull out my red shawl. "Well, if you want my two cents, I think you were right to dump Aidan. Fang is clearly the guy you should be with, and he obviously has the hots for you."

I stared at her. I don't know who she had been listening to for the last ten minutes, but it hadn't been me. "What, are the voices in your head talking again? Fang is up in the north somewhere doing vet things to livestock. It was Devon who brought me home, via the lesbians, and he—*Devon*—doesn't have the hots for me. He barely noticed me, to be honest, and clearly, he has lots of other interests. How many lesbians do you know who want to bring a man into their fun time? He's just a nice guy who realized his buddy was too snockered to think straight."

"Uh-huh. Right. He was so worried about his friend that he left a club to take you home. Sure." She leaned over and patted me on my cheek. "One day you're going to open your eyes and you'll see what sort of guy is really worth your time. Until then, keep waving the banner of womanhood. No man has the right to do anything to you that you don't want."

"Preaching to the choir," I said tiredly.

"You know …" Bess stood in the middle of my room and tapped a finger on her chin. "I think you should come with me when I go to the Womyn's Festival and Celebration of Self. Monk's sister is holding an awareness hour at her house over in Alling. I think it would do you good."

I hugged Chris Hemsworth to my chest. "I've already told you my life is too busy to join in any protests right now."

"This isn't a protest. It's a festival of empowerment, to get in touch with your inner goddess."

"No blockades?" I asked her, suspicious. You know how she tricked us into going to that Greenpeace rally in Seattle, and we ended up with red paint on us from where they were throwing it on the gillnetters. Not that I like them, but it took me a good week and a half to get the paint totally out of my hair. "No paint or air horns or anything like that?"

"Just a bunch of women getting to know their deepest, innermost selves."

"Like I need that?"

"Can't hurt."

"Hmm." To be honest, it didn't sound too bad. They'd probably play Sarah McLachlan songs, light incense, and meditate a lot on the joy of the yang. Or yin. I never can remember which is the feminine part.

"You can bring your friend, the one with the rabbit teeth. What's her name?"

"Holly," I said, bristling a bit on Holly's behalf. She's only been over to the house once, but looked worried the whole time. "Hmm. You know, that might not be a bad idea. I've been working on her to realize her self-esteem is important to her mental health, and perhaps a good old-fashioned Celebration of Self might help show her that everyone has crap they have to cope with."

"Do you both good." She threw one last piece of advice over her shoulder before she left. "If this Aidan has any feelings for you, he'll be on his knees groveling before you, apologizing for his behavior. If he doesn't, he's not worth it."

"Amen to that, sister," I said with a sigh.

EM You still there? Did you fall asleep again?

DRU No, was getting coffee.

EM So, thoughts?

DRU On Aidan? Gotta say that if you don't super fancy him, I think Bess is right.

EM The problem is, he's so nice when he's not drunk.

DRU 'Tis a puzzle.

EM What on earth did you put in that coffee? Your normal pollutant?

DRU Baileys. Ran out of creamer, and Baileys is cream, right?

EM Yeah, with a punch in it. Crapbeans, I'm going to have to go. I promised Holly I'd go with her to the local library so she can do her research project. Oh, I forgot to mention that I bought a mousetrap and put it in my undie drawer.

DRU Go, you, with your bad scientific self!

EM Don't drink too much "coffee."

DRU Heh. Laters.

EM Hugs and kisses.

YOU LOGGED ON

DRU It's tomorrow. That is, it's today. Monday. And you are eight hours ahead. What did Mr. Gropey say when you saw him?

EM Hi.

DRU Hi. What did he say? And where have you been all day?

EM Phone battery died. I had to get a new one after class.

DRU So?

EM Aidan wasn't at school. No one knows what's happened to him. You can't die of an almost broken nose, can you? Devon said he's not answering his phone, and no one has seen him since the club. I asked Peg and Lalla where they thought he was, but they had no idea what he's up to. Even Brother is annoyed at him for not showing up for work without an explanation.

DRU Oh lordy, you killed him with the punch to the huevos!

EM I can just see the headlines now—"Emily Williams: Dates with Her Are So Horrendous, Men Don't Recover from Them."

DRU I doubt if you actually killed him.

EM Then where is he?

DRU Dunno. He might be hungover, or maybe he just doesn't want to face you after he acted like such a douchecanoe.

EM Meh.

DRU How are things other than that?

EM So-so. Undie ghost was at it again.

DRU That is so insanely weird. Have you looked at your parents' fingers closely? No signs that they are tripping the mousetrap?

EM Nope. I don't see how they can be setting off the trap, but almost every day when I come home, my underwear is all over the place. I'm going to have to take the next step and coat the drawer handle with itching powder or something. Oh, how's the walking cast?

DRU Liberating! I drove to Starbucks this morning. It was a bit clunky walking, but I'm just so relieved to be out of the house.

EM I bet. Do you have any plans now that you're mobile again?

DRU So, Vance and I were supposed to go to Whistler, but that's not happening.

EM It's the wrong time of year for snow, and even if there was some, you can't exactly ski.

DRU Just my luck I'd break my other leg.

EM So are you and V doing anything else, then?

DRU Nope.

EM Um. Is everything OK?

DRU With me? Of course.

EM It's just that you don't sound disappointed or anything about the trip to Whistler being off.

DRU I'm not disappointed.

EM ...

EM OK, now I'm worried. What's up, girlfriend?

DRU With what?

EM You're evading the question. You only do that when you have something to say but don't know how to say it. Do I sense things are a bit iffy with the V-man?

DRU We're ... apart, yes.

EM Wait, what? You are? What happened?

DRU Not much, really.

EM Dru! Spill your guts! You know I'd do the same for you.

DRU It's just that V feels like a stranger whenever we talk. He was planning on spending the long weekend with me, but then his plans changed and he was going to spend it all with his cousin. They were going to go diving at some underwater park. We just don't connect anymore, you know?

EM Holy crapballs! I'm so sorry. Do you want to vent about him? Is he being an ass, or do you think you guys have just grown apart?

DRU Definitely grown apart. That business with Tabitha was the warning that things couldn't get patched up.

EM But you said he apologized and you were all cool with it.

DRU That was before he took Tab out to see the new Marvel movie last night.

EM *wide eyes*

DRU #eh #it'sok #overhimagain

EM Do you need hugs?

DRU No, I'm fine.

EM ...

DRU ?

EM Why are you fine? You shouldn't be fine. You should be having a hissy fit to end all hissy fits. Something is up. Did he say mean things to you? No, he couldn't have done that, because you'd be swearing up a blue streak if he had, and making threats against his private parts.

EM Dru.

EM Why are you fine?

DRU You're the only person I know who would question why I was happy about breaking up with my boyfriend.

EM !!!

DRU Dude, I'm peachy. I decided, in a mature and insightful manner, to take a long look at our relationship and where it was going, and decided that we really were not meant to be together. I'm not mad at him. I'm just relieved that I don't have to spend my time worried about what he's doing, to be honest. This was the best choice for us. Now we can both start building meaningful relationships elsewhere.

EM WHO ARE YOU AND WHAT HAVE YOU DONE WITH DRU?

EM Seriously, you decided this when? Last night?

DRU Yeah. You were asleep or I would have asked you what you thought. So ... what do you think?

EM I ... well, I guess if you are happy, then it's a good thing.

EM I'm just a little surprised.

DRU Why? You said Vance was a weasel.

EM Not that you decided to kick his ass to the curb, but that you're ... well ...

DRU ???

EM Fine, I'll just say it. You're being way too calm.

DRU I'm the same as I've always been. You make me sound like I'm a big ole drama llama.

EM If the llama fits, wear it.

DRU I bah at you.

EM This from the girl who threatened to burn down her house the day she found a spider nest in the basement.

DRU Spider. Nest. *In the house.*

EM It was three spiders.

DRU THAT WE KNEW OF! There could have been more.

EM And they'd been dead for at least a year, according to the exterminator.

DRU I still think Mom was insane for believing him. Once spiders have set up a nest in your house, they will never leave. NEVER!

EM That's the Drama Dru I know and love. Now tell me how you feel about Vance.

DRU Meh.

EM Something is going on. Why are you so calm about this? Why are you all meh when you would normally be ranting and wailing and threatening to cut off your hair and joining some weird back-to-nature cult that sells pink Himalayan salt at roadside stalls? Wait … you're not … you haven't … oh my god, you have someone else!

DRU The way your mind works is frightening.

EM AHA! You didn't deny it! You've met someone and you haven't told me! DRU! You have to tell me everything! Who is he? Where did you meet him? What does he do? Do you want me to send you my erotic massage book? It's not like I'm going to get any use out of it at the rate I'm going, and to think I went to all the trouble of getting it from India. Tell me every single thing about this man you have lined up.

DRU Well …

DRU If you must know …

EM Oh, hell yes!

DRU He happens to be a UPS driver.

EM How did you meet … oh!

DRU Yup. Mom's addiction to subscription boxes has finally paid off.

EM Wow. I want to say that's romantic that he wooed you with packages for your mom while you were housebound, but it's kind of … hmm.

DRU Anyway, we've chatted a few times, and seem to hit it off pretty well.

EM You didn't tell me!

DRU I didn't know how I felt about him. And I thought Vance was still with me.

EM Gotcha. You didn't want to be leading him on. So, tell me everything about him!

DRU We're going to get together on Wednesday.

EM On a date? All right, first of all, I know he knows where you live, but do not meet this guy anywhere private. Go to a Starbucks or somewhere like that, and be sure to tell everyone where and when you are meeting him. And then text me when you're done with the date, so I don't have to call the cops from England.

DRU LOL!

EM I'm serious, girlfriend!

DRU As a matter of fact, we are meeting for coffee, and I promise not to get in his car and go anywhere with him, all right?

EM OK, but you have to text as soon as you're done. Now, tell me everything there is to know about him. What's his name? Do you have a picture of him? Have you done a social media investigative background search on him? What's he like? TELL ALL!

DRU Er …

DRU Not right now.

DRU You're not hurt, are you?

EM Kind of. Why don't you want to tell me about him?

DRU It's still too … you know … new.

DRU You understand, right?

EM Well … not really, because I always want to tell you everything about the men in my life—not that I have any at present until my friend with bennies rolls back into town—but I can respect your need for privacy. Just let me know when you are ready to talk about it.

DRU You'll be the first one. I just want a little time to process things.

EM Gotcha. Can I be excited for you, though?

DRU Yes. How's Holly doing?

EM Nice change of subject.

DRU I thought so.

EM She's maintaining. Her gym class had their first hockey practice today. Well, I should say *our* first hockey practice, because somehow, Holly talked me into donning the pervy games skirt (as they call it—well, not the pervy part), and the next thing I knew, I was running around in tennis shoes and shin guards, with the ever-so-attractive gum guards firmly clenched between my teeth.

Honestly, if I ever imagined this tutoring job would force me to relive high school, I would have run, far, far away from Mum A. Although I will admit the paychecks are nice. I was able to send a big wad to drop on the amount I owe for that car I totaled.

You know me, Dru: I'm not the most athletic person in the world, although I like tennis and I can do Pilates so long as I don't try to use the ball, but the purpose of field hockey escapes me.

DRU You and me both.

EM At least with real hockey, you get to ice-skate, but with this sort of hockey, all you do is run around with your shoes squeaking on the gym floor as you chase after a stupid ball. Of course, I got stuck with a bunch of the Snickerers on my team, and despite the fact that the gym coach told me to stay in the rear and try to pick up the game as it was played, Snickerer Ann made sure she messed with me every chance she got.

"Hey!" I yelled the first time she whacked me on the shin guards. It hurt! "Knock it the hell off!"

"Don't be such a crybaby," she sneered, then said loudly to the coach, "Miss! Williams is swearing again."

"Is there a problem, Williams?" Ashley the gym coach asked.

I glared at Ann and fired up Emily, Weapon of Vengeance. "No problem that I can't solve," I said, gritting my teeth.

Ann and Bee double-teamed me after that, taking turns to smack me on the shins, or "accidentally" hit me with their sticks. You'll be glad to know that I got in a few good smacks to both of them, but got called out for high-sticking each time.

DRU *Bastardos. Bastardas?* Which is right for plural females?

EM Bitches.

DRU That's so mundane. We can do better. I'll think about it.

EM Holly was thrilled each time I got one of the two asswipes, and just at the end of the game, Bee waited until Coach Ashley was looking away; then she stuck her stick out as Holly and I ran past, which made us both fall. Ann saw me on the floor and hit the ball straight at my head. I curled up to keep from being brained by it, and waited until Bee charged forward.

DRU Holy crapballs!

EM As soon as Bee was a foot away, I lunged up, twirled my stick in the best gunslinger manner, caught Bee in the gut with the stick, and then swung it around to nail Ann smartly on the shins. They both went down, crying foul.

DRU WOOT! You are da man!

EM "Williams! You're out!" Ashley said, clapping her hands. "And you should be ashamed of yourself for attacking those girls in that manner."

I grinned at the two weasels in question. They snarled in return.

DRU Bitchitas! That's the word I was looking for.

EM It fits them. Holly hobbled over to stand with me. "It wasn't her fault, Miss Ashley. Bee and Ann deliberately tripped us."

"That will do. Williams, you will report to the headmaster's office."

The Snickerers snickered. I sighed heavily, and headed toward the locker room to change into my normal clothes, because I was damned if I was going to put that foul uniform on after spending an hour in the perv skirt. I know the gym teacher thought she was punishing me by sending me to see Russell Crowe, but I didn't mind. We were developing quite a rapport, and spent our time together talking about his honeymoon trip down the West Coast. Honestly, if he was ten years younger, and didn't have a wife and two kids, all of whom he clearly adored, I might have put him on my Make Mad, Passionate Monkey Love To list.

DRU Ew!

EM What ew?

DRU He's Holly's uncle. That seems just too incestuous.

EM Your sense of weirdness has gone off. He's not related to me. He's a bit old, but eh.

DRU There's nothing wrong with an older man. But the relationship with Holly … *shudder*

EM It's a moot point. I don't really have the hots for him, and he has a wife and kids, so you don't need to work up your sister-wives lecture.

DRU Seriously! How can those women live like that? How can they buy into that whole "man must have multiple women" crap?

EM I'm going to toddle before you get into full rant mode. I'm meeting with Holly's parents to give them an update on how things are going (she actually volunteered to join the Halloween party group, which has expanded to be a community thing). Evidently they want to talk to me about taking a trip with Holly in January, which might be fun, assuming it's somewhere warm, with lots of dishy men just waiting to be ogled.

DRU Oooh. I vote for the Riviera.

EM Me too. Smooches and hugs, and call if you need me, OK?

DRU Backatcha.

CHAPTER ELEVEN

EM I return, filled with news of my sad and pathetic life.

EM Pooh, you aren't here yet.

EM I'll just dump this here for you to read when you come back.

My big news concerns Aidan. I saw him heading into the library at Gobbottle, and since everyone says he owes me an apology, I just looked through him and continued my way to being diverse. He said something, but I couldn't hear what.

The whole time I was in class, I worried. What if he'd tried to apologize, and I denigrated his attempt to make things right? That wasn't fair. If the man wanted to apologize, then I should let him do so. After all, we were civilized beings, even if one of us got his balls whomped.

After class I toddled off to the library, and then suddenly realized I had nothing to do there. I mean, I could stroll around looking for books, but I didn't need anything, and besides, I didn't want to be too obvious. So instead I went over to the computers, and parked myself next to a rack of career pamphlets that looked like they'd been left over from the 1970s.

"There you are. I've been hoping to see you before lunch."

I grabbed a pamphlet, then spun around with a nonchalant expression. "Hello. Aidan, is it?"

He grimaced. "I deserve that. Hello, Emily."

"I didn't see you. I just stopped by for a quick look at info on being a"—I looked down at the pamphlet in my hand—"mortician."

He gave a little laugh and tucked a strand of my hair behind my ear. "Really?"

"It's a lost art," I said, and waited.

"I'm glad I found you here. I've wanted to talk to you, but I was sick with a cold for a few days—"

A cold! Why didn't I think of that?

"—but I wanted to apologize for the other day. I had a bit too much to drink, and you know how it is—you're out with your mates and things get a bit fuzzy."

"Fuzzy?" I said, squinting at him. "Dude, you had your fingers in an area they hadn't been invited to, and that's not due to you being fuzzy."

"You're right, you're absolutely right. I was way out of line, and I can only say that I thought you were as interested in me as I was in you. Forgive me?" He tipped his head and gave me a little smile when he said the last bit.

I waffled. On the one hand, he'd treated me horribly. On the other hand, not only did he get punched in the balls; he admitted he was wrong, and apologized. I decided, after a moment of staring in thought at the mortician pamphlet, that I would give him the benefit of the doubt.

"Sure. Just … don't let it happen again, OK?"

"Never," he said, rubbing his thumb over my bottom lip. "Maybe we can go out to the club again. I promise I won't give you any reason to give me a nosebleed, or make me walk funny for a day."

I refuse to apologize for taking action to protect myself, but I did acknowledge the damage I might've done. "Is everything all right down there?" I asked, waving toward his crotch.

He gave me a look that made me blush a bit. "You'll have to find that out for yourself."

"Uh … OK. So, speaking of things you can do to make up for behaving so atrociously, in a bizarre way that is too unbelievable to mention, I've been put in charge of my tutoree Holly's school Halloween party. They decided to open it up to the community as a fund-raiser for a group of special-needs kids who need some equipment to go for horse rides. And I thought you might want to come along to the party and help out."

"A *high school* party?" he asked, looking downright horrified.

"Not just high school; there will be kids of all ages attending. We need chaperones to make sure none of the older kids get up to anything they shouldn't be doing, as well as people to handle the haunted house for the younger kids, and people to decorate for the dance part of the party, and that sort of thing. What shall I put you down for?"

He grimaced. "I suppose I could help out at the dance if you really needed me."

"Excellent. Everyone will be in costume, so you'll want to find something for yourself."

He made another face. I waited for him to ask me what costume I'd be wearing, but he said nothing else about it.

Later, I met Aidan and his cronies for lunch at the dining hall. I mentioned the Halloween party to Lalla and Peg, both of whom instantly volunteered to help. Even Lalla's boyfriend, Digger (who was not an archaeology student despite having the perfect name for it), said he'd help.

"What's your theme going to be?" Peg asked, poking her fork through a sad-looking salad.

I sighed dramatically. "Vampire Ball."

She gave me a look.

"Oh, don't even go there," I told the look. "It wasn't my idea. The school insisted that the kids got to pick the theme, and that's what they went for. I told them it was so 2010, but no, they insisted on it. I figure any costume, Goth or historical, will qualify."

"Oooh, costumes," Lalla said, poking Digger. "We can go as Bella and—"

"No," Peg interrupted, giving Lalla a hard look. "Don't say it. If you do, I will have to stake you."

Lalla made a face, then looked thoughtful. "I guess we could pick something a little less obvious."

"What will you wear?" Peg asked me.

I glanced at Aidan to see if he noticed the question, but he was too busy talking to Digger about some football (aka soccer) game that had just been played.

"I'm not sure. Holly—she's my tutoree—wants to go as a wraith, but I think we can do better than that for her. If you have any ideas for a couple of good costumes, lay them on me."

Peg murmured that she would put her mind to it, and that was the end of the Great Aidan Apologizes Event.

Man, I'm pooped. Going to bed now.

Hope you're back online by the time I get up tomorrow.

Miss you.

EM Notice I haven't once asked about Mr. Mysterious?

EM I think I should get a tiara for that.

YOU LOGGED ON

EM OMIGOD OMIGOD OMIGOD!

EM I just got into bed and Holly texted. Her non–Russell Crowe uncle works for a paper in London, and he told her that he'd heard that Chris Hemsworth will be in Hartford Forest (about two miles north of here) the week after next. Holy schnitzballs, girl, I have to be there! I will have my picture taken with him, or I will die in the attempt.

EM She who would be the future Mrs. Hemsworth except that he's happily married, and I probably wouldn't like being married to him despite his glorious six-pack.

YOU LOGGED ON

EM I'm going to kill my sister.

EM Sigh. Still not here?

DRU LOGGED ON

DRU Hellos.

EM There you are. Where've you been?

DRU Went shopping. Had to go with Mom to see my grandma. Had "I can walk again" celebratory high tea with Evans. Picked up new contacts. Yay about the Hemsworth thing. Why are you going to kill your sister?

EM How's Ev?

DRU Fine. She dumped her girlfriend, so we consoled each other over nommy tea and scones. What's up with Bess?

EM When you didn't show up after my Aidan bit last night, I thought you might have gone off with your mystery dude. I was trying to decide at what point I call your mom and ask if she knows your whereabouts.

DRU I snort at you. Besides, our coffee date is tomorrow.

EM Whew. I was worried.

DRU What. Is. Up. With. Bess?

EM What isn't? Lordaloo, Dru, I'm so going to have to kill her, bury her in the backyard, and then brainwash the Oldsters into forgetting she was a family member. At the very least I have formally disowned her.

DRU Gah! What did she do to you? Stop tormenting me and just tell me!

EM OK, but this is going to be lengthy. I have my phone plugged in so using the voice-to-text doesn't kill the new battery.

Where to start ... well, you remember that the other day I was going to take Holly to some woman's shindig that Bess recommended? A get-in-touch-(HA!)-with-yourself kind of thing? Well, we went to Bess's BF's sister's house (the BF in question being Monk), and everyone was sitting in the living room having healthy snackies, and drinking expensive waters, and chatting about auras and chakras. There was a chanting CD on the stereo, and lots of big pillows were scattered on the floor. I figured it would be a couple of hours of "inner goddess" time, and then we'd be off for home so I could figure out a way to get Holly off her idea of wraith costume, and into something where she wouldn't be covered by layers of gauze.

DRU *It* clown?

EM Ugh. No. She'd be freaked out by it. And so, for that matter, would I.

DRU Mina what's-her-face from *Dracula*.

EM That might be better. Especially if I could get her a black leather corset.

DRU Feral Sailor Moon. Werewolf's victim. Grandmother of dragons (instead of mother—get it?).

EM I'm going to have to ask you to put down the crack pipe now.

DRU I'll think more on the perfect costume while you tell me what embarrassing thing Bess did at this chakra party.

EM You do that. So, Holly and I sat down on pillows near a corner, and all of a sudden, rather than the lights dimming, a bunch more were turned on, and Monk's sister came out with a big box. She started handing stuff out, but while she was doing that, the women around us began taking off their clothes. Holly made kind of a choking sound. I thought her eyes were going to pop out of her head.

DRU Oh my fucking god!

EM "What on earth …" I watched in horror as clothes went flying. "Dear god. My sister has become a lesbian and she wants us to join an orgy with her. And you're *so* underage. Quick, Holly, run for the door. I'll distract them until you get out. Call my mom if I don't come out right after you!"

DRU Holy cheezeballs!

EM Holly jumped up and stood like a deer in headlights. I scrambled to my feet and prepared to fight off anyone who was going to try to stop her, but just at that moment, Bess came over waving a couple of clear plastic things that looked like deranged nutcrackers with long bills at us. "What's the matter with you two? You look like you've seen a ghost."

DRU!!!

EM "Ghosts I can deal with, but this little orgy you've planned will have to go ahead without us. We're not into that sort of thing, and Holly is very underage. You're lucky if no one calls the police! And you can just bet I'm going to be telling Mom what sort of stuff you are doing behind her back."

DRU You go, girl!

EM Bess rolled her eyes and shoved a plastic thing at each of us. "It's not an orgy, stupid—it's a self-awareness party. I told you that."

I looked around. Everyone was laughing and chatting and acting just like they weren't all naked. "You are too strange, Bess. We don't need to get naked to be self-aware. You can have your plastic thing back. I won't need it."

"Problems?" Monk's sister came up, the only one besides Bess and Holly and me who still had her clothes on. Holly was staring over my shoulder in horror at a woman who was on a floor pillow. She had the plastic thingie and was shoving the bill part up her Glory, Glory, Hallelujah.

DRU I just don't have any words left.

EM "Don't look," I whispered to Holly, and had to forcibly turn her around so she wouldn't see the orgy. "I'll get you for this, Bess, so help me god, I will. Holly is young, and sensitive, and has enough self-esteem issues without you deliberately shocking her with images of women sticking sexy things up themselves."

Holly squawked her agreement.

"Stop being such a little twit," Bess said to me, then turned to the M's sister. "No problem, they just don't understand what the purpose of the evening is."

The M's sister laughed. "No wonder you have those surprised looks on your faces. You're holding a speculum, a tool used by gynecologists to examine your vagina and cervix."

I turned about a hundred shades of red.

DRU You're right. You have to kill her and bury the body.

EM "Jeez, Em, haven't you ever been to a gynecologist?" Bess frowned at me, and waved a duck-billed speculum in my general direction. "Stop making such a big scene. You're embarrassing me."

"Of course I've been to a gynecologist, but I don't examine all the stuff she uses on me," I said in a vicious whisper. "And let's not be casting the embarrassing blame around, because you take the cake on that, you really do. Look at Holly, just *look* at what you've done to her!"

Holly weaved where she stood, like she was going to pass out or something. I grabbed her arm and held her upright.

"The purpose of this evening is to examine our cervixes, and become familiar and comfortable with our femininity and reproductive organs," Monk's sister said, patting Holly on the arm. "It's very empowering, you know, and something that is recommended for women of all ages. It'll give you confidence."

"How?" Holly asked, and I had to admit I was proud of the way she managed to put her horror aside in order to ask a question. I made a mental note to share that with her parents, then decided that perhaps I'd leave out the context of it.

"More importantly, why?" I asked. "I get that you want to look at that part that we can't really see, and only doctors and lovers really get to explore, but why for all that's good and green on this earth would you want to stare at it?"

The M's S smiled. "The pelvis is an area of a woman's anatomy that is often a mystery to us. Self-exams offer us the ability to really know our bodies, even that part that we don't normally see. As your knowledge of yourself and your body grows, you will take back the power to care for yourself, to know what your body is going through, and to understand the changes that happen over time. No longer will you have to rely on others to diagnose what's happening in your own body—you'll be able to tell for yourself, because you'll *know* yourself."

Holly sank down onto the floor into a blob-like shape, whimpering quietly to herself.

"If I wanted to see cervixes, I'd be a doctor," I told Monk's sister. "What you're talking about is just flat-out weird. Especially in this situation."

"It's fascinating, Em, it really is," Bess said. "You can see everything. It's amazing down there. Did you know that the walls of your vagina are a pretty, glistening pink?"

"You keep your eyes out of my vagina," I said quickly, clutching my hands in front of my crotch, which was silly, but she was still holding the duck bill, and I wouldn't put it past her to wrestle me to the ground and force me to look at my innards.

"Don't be such an idiot, Em. You have to take back your own body!"

I grabbed Holly and pulled her up to her feet. Her eyes looked wild, like she wasn't aware of her surroundings. I pushed her toward the door. I had no idea how we were going to get home, but I didn't care. I just wanted out of that den of cervix-peekers.

"The medical industry has hijacked our bodies," Monk's sister said, following with Bess as Holly and I stepped over naked women on the way to the door. "They've stripped us of our autonomy. We have to take back what's our due."

"Ignorance is enslavement," Bess added. "Don't rely on someone else for knowledge about your body—learn to love yourself. Empower yourself. Examine yourself. Touch yourself!"

"Eek!" Holly shrieked as she saw what the woman with the plastic speculum was doing. She had a flashlight and a mirror and was looking up inside herself. Hell, we could all see up inside her.

"And that's it," I said, holding my hand over Holly's eyes. "We are so out of here. Stop trying to empower us. We would rather be ignorant."

"Yes," Holly whispered. "I want to be ignorant."

"Ignorance is bliss! Bess, so help me god, stop touching me with that thing, or I will not be responsible for what orifice you find it stuffed into!"

Holly made a gabbling sound that warned she was close to ralphing, so I flung open the door and shoved her through it.

"Emily, come back here!"

"I'm going to tell Mom!" I yelled at Bess, then turned and ran after Holly as she raced down the path to the street.

DRU I am utterly and completely speechless. Well, except for this. But other than this, speechless!

EM It was raining, but honest to Pete, Dru, neither Holly nor I noticed it. She was half crying, and gasping, and babbling about never wanting to see inside herself, and it took me a good half an hour of telling her that Bess wasn't really my sister before she calmed down enough that I got us on a bus back to POTW.

DRU If it wasn't so illegal, I'd suggest pouring booze in her and getting her so drunk she forgot everything that happened.

EM Don't think I didn't consider that. Luckily, by the time I got her home, she was seeing the humor in the situation, although her laughter was a bit shaky.

"Thanks for ... uh ..." She stopped when we got to her front door.

"No," I said, shaking my head. "There is no thanking me for a fun outing. That was atrocious, and we both know it. But hey, look at it this way, you faced the cervix head on, and survived!"

She giggled at my punny sentence, and then did something that took me by surprise—she gave me a hug, and said quickly, "Thank you for being my friend. It means a lot to me, even if we have to face vaginas together."

Then she dashed into her house, and I walked home feeling pretty damned good, like I'd made a difference in someone's life.

DRU You are my hero.

EM Awww. Thank you. That means a lot. I'm really trying to be supportive in whatever she wants to do, so long as it's not harmful.

DRU I sniffle at you.

EM After I got home, I filled Mom in about what happened.

"Those sorts of things go on," she said, stirring a pot of mushroom and wild rice soup. "I don't see anything wrong with it, even given Holly's age, although I agree Bess should have asked the Altons' permission first."

"If you had seen the way Bess came at us with that speculum," I said, shuddering. "I'd say that I thought it was a clear sign she's a lesbian, except no lesbian I know would ever dream of doing that."

"Not to mention the fact that she has a boyfriend," Mom pointed out.

"Then she's certifiably insane. I would be happy to draw up the papers to formally throw Bess out of the family."

Mom cocked an eyebrow at me.

"Too far?" I asked.

"Very much so."

"You realize that simply confirms the fact that she is your and Brother's favorite."

DRU She so totally is.

EM "Emily," Mom said with a warning note in her voice.

I sighed and got to my feet, snagging a piece of celery as I did so. "Fine, but I bet if I ran around shoving speculums up myself and showing everyone my cervix, you'd kick me out of the family pretty damned fast."

Bess came down the next morning and started to read me a lecture about how I embarrassed her in front of her friends, but I told her I was de-sistering her, and therefore she was a stranger, and since I didn't know her, I didn't have to listen to her. So I didn't.

The only bad thing about this is that I was counting on Bess to head up the haunted-house decorating committee. Now we'll have to find someone else.

DRU I hope you do. You have horrible decorating sense.

EM I do not! I'm awesome at decorating.

DRU Two words: SimEmily's house.

EM That doesn't count—it's virtual. Besides, I was thinking of getting a fog machine. It'll be a kick-ass party with a fog machine, don't you think?

DRU I fear for Piddlington.

EM Gah.

YOU LOGGED ON

EM Hey.

EM It's after five your time.

EM Why haven't you texted me? What are you doing? You aren't gettin' it on with this UPS dude, are you? Not that it's any of my business, only I want to make sure you haven't been murdered and dumped by the side of the road.

EM Let me know when you're done having steamy UPS sex.

DRU LOGGED ON

DRU I'm here, I'm here. Stop worrying that Richard murdered me and chopped me up into little bits, then force-fed me to his hogs.

DRU Not that he has any.

DRU Hogs, that is.

EM Oh, thank god, you're alive! Richard, did you say?

EM Richard who?

DRU Richard Gatling. Yes, like the gun, and no, he's not related.

DRU He's … oh, it's hard to put into words. He's very sweet, very thoughtful, and was so interested in me.

DRU What a change it made from He Who Shall Not Be Named.

EM Voldemort?

DRU No, silly, Vance.

EM Oh, that he.

DRU Anyhoo, Richard has two beagles named Darwin and Edwina that he takes running with him every morning.

DRU He asked me to go running with him just as soon as I get the cast off, and my leg can take exercise.

DRU Naturally, I said I'd love to.

EM You hate running.

DRU That's neither here nor there. He's a wee bit … older … but not so old that he's ancient.

DRU And he likes the same things I like! He loves an Americano extra hot, and likes to people-watch, and loves indie rock.

DRU He's perfect for me, he really is.

DRU Um.

DRU Em?

EM Hmm?

DRU You're googling him, aren't you?

EM Would I do that?

EM Is he the Richard Gatling who lives in North Seattle, is thirty-three, and recently sold a condo in Bellevue, or is he the Richard Gatling who was up for felony assault seven years ago, and has a panorama tattoo of the Seattle skyline around his neck?

DRU I knew it!

DRU And he wasn't convicted of the felony assault—it was thrown out of court for lack of evidence.

EM I GASP AT YOU!

DRU Ha! Gotcha. He's the first one, naturally.

EM I kind of figured. He is a bit old, isn't he?

EM But I suppose if you guys really have things in common, then you can cope with the age difference.

DRU We'll see. I'm taking it slow. We're going out tomorrow night for pizza, but I told him I had plans the following morning, and couldn't stay out late. Just in case he had hot lovin' ideas.

EM Smart thinking. Does V know?

DRU About pizza date? No, but he knows I'm seeing someone.

EM Good. I think you'll be happier without him.

DRU That's all the news I have. What's going on in your soap opera life?

EM Sheesh. You don't want to know.

DRU Fang dump you?

EM Fang? What does Fang have to do with anything?

EM Why does everyone keep bringing up Fang?

EM No, he didn't dump me, not that we're a couple to begin with.

EM I got an e-mail from him that he's gone to Ireland to help with some dire outbreak of … shoot, now I can't remember it. Something to do with sheep innards. Whatever it was, it's bad enough to keep him from heading back down here to sex me up as is right and proper.

DRU Either he really likes his vet stuff, or …

EM Oh! You did not just ellipsis what I think you ellipsised!

DRU Is that even a word?

EM I don't know, but I don't care when my best friend in the whole entire world implies that a man would go to Ireland to mess around with sick sheep just to avoid gettin' it on with me.

DRU OK, OK, I take back my ellipses.

EM I should think so. Anyway, Holly and I were in town to pick up some dye to put on the handle of my undie drawer, and we ran into Devon.

DRU How is she? Has she recovered from the Great Vag Invasion?

EM You seriously need to rethink that title. But she's fine. Actually, she seems to be much perkier, and I haven't had to go to quite so many of her classes, because she says she's OK in them on her own, which is nice. Although I miss the school-time money.

DRU What's new in the world of hunk-of-burnin'-love Devon, aka possible bunnymuffin lovetoy?

EM Ha. I wish. He invited me to a party he's throwing for his birthday. And because Holly was standing with me, he invited her.

DRU Oh dear.

EM Yeah. I have to find a nice way to tell her that it's not going to be appropriate for her to be there, without crushing her newfound self-confidence.

DRU Ouch. Good luck.

EM Then there was … um …

DRU Um?

DRU Spit it out, girlfriend.

EM Sigh. OK, but I don't want to hear any I-told-you-so comments.

DRU Uh-oh. What happened?

EM While Holly and I were yakking with Devon, I asked if he'd seen Aidan around. And he said no, but he wasn't surprised if he (Aidan) was still tired from his visit to London.

DRU Did we know about this visit to London?

EM I certainly didn't. He told me he had a cold. So I said, "Oh, he went to London?"

And Dev said, "Aid went up with Quint and a couple of birds."

DRU Before I put on my shocked face, who is Quint?

EM Aidan's older brother. He's some sort of producer for the BBC or one of those networks.

DRU *shocked face*

EM So I, like the boob I am, looked all confused and said, "When did he do that?"

"Earlier in the week," said Devon. "I did warn you he's a mixer."

DRU Wassit?

EM Someone who mixes around a lot. Aka a dawg.

DRU Gotcha. So Aidan lied to you.

EM *headdesk* Why is finding a man so frigging hard?

DRU Well, you did find one—he just wanted to be a friend with bennies.

EM Bennies that I can't even enjoy because he's never around.

DRU Yeah, you need a man who can attend to your needs, not drive you to your purple passion maker.

EM It's a hippo.

DRU A sad, sad hippo.

EM You said it, sister.

YOU LOGGED ON

EM I can't sleep.

EM You still up?

DRU It's only nine here.

EM What are you doing?

DRU Watching the latest ep of *Doctor Who*, making cookies, and trying to decide if I want to get a labia tat.

EM *blink*

DRU You don't think a little sugar skull would be pretty there?

EM Did you learn nothing from my retelling of the horrible events at the vulvathon that Bess held the other day? There are some parts of the body I don't want to have to stare at, and anything to do in the crotch department qualifies for that. Plus, it would hurt like hell. Double plus you'd have to have some dude holding your glitter biscuit while he tatted you up.

DRU *Glitter.*

DRU *Biscuit.*

EM I thought it was cute.

DRU Regardless of what odd euphemisms you use, I could get a chick to do the tat.

EM Does that make it any better?

DRU Well …

EM Mmmhmm. I wish I could sleep. I'm tired, but my brain won't shut down.

DRU What's it going on about now?

EM A lot of things and nothing. At the same time.

DRU Cryptic.

EM Oh, I know you are dying to hear how the plans are going for the trip out for the Viewing of the Hot Movie Star and I am nothing if not obliging.

Since I am still limited funds-wise (with almost every last little bit going to the court-ordered repayment schedule, damn my ex-boss's hide), and thus have still not taken the driving test in order to get a UK license, Holly and I will have to ride bikes the five and a half miles to where the film crew will set up.

DRU Would you be offended if I said that I feel sorry for the film crew?

EM Dude! I am not a blight. Or a curse. Or a jinx.

DRU I didn't say any of that.

EM No, but you thought it.

DRU *cough* Go on.

EM I'm gonna remember that attitude when the Hemsdude begs me to be his.

DRU Snort!

EM It could happen. Stop rolling your eyes, and yes, I know you are.

"But, Emily," Holly said yesterday when I told her the game plan. "We'll only be able to go after three, when school is over, and I'll have to be home by five or Mum will want to know where I've been. And with travel time, that only leaves us an hour to find Chris Hemsworth."

"So? Tell her you're with me on an educational thing."

She frowned at me. "I couldn't lie," she said, sounding scandalized.

I sighed. "All right, then, we'll simply have to go earlier."

"How can we? I'll be at school."

"And we're going to make that work to our advantage." I smiled a smug little smile at myself, and applied eyebrow pencil to my freshly waxed brows (no Unibrow on this girl, no sirree!).

"How?" she asked.

"You're a key member of the Vampire Ball planning committee, aren't you?"

"Yes," she said slowly, watching me carefully.

I pointed the eyebrow pencil at myself. "And I'm the head of the very same planning committee."

She thought for a minute. "Yes."

"I am allowed to call meetings of the planning committee if they have free time, right?"

"Right."

I filled in her brows a bit with the pencil and waited for it to sink in. Evidently she needed a little help. "So I'll just call a meeting between you and me, and we'll do some party planning on our way to see the gorgeous Mr. Hemsworth! Brilliant, isn't it?"

Her eyes got really big, and she squeaked a bit when she talked. "But that would mean leaving the school grounds."

"Yeah, so?" I pulled out some blush and gave her a hint of cheekbone.

"That's against the rules."

I smiled at her in the mirror. "Rules are for sheep, Holly. You and I aren't sheep—we're stunningly sexy women who refuse to be tied down to mundane rules meant for people like Ann and Bertrice."

"But—"

"No one will know. Now stop being such a wuss and repeat after me: Chris Hemsworth makes me sigh."

"Chris Hemsworth makes me sigh," she said, looking miserable.

"He is drool-worthy."

"Drool-worthy?"

"Drool-worthy."

"He is drool-worthy."

"He is mine. Well, technically he belongs to his wife and kids, but a girl can dream, right?"

"A girl can dream," she duly repeated, but she didn't look like she believed it. She'll soon learn that nothing stands in the way of me and a picture with a handsome movie star.

DRU Poor Holly. Poor, naive Holly. She has no idea what force she has run into.

EM If you're talking about me, I'd like to point out that just the other day you were saying what a good influence I was on her, and how nice it was that she had me for a friend.

DRU Doesn't mean you can't be a chaotic force, too.

EM Mmm. All right, I'm going to give sleep another whirl. Let me know about your date today with Mr. Package.

DRU His name is Richard, and will do. Nighty-night.

EM Hugs and kisses.

CHAPTER TWELVE

DRU Let's see. … It's eleven thirty at night here, which means its seven thirty for you. Wakey wakey!

EM Nnrng.

DRU Don't tell me you had another insomnia night?

EM Yeah. Made mistake of nap yesterday afternoon. No sleep until three a.m. Had to get up at seven. Am a zombie. How was date?

DRU It was … um … well …

EM Take pity on zombie brain. Why ellipses? Use words.

DRU Richard is really sweet. Like I said, we have so many interests in common.

DRU What???

EM Didn't talk.

DRU No, but I could feel you thinking.

EM Zombie brain no think. Go on.

DRU So, we went down to Fabioso's and ate pizza. He didn't mind that I asked for gluten-free crust, fake cheese, and no meat on my side of the pizza. We talked and talked and talked, and it was super nice. V never talked to me like R does. He treats me like I'm a real person.

EM You are person.

DRU Yes, but Richard asks me what I think about things, and discusses things, not just tells me what he thinks and likes. So anyway, we went to the lake and kissed. A lot. And things got a bit touchy-feely.

EM Thought you were taking things slow?

DRU I was. Until, well, you know how long it's been since V and I were together in the same room, let alone same state. Anyway, he was touching and kissing and seemed to enjoy himself, but then I decided to reciprocate, and … well …

EM Ellipses again. Bad. Bad ellipses.

DRU OK, I'm just going to come right out and say this, but NO JUDGMENT, all right?

EM *blinks*

EM 'K.

DRU Like I said, I thought I'd reciprocate some of the finger dancing, and he just … did nothing.

EM He didn't finger dance you in return?

DRU No, he did that first, but when I tried to inflate the balloon, so to speak, he didn't respond. You don't think it's me that's making him floppy, do you?

EM 1. No.

EM 2. You don't get to pick on my euphemisms anymore.

EM 3. What did he say?

DRU He said he didn't perform well in a car, and we could go back to his place if I wanted.

EM Ah.

DRU I didn't go, if you were going to ask. And I know you were.

EM Wasn't, but thought about it.

DRU I'm just worried. What if I've lost my ability to drive a man wild with my sensuality?

EM You mean your boobs.

DRU My boobs are my best asset. No boyfriend has ever been able to resist them. Richard liked them, but didn't go gaga like the others have.

EM Hmm.

DRU It's me, isn't it?

EM Could be just performance issues. You guys don't know each other well.

DRU That's a good point.

EM Zombie advice: Cut Mr. Floppy a little slack. For one, if you guys want to get your jollies, you can still do that, just without involving his naughty bits. And for another, some men don't like that whole expectation thing. Maybe rather than planning for a hot sexy time, you can do so spontaneously.

DRU Wow. That's actually really good advice. Your sleepless zombie brain is awesome! You get ten out of ten.

EM Then again, given his age, you might want to think about Viagra. Maybe it would help? I'll ask Mom about it for you.

DRU Minus five points.

EM Ugh. Gotta go. I have to record some people in a local women's shelter for this stupid diversity class. Because that's what frightened and at-risk women and kids need, right? *shakes head*

DRU Smooches. Thanks for the mostly good advice.

EM Smoochback.

YOU LOGGED ON

EM Mom says Viagra is supposed to work, so if Richard can get some, I think it would probably help. If I get another Viagra spam on my Gmail, I'll forward it to you so you can send it to him. And maybe one about the prostate, too. Not sure when that starts kicking in for men, but thirty-three sounds about right. Better safe than sorry!

YOU LOGGED ON

EM Oy. I'm here.

DRU Yay. Did you get to see the movie set? Did you kill anyone?

EM Really, the way your mind thinks!

No, no one was killed. We did get there, but Day One of the Hemsworth Hunt was pretty much a scratch. Holly and I rode out to the forest where they were filming despite the fact that it was raining and we got totally soaked. Once we got there, I suddenly realized the mistake I'd made—I was still in the school uniform. I'd have died if he saw me and thought I was a schoolkid, so all in all, I'm glad we didn't see him, although we did see his trailer. Attached is picture of Holly kissing the side of the trailer.

We saw a few actors in medieval garb, cameramen, and other technical types. I wanted to ask them when Mr. Hunky would be there, but Holly had a panic attack at the mere thought of that, so I had to make her sit down and breathe until she calmed down. After that, we rode back. My ass hurts from all that bike riding, but it will make my legs look fabulous!

DRU That's pretty anticlimactic. You didn't get to see him at all?

EM Nope. I got Holly back to school safe and sound, but I was caught coming in and was expelled.

DRU Again?

EM Yup. I've been kicked out of that place at least seven times in the last month or so, which I think has to be a school record. I believe the next time I get sent to Russell Crowe, I shall mention that, and ask for a tiara.

DRU I'd ask for a cake.

EM I made a mistake, Dru.

DRU This surprises you how?

EM No, I'm serious.

DRU Uh-oh. What's going on?

EM One of the things that I've been encouraging Holly to do is to take on little projects that she's perfectly capable of doing, in hopes they bolster her ego, and keep her from being in that scary, depressed place that she seems to drift toward if left alone.

DRU Smart thinking.

EM So I encouraged her to volunteer to help with a student-created website for the school, and do some grunt work—basically, reformatting text and slapping it into the template provided.

Easy peasy, right?

DRU Um. Knowing you? No.

EM It would have been simple except one night Bess and I had got into a Mai Tai Off, where we were trying to top each other's mai tai recipes, and of course, we got snockered pretty fast. Holly came by to ask me for some help on writing some basic descriptions of the school purpose, etc.

DRU Oh lord.

DRU She didn't.

EM Yeah. Not a good idea. Not while Bess and I were mai taied. Tai'd? Taied, I think.

DRU I forgot you can legally drink there.

EM "What's that?" Bess said when Holly went off to the bathroom. I was sitting with her laptop, singing a happy little song to myself (as I am wont to do when slightly squiffy). Bess weaved her way into the room, giggled at absolutely nothing, then fell facedown on the couch and tried to swim over to where I was.

"It's Holly's lappy. She's having me read over her stuff so she looks good. The stuff. Looks good. The stuff she has looks good. Snotballs, I can't talk. I think my numb is tongue."

DRU Hahahah.

EM "Well that sounds boring as hell," Bess said, and gave up trying to swim the mighty couch river.

"It is. See? School policy page. Bleh. School honesty policy. Staff bios ... oooh."

"Hmm?" Bess sounded sleepy.

"Weeeeeeeell, what have we here? My archnemesis! Or rather, nemeses. Is that the right plural? Damn, now I can't remember."

DRU Oh man oh man oh man. You didn't!

EM "What can't you remember?" Holly asked as she eyed Bess, and took a seat in the chair.

"Plural of archnemesis," I said, busily typing away.

"What is it you're doing?" She tried to see what I was typing but couldn't see over the screen.

"Just perking up a couple of bios."

Her eyes got massive and she sucked in a huge amount of air. "Emily! You can't do that! I'll get into trouble!"

DRU Run, Holly. Run far away. Change your name. Maybe become a man.

EM "No you won't. See? I'm saving it to a temp file so it won't get uploaded to the cloud. Hee. Hee hee and hee again."

"What are you heeing about—gark!" She moved over to the arm of the couch and read what I had typed.

Which, for your perusal, I'll slap in here.

DRU I don't … I almost don't want to see. And yet, I have to. It's just like a horrible car accident.

EM Martine Ashley

Physical Education

"I believe the key to a good grounding in life is found by playing hockey. Not only will the pervy skirts teach you what it's like to be ogled by everyone with a pair of eyes in their head, you will also understand better the nature of sport and sportsmanship, and learn that the only way to succeed is to lie, cheat, and in general stomp all over your teammates."

Elizabeth Spreadborough

English

"WHAT? WHAT'S THAT YOU SAY? SPEAK UP, WILL YOU? WHAT DOES TEACHING MEAN TO ME? ORGANIZATION! ORGANIZATION IS THE KEY! WITHOUT ORGANIZATION, YOU HAVE NOTHING, NOTHING AT ALL! AND MOBILE PHONES! HATE THE LITTLE BUGGERS."

Emmeline "Horseface" Naylor

Physics / Head of Year 11

"Students should be humiliated at every opportunity so they don't discover that they're smarter than we are. And they shouldn't be allowed to talk back. Or neigh in the hallways when I walk by. Particularly the neighing. Stupid students."

DRU Wow. Mai Tai Emily really unleashed her frustrations.

EM And how. Holly, once she got over her fear, had a good laugh with me about the revised bios. And yes, you guessed it. … In my mai tai haze, I didn't actually save the bios to a temp file—they went straight onto the website. Luckily, Russell Crowe realized his innocent niece Holly could never do anything so horrible, and called me in to ask if I've been messing with the website.

DRU Thank god it didn't go out so anyone else could see it.

EM Oh, they saw it, but Russell Crowe told them someone hacked the site so as not to get Hols into trouble. But he chewed me out royally.

What have you been doing? Did you see Richard the Floppy again? Oh, did I tell you how much he sold that condo for? This guy has some bucks, babe. I say it's sugar daddy time!

DRU So.

EM Mmm?

DRU About Richard. I told him about the info you found out re Viagra.

EM And?

DRU Big mistake. He got all hurty and told me that if I didn't think he was enough of a man for me, he'd let me find someone else, etc., etc. It took me forever to get him back in a happy mood.

EM Man. I have two things to say to that.

DRU I have absolutely no doubt that you do, although I'm surprised at there only being two things.

EM First of all, I'm sorry if my advice upset your BF.

DRU Thank you. I accept your apology.

EM Second, who died and made you responsible for his moods, happy or otherwise?

DRU Wha'?

EM You're not responsible for his moods, babe. Yes, I can see where he could get upset (although honestly, I bet it's a case of it hitting a bit too close to home for his comfort). But that doesn't mean he gets to be all bent out of shape and blame it on you. He needs to own his own emotions, not push them off on you.

DRU I get your point, but he's not like that. He was hurt. He thought that I thought he was impotent.

EM Well … he is, isn't he? I mean, you guys haven't had sex, have you?

DRU Not as such, although we did … last night … oral.

EM You know, I think I'm just not going to say anything more about this, because all I'll do is make you mad.

DRU I'm not mad at you, Em. I'm just … I don't know. Frustrated, I guess. And yes, I think you're right that this is something I need to work out with Richard.

EM That sounds like the smartest thing to do.

DRU Unrelated: when do you go to see the Hemsworth again?

EM Hopefully tomorrow.

DRU Happy hunting!

EM Thanks. I'll let you know how it goes. I should toddle. Laters.

DRU Ciao, bella.

DRU LOGGED ON

DRU Boo!

EM Hiya. How be things?

DRU Meh. Nothing interesting. You? Did you stalk the wild Hemsworth?

EM Sigh. Not today. I met Holly at her school, but we got a late start because she was freaking out again that people would notice she was leaving during her study class time, and it rained again the whole way there and back. No one was around the film site but a couple of maintenance guys.

DRU Were they at least cute?

EM Not even remotely. I'm going to be seriously depressed if I come halfway around the world to see the Divine Mr. H. and not actually get to lay my eye peepers on him.

Hang on a mo, Brother wants to talk to me about something. BRB.

DRU I have to run for a bit, but you can pop the rest here. I'm meeting my mom for dinner so I can vet her latest boy-friend. Smooches!

EM I have, without a doubt, the most bizarre parents in the world.

While I was chatting with you, Brother said he wanted to talk to me. So, being the thoughtful daughter who suffers silently just to keep her parents happy, I toddled into the small room Brother calls his study (he's getting *so* lord of the man-

or). Mom was there, too, which should have been a big red-light warning, but all I could think was that Russell Crowe told them I had messed up the school website, and that I'd have to pay to have it put back the way it should be.

"Sit down, Emily. Your mother and I thought it was time to have a talk with you. Er … another talk with you."

Crap. This couldn't be good. Was there another lawsuit against me? I'd never be out of debt at this rate!

Brother sat opposite me, on a leather couch next to Mom, who was smiling in that bright, chirpy, *I've got some bad news for you* sort of way. "Your mother told me that you were inquiring a few days ago about … er … a substance used to give men stamina."

Huh? I blinked at him and wondered if he was hallucinating, or if he'd finally just gone dotty.

"Sexual stamina," Mom said.

I moved my blink to her. Why on earth would I be asking her about sexual stamina?

"Viagra," Brother added.

"Oh, that. Yeah. What about it?"

Brother jumped up and started pacing around the room, clearing his throat and tugging at his shirtsleeves. "You asking about the Viagra brought to our attention that you're of an age now where you might wish to … er … experiment."

"Not really," I said, wondering what bee got up his butt. Boy, you ask someone about a little Viagra, and they go all psycho on you. Obviously, they figured I had an older man who I was dating, and he needed help doing the deed. "Currently, I'm still perusing the offerings, if you really must know, and I don't see that it's much to do with you except insofar as I might someday pay off enough of that stupid car that I have hopes of an actual future."

Brother stopped and stared at me. "Emily, what are you talking about?"

Honestly, was the man losing his hearing, too? "An older man."

His Unibrow got all scrunched together as he stood at the end of the couch and frowned at me. Mom started snickering. "What older man?"

"I don't know. I don't have him yet," I said, confused by why he was making such a big deal about possibly dating an older man.

"Does this man you don't have need the Viagra? Is he asking you to take drugs to another country for him?"

"What man?" I asked, thinking seriously of banging my head on his desk.

"Exactly!" Brother said, all exasperated.

"Dear, she doesn't understand—" Mom started to say, but Brother interrupted her.

"Well, that much is obvious, Christine. How can a girl have such a high IQ but be so clueless about real life?"

"Clueless!" I gasped. Me? Was he *mad*?

Mom smiled and patted him on the arm. "Sometimes the smartest girls are the ones who are the most naive."

"I am so not naive! I am the least naive person I know! And for the record, the term *girl* is derogatory and belittling. I'm twenty! I can vote, and drive a car when I have a license, and buy a house if I want to."

Brother did a little nostril flare that you really don't want me to describe. "Now, listen to me, Emily. I'm trying to be sympathetic and understanding and all that rot. I am trying my best to give you both space and respect, but you are living under my roof, and by that fact, I claim the right to know if you are consorting with a man who is asking you to smuggle drugs."

"Fang, you mean?" I asked carefully, concerned that he was about to burst a blood vessel. "He's out of the country, but he hasn't asked me to bring him any drugs, and if he did, they'd probably be vet drugs, because he's helping with some sheep-innards epidemic."

"God above, she's trying to drive me mad!" Brother yelled, running his hands through his hair and instantly forming the hair horn.

Mom laughed.

"This is your doing, isn't it?" he asked, rounding on her. "This is all part of that women's lib you've taught them, isn't it? One daughter is out gallivanting around the country, protesting everything that takes her fancy and talking about shacking up with a noncelibate monk, and the other is calmly inquiring about Viagra!"

Now, that was interesting. I had no idea Bess was thinking about moving in with Monk.

"Brother, calm down," Mom said, still laughing. "If you'll just tell her what you're talking about—"

"Do you want to do this?" he asked, kind of snapping the words at her, his hands on his hips.

She shook her head and laughed even harder. "You wanted another child. We made a deal—I'd talk to Bess; you talk to Emily."

"I didn't know I was going to get the Viagra daughter! The deal's off."

"Hello," I said, waving my hand. "Is anyone aware of the fact that the Viagra daughter is sitting right here in the room? Isn't it bad for my psyche for you to be talking about me like that? You don't want to scar me for life. I'll need therapy."

Brother took a deep breath and let it out slowly. "Emily."

I tipped my head on the side and looked at him. I suppose in a father kind of way he looked cute, all hair-horned and Unibrowed, and with a twitch that had appeared out of no-where. "Yo, big daddy."

"You are of legal age."

"You remembered! I'm so proud of you."

"Just barely, though. And you have asked about Viagra."

Weasels feasting on my tender flesh would never pry from my lips the fact that I was asking about Viagra because your BF is also known as Mr. Floppy. "You're two for two—would you like to risk it all for the grand-prize round?"

He closed his eyes for a minute, then opened them up again. They were bloodshot. "Your mother assures me that you have learned the pertinent facts, and that during the time you lived in that horrible apartment building, you no doubt had male friends visiting you. *Overnight.*"

A horrible suspicion started to grow in the back of my mind. He couldn't be talking about—oh, god, he couldn't, could he? The very last thing I ever expected him to talk to me about?

"You are a young woman, a young woman with a lively and naturally curious mind, one who enjoys new experiences."

Maybe I was wrong. Maybe I was imagining it. "Yes, but where does the older man come into it—"

"SEX!" he bellowed suddenly, making my eyes almost pop out with surprise. "Dammit, I'm talking about sex, girl! Sexual intercourse! Between you and a man ... er ..." He looked at Mom. "It is men she's interested in?"

Mom nodded.

"That's good. Although if it was the other, at least we wouldn't have to worry about her getting pregnant—"

"Argh!" I screamed, unable to stand hearing them talk about me like that. Sex! Brother was talking to me about sex! "Stop it! I don't want to hear this! I had the sex talk with Mom donkey's years ago, when I was still in middle school! Isn't it illegal or something for you to be talking to me about it now? It has to be. There has to be some human rights law against an elderly father speaking to his adult daughter about sex."

"Emily, behave yourself. You're upsetting Brother."

"I'm upsetting *him*?" I stared at Mom, my mouth hanging open, which just goes to show you how upset I was, because I make it a policy to never let my mouth hang open. "What about *me*?"

Mom sighed, pulled Brother down to the couch, then leaned forward. "We're concerned that you might be involved with someone who isn't of an appropriate age for you. There are a lot of professors around the college, and I know how attractive some of them must seem to you. I, myself, had a raging crush on my chemistry professor, but that's all it was, and all it ever should have been. Do you need more supplies?"

"Supplies? What supplies?" Brother asked, all suspicious-like.

"No, I have plenty of condoms, Mom," I said, wanting to both laugh and run away screaming. Honestly, at my age! Brother decides to have a sex talk with me now?

"You offered the girl condoms?"

"Woman," I corrected him, but it did no good.

"You gave our daughter condoms before I could have the sex talk with her?"

Mom gave him a look. "Dear, I think you've let a few years slip past you. She has a point in that she is an adult now, and fully capable of making her own choices. Emily, I know money is tight, so I want to make sure you have plenty of condoms to use if you need one. I will give you another box."

"Two condoms," Brother said, still running his hands through his hair. "One can break; use two. Maybe three would be better. That's not too much to ask, is it?"

Mom reached over and patted my knee. "So there is no older man?"

"Well, there's Fang. He's a few years older than me, but not Viagra older. And Aidan is the same age as me."

"Aidan." Brother shuddered at the name. "Four condoms. I couldn't bear to have my first grandchild sporting that goatee."

"You know you can ask us anything, or Bess, if you don't want to talk to Brother or me," Mom said in a sympathetic tone that made me get a bit teary-eyed. I mean, how many women our age get bonus sex talks by their parents? It was really rather sweet—albeit in a creepy way. "It's not like you can shock us. I know you think we're older than the hills, but your father and I have a very healthy sexual relationship, so don't be afraid to ask us about things that might seem strange to you."

"TMI, Mom!" I said, giving her a look.

"TMI?"

"Too much information. I'll make you a deal—I won't tell you about my sex life if you don't tell me about yours."

"Very well, but it's a natural part of life—"

"And here is where I draw the line." I jumped up and ran for the door. If she was going to start talking about the sort of things she and Brother did, I had to get out of there.

"You've been giving her condoms?" Brother asked as I ran out the door. "Just like that? You didn't talk to me at all—you just offered the girl condoms?"

"She *is* an adult, Brother."

"She's not *that* adult. She's getting expelled weekly from

that high school she's pretending to go to, for the love of all that's holy!"

Now I can't even remember what I was going to tell you, so I'm going to bed and try to erase the words "your father and I have a very healthy sexual relationship" from my mind.

Hope dinner with your mom and her new BF goes well.

Hugs and kisses.

Subject: Details of the ghost or entity at 249 Basque Close
From: TheEmster@oxwills.gobbottle.co.uk
To: enquiries@prs.org
Cc: Dru@seattlebikerchix.com
Date: 8 October 11:19 a.m.

Dear Psychic Research Society,

I am an American woman living in a house at 249 Basque Close, Piddlington-on-the-Weld, Oxfordshire, and my underwear drawer is haunted by some sort of ghost, entity, poltergeist, or other being that would be likely to haunt an underwear drawer and routinely throw underwear around the room when I'm not around.

At first I thought it was my parents having a bit of fun, but after extensive tests (see attached spreadsheet), it has become crystal clear that nothing human could be rummaging around my undies. It's getting a bit old having to pick up everything almost every day. I heard on the television (aka "telly") about your ghost-hunting team that goes around England trying to get proof of ghosts, and thought you might want to send them out to investigate my underwear drawer. Frankly, given the appearance of the house, I'm willing to bet there's more than one ghost present. Your investigation team could have a field day with it. The basement alone is probably home to at least a couple of deranged ax-murdering spirits.

Thank you.
Emily Williams

Details of Investigation into Underwear Ghost
Date: 15 September

Action: Duct tape X across front of drawer

Reaction: Undies removed without apparent movement of the duct tape

D: 18 September

A: Loads of duct tape slathered all over the front of the drawer, making it impossible to open drawer without a pair of scissors

R: Undies scattered around room. Wad of duct tape still plastered across drawer. Upon opening of drawer, strange cold spot was felt inside drawer where undies usually reside. Remains of spirit?

D: 20 September

A: Mousetrap hidden in left cup of WonderBra (worn only on special occasions)

R: Trap triggered, undies strewn about, but no signs of injured fingers on anyone in the family (Christine Williams, Dr. Williams, and Bess Williams). Proof that entity has the ability to conduct physical interaction with objects.

D: 25 September

A: Powdered paint applied to handle of drawer in case one of the occupants of the house is pulling a fast one

R: Not very successful. Hopes were that paint would dye hands of culprit, but powdered paint didn't cling to the brass handle very well unless first wetted, which pretty much defeated the purpose of using powder. Could this be evidence of ghostly interaction?

D: 29 September

A: Consultation with Rev. Brand Miller, Piddlington-on-the-Weld church

R: Rev. Miller refused opportunity to conduct exorcism on underwear drawer, stating it was against Church of England policy to conduct exorcisms. Rev. Miller suggested researching history of house for possible information on ghost known to haunt undie drawer. Research on house history will commence immediately after the end of current Oxwills semester.

DRU Houston, we have touchdown!

EM Ooooh. As in no more Mr. Floppy?

DRU That's right. I "borrowed" some of Mom's massage oil, and Richard really liked it.

EM That's kind of ew.

DRU Richard's erection?

EM No. Well, yes. I mean, not ew to you, but to me, because I don't know him. I meant using your mom's slicky-slicky oil.

DRU It was a new bottle. I told her I'd buy her a new one. I have to say, Em, at one point I might have giggled to myself. I mean, there he was, grunting and groaning and thrashing his head around while I groped him, and I suddenly had a mental picture of what we looked like. It was hard not to laugh out loud.

EM Thank god you said that. I thought something was wrong with me because I think penises … penii? … are downright funny-looking. I have never understood why men are so proud of them, and want to show them to you. OK, they're fun when they're on the job and working as usual, but when they're standing around waving at you … yeah. Not going to go on. I'll start to laugh if I do.

DRU I'm right there with you.

EM Oh, and for the record, the above was not a denigration of Fang's willy. While I didn't get a super-good look at his, I'm sure he had a more manly dick than a lot of guys. Just because Fang is pretty manly.

Now I'm curious what Aidan's looks like. Dammit, now I want to compare and contrast, and that's wrong, isn't it? One should never compare lovers (or potential lovers). Forget I said anything. Moving on …

DRU I have to admit I kinda want you to get it on with Aidan, too. Just, you know, so you can make a decision about which guy you want more.

EM What excellent timing you have. Guess who rolled into town last night?

DRU Is Fang back from the wilds of sheep innards?

EM Yup. He called me this morning to say that he's here for a couple of days, and would I like to get together with him? I said that I'd love to, and mentioned Devon's party. End result: he's coming to dinner tomorrow night; then we're going to Devon's party together, since a certain Mr. Aidan the Mixer hasn't bothered asking me if I'm going or not.

DRU Ha! That'll teach Aidan. And yay for Mr. Benefits returning to town. BRB, have to get dressed. Richard is taking me to dinner. A special dinner, he said. Do you think he's going to propose? We've only been on a couple of dates.

EM Wow, he works fast. Maybe he's feeling his mortality due to his advanced age, and figures he doesn't have time to live together for a few years before you get married.

DRU He is not that old!

EM Mmmhmm.

DRU Fang's older than you, and you don't see me making references to him being as old as the hills. Regardless, BRB. Must get dressed.

EM Fang is only a couple of years older than me. Oddly enough, I ran into him at the store while I was shopping for the dinner (I'm going to make lasagna, since it's one of the few things I can cook without making it taste weird). He was buying a few frozen-food items for himself, and had two huge bags of dog food for his hounds.

"Fancy meeting you here," I said, giving him a quick kiss because there were other people in the aisle.

His eyes went from kind of sad to happy. "Just who I need to see—you look wonderful."

"Thanks. It's all the bike riding I did to try to find Chris Hemsworth." I held out a leg and wiggled my toes.

He duly admired my leg. "How are your classes going?"

"Which ones, my college ones or the ones I'm taking with Holly?"

"Holly?"

I spent ten minutes catching him up to what's been going on in my life, after which I mentioned the Vampire Ball.

"A Halloween party?" he asked, holding a package of frozen fish sticks.

I handed him one of stuffed sole instead. "Yuppers, I got sucked into being head wrangler for it. The high school kids picked the subject, not me. It's going to be pretty fun, though—I booked a local metal group for the band, and the younger kids will have a haunted house to go through. Oh, and everyone will wear costumes."

"A fancy dress ball, eh?" He looked at the stuffed sole.

"It's better for you. More healthy. The fish sticks are loaded with nitrates and stuff."

He grinned and put the sole in his basket. "We wouldn't want that. About this Vampire Ball—is it a school party, or a community one?"

I picked out a package of frozen stuffed peppers. "You like these?"

He nodded.

I handed them to him and moved down to the next section. "It's open to everyone."

"I see. Are you going with anyone?"

"No, I'm organizing it." I gnawed on my lip for a second. "Mac and cheese OK?"

He looked at the package. "Sure. Would you like to go to the ball with me?"

I stared at him for a second, not sure if he had really asked me or I had imagined it. "That would be fabulous."

"Unless you wanted to go with someone else," he said, looking back at the frozen foods. "I got the idea you were interested in Aidan."

"I'm interested in a lot of people, but it doesn't mean I want to go to a costume ball with them." I put my hand on his arm and squeezed until he looked back at me. "I'd love to go with you, Fang. But will you be here then?"

"I will make a point of it. I'm due to go back up to Scotland on Monday, but I will have a couple of days I can take off."

"That would be awesome, then. You really are the best of friends, you know that?"

"With benefits," he said with a little twisty smile.

"Amen to that." I waggled my eyebrows at him in a *let's get it on tonight and every night you're here* way. "What about some turkey?"

He looked at his basket. It was full of frozen food. "I think I have enough for three days."

"Oh, sorry, I didn't mean to do that. I guess it's my mom's genes. She likes to feed people. So we'll see you tomorrow at six. Unless you're free tonight … ?"

"I wish I was, trust me. All I could think of coming home was seeing you again. And spending my days not having my hands up to my elbows inside a sheep. Unfortunately, I can't see you tonight. My dad is a bit poorly, and I promised to see him."

"Sorry to hear that about your dad. I hope he's OK."

"He will be. He has these attacks regularly a couple of times a year so the whole family descends on him." He flashed me a grin. "I'm looking forward to eating something that's not been frozen first."

"My lasagna has been known to make vegetarians reconsider," I bragged. "I'm afraid you're going to see my family at full force, too, though. Bess is having her Monk over tomorrow, too, so you'll get to see him."

"I look forward to it."

I gave him another quick peck (wishing like hell I could have snogged him the way I really wanted to) and dashed off to finish my shopping.

Gotta run. Fill me up with gossip, buttercup!

DRU Back! Oh, you're gone. Rats

DRU LOGGED ON

DRU I'm cursed. I am simply cursed. There's no other explanation for it. Dinner was awful. Instead of him proposing to me—as I didn't really expect, but it might have happened—he came out.

Of the closet.

That's the reason why he was Mr. Floppy.

I was his rebound from breaking up with his boyfriend.

Sigh.
My curse and I are going to bed now.

CHAPTER THIRTEEN

EM Holy shitballs! He's gay? Bi? Whatever, that was just rude to make you think he might be about to propose and instead tell you he bats for the other team. Are you heartbroken? Are you crying? Do you want to talk about it? I'm assuming you don't; otherwise you'd have a lot more to say to me. Just let me know if you want me to bad-mouth him for you. Or offer you virtual hugs and scathing comments about men who play the rebound game.

EM I got on just to tell you that my life is over. You awake? It says you're here.

Well, since this is going to take a half hour to dictate, I'll start. Let me know when you're back.

I know I've said my life is over before, but this time I mean it. I'll never have a life again. I'm not ever stepping foot out of this house. Mom and Brother and Bess will go back home next year, and I'll have to stay with the underwear ghost, because I can't possibly ever face anyone again after what happened last night. I hope the professor that Brother did the job swap with doesn't mind me hanging around until I'm thirty or so. I should be able to face people by then. Maybe.

In an attempt to make you feel better about your life, allow me to tell you just what a horrible turn mine has taken. I'm going to do this properly so you can relive the horror with me.

First of all, I had a bit of a problem with my makeup. Now, you know that I'm really good at evening makeup—you told me that no one does cat's eyes quite like I do. Well, my eyeliner would not go on right. It kept smudging and making big blots, and eventually dribbled down my face so that I looked like the clown from *It*.

So not the look I wanted to spring on Fang, especially since I was looking forward to major benefit time after Devon's party.

I ended up removing all the makeup, which is fine if you're naturally pretty (like you) or are just hanging around college and don't care who sees you, but when you're trying to impress your friend with bennies, you want to look less like a pale rabbit and more like a voluptuous temptress.

In the end, I reminded myself that I wouldn't want a man who valued appearance more than anything else, so I made do with a little mascara and powder.

Then my dress (the red velvet one) had a tear in the armpit, which meant I had to get Mom's sewing kit so I could fix it. I managed to stab my thumb three different times while mending it, and bled on the fabric. You wouldn't think blood would show up on a red dress, would you? I'm here as proof that it does.

Then Fang arrived for dinner. All good, right?

Sigh.

I managed to beat Mom to the door, and hauled Fang into the downstairs loo to kiss the bedickens out of him.

"Ah … Emily … " he tried to say, but I had possession of his tongue by that point, and was trying to get my hands in his shirt, while at the same time wiggling around on him so he'd touch any part of me that he desired, and kissing every part of his face that I could reach.

"Ah, Emily, what?" I said when I came up for breath. Fang was panting by that point (I might not have been letting him breathe much), and my desperate attempt to touch and kiss and rub against him meant his hair was all standing on end, his tie was halfway undone, and his belt was hanging open.

"Ah, I think perhaps this activity had better wait, Emily." He flashed a smile, then dove in for another kiss, this time one he was in charge of.

"Emily? Did I hear someone knocking?" Mom called from just outside the bathroom door.

I poked my head out of the bathroom. "Yes. Fang's here."

She looked startled for a moment. "In the bathroom?"

"Yes." I realized what she was getting at. I coughed delicately. "He's … uh … I'm helping him with his tie."

And at that moment Fang appeared, his buckle tidy, his tie back in place, and his shirt buttoned. Only his hair still looked rumpled, and I just figured Mom would think that was his do.

"There you are. Welcome to our home, Fang."

We went through the niceties of Mom asking him how vet school was, and he asking her how her artsy-fartsy classes were going, and then Brother entered the room.

The only explanation I can think of for what Brother did is that he's obviously going senile. That, or he's started drinking and no one knows it yet.

"This is Fang Baxter," I said, introducing him to Brother. Mom was out in the kitchen with Bess making a salad, since you know I suck at that. Bess's BF, Monk, was slouched in a chair watching TV. Brother was watching Monk with the same look on his face that he has when Mom makes brussels sprouts.

"Fang?" he asked, looking even more brussels-sprouty.

"It's actually Francis, but my mates call me Fang," Fang explained. Brother shook his hand and did man chat for a couple of minutes before Bess came in and dragged Monk off to the dining room.

"Dinner's on. Hi, you must be Fang. I'm Bess. This is Monk. I hope you like Emily's lasagna with dead animals in it. I tried to tell her how beef is processed, but she just ran away and refuses to listen to the value of a Paleolithic diet. Do you have any idea of the amount of mercury that's contained in English chickens? It's appalling, let me tell you. We're having a chicken protest next week. You're welcome to come with us."

"She's adopted," I told Fang as we toddled off to the dining room. "I don't share any of her genes."

He laughed.

Everything was fine until the food stopped being passed around, and we started eating. Then the man who claims he is my father started the dinner conversation out by looking over at Fang and asking, "So, do you plan on having sex with my daughter?"

I shot the piece of lasagna I was eating out of my nose. I swear to you, it shot out my nose!

"BROTHER!" I screamed, dabbing at my nose. It came away red, and for a moment, I thought it was blood, but quickly realized it was tomato sauce.

Do you know how badly tomato sauce in the nasal passages stings? Let me tell you, it's seriously unpleasant.

"Erm—" Fang looked more than a little startled. He just blinked at Brother, his fork halfway to his mouth. "Eh—"

"Dear, perhaps now is not the best time for this conversation," Mom said.

"Yes!" I said fervently, nodding like mad and wiping my nose. "What she said. In fact, never is a good option."

Brother hoisted the Unibrow and looked at Mom. "She is my daughter. I believe that I have the right to know if this young man plans on copulating with her."

"As if the Viagra talk wasn't mortifying enough," I told him.

"Viagra talk?" Fang asked in a kind of strangled voice.

"You do not want to know what sorts of things that man"—I pointed at the parental being—"chooses to discuss with me, an adult. He's under the delusion that I'm sixteen and a virgin."

"You're not?" Brother asked, his Unibrow smooshing up in a frown. "And just when—"

"Brother," Mom said sternly. I could have sung praises when she stopped that particular line of discussion. "Emily, the lasagna turned out quite nice. Isn't it nice, Bess?"

"It is filled with the suffering of countless animals."

"It's not as if I'm being unreasonable in asking," Brother insisted to Fang. He nodded toward Monk. "After all, I know the other one is having sex with Bess; she told me so."

"That's right, isn't it, my little stud muffin?" Bess asked, sliding her hand up Monk's thigh.

"Bess, not at the dinner table. Brother, there is a time and place for this discussion, and it's not while we are eating. This can wait until later."

Brother eyed Fang carefully. "What do you say, Fang? You planning on getting lucky with Emily?"

I seriously contemplated sliding off the chair and curling up into a fetal ball on the floor. "I didn't think you could go much lower than the Viagra talk, but you, Brother, have taken humiliation to a new high. I can die now secure in the knowledge that you have reached the zenith of ways to humiliate me."

"Humiliate you? I'm not trying to humiliate you; I'm just trying to stay in touch with what's going on in your life. Your mother made a deal with me when you were born. Of course, I didn't know you were going to be asking about Viagra, and running around with condoms just waiting to pounce on unwary men."

It was at that point that I did slide off the chair. I lay flat out on the floor and prayed for it to open up and suck me in, prayed for a hurricane that would destroy the house instantly, prayed for a bolt of lightning to come down and strike my father dead.

"Actually, I don't think that what Emily and I do with regards to sex is anyone's business but our own," Fang said.

I got to my knees and peered over the table at him. "Did you just tell my father to mind his own business?"

Fang looked disconcerted. "I tried to be polite about it."

"You are the bravest man in the world," I told him, and got back onto my chair.

Brother was contemplating Fang, who, after waggling his eyebrows at me, returned the gaze.

"I see," Brother said finally. "I take that to mean you aren't, because evidently young men these days are the first to flaunt their relationships with my daughters." He waved a fork at Monk.

Monk growled, and pounced on Bess, who squealed with joy.

"You see?" Brother shuddered a little. "In my day—"

"No, dear," Mom interrupted. "None of the 'in my day' stories. Not now."

"Ah. Yes. Perhaps not." Brother lined Fang up in his sights again. "Where did you say you're going to school?"

"Oxfordshire Agricultural College."

"He's going to be a vet; isn't that nice?" Mom said.

"Good," Brother said, and smiled at Mom. "You see? There's never a wrong time to discuss these things."

I breathed a sigh of relief and picked up my fork. Brother had embarrassed me, but it wasn't a mortal embarrassment. I had survived it, and Fang didn't look shocked anymore.

Suddenly Brother looked up and pointed his fork at Fang again. "You include oral sex in that statement, too, correct? And … er … the other kind? Not vaginal, if you get my drift."

"And that has been your mortifying event of the evening," I said, standing and grabbing first my plate and then Fang's. "Thank you for attempting to kill me with embarrassment. I will see you tomorrow. Possibly. If Fang and I aren't too busy having oral, anal, and vaginal sex. Come along, Fang. We're going to eat in the library, where there are no sex-obsessed deranged old people trying to ruin the shreds of what's left of my life."

Be back in a mo. Have to get some aspirin. Just thinking about last night has made my headache worse.

DRU Ohai.

EM There you are. *gentle hugs*

DRU Thank you. Let me read back.

DRU Holy shizznits! What is up with Brother?

EM I thought my hellish life would make you see just how good yours is. And you haven't even heard the half of it.

DRU Dear god, girl! What happened? Tell all!

EM I will, but do we want to discuss your evening first?

DRU No. Not now. Not tomorrow. Possibly never.

EM OK, but if you do want to, I'm here.

DRU Thank you. Go on with your evening. I take it Brother followed you into where you and Fang were eating?

EM No, thank god. Fang and I had our dinner in the library, and he actually told me that his dad once threatened to cut off his balls if he got a girl pregnant, so that made me feel better. That I'm not the only one whose father is sex obsessed, that is, not that Fang's dad threatened to cut off his noogies.

Anyway, we managed to avoid the Sex Fiend for another hour, during which time Fang caught me up on all the things he'd been doing since I last saw him, and then I had to kiss him a bit more, but since he said he wouldn't be able to walk if I didn't stop, I had to peel myself off him.

DRU Sigh. I like him.

EM So do I.

DRU I kinda got that idea.

EM "Where are the dogs?" I asked when he helped me into the car (you have to close the door from the outside).

"At my cousin's farm. They've been staying with him while I've been out of the area. I'll pick them up in November, when I'm done with all the fieldwork."

"I bet you miss them."

"I do." He smiled at me. "Amongst other things."

Devon doesn't live too far from us, but in an expensive neighborhood. The houses are all set way back off the road, and surrounded by big stone fences with iron gates. You know, the kind of houses that have names. Devon's family has some big house somewhere in the east, but this one—Penhallow—Devon said was left to him by his grandma. It was a huge pink stone house with lots of windows and a separate five-car garage. It was really impressive, and I was glad I'd shaved and pruned earlier, because it was the sort of place that you don't want to go into knowing you have hairy armpits and rampant pubes.

DRU *nods*

EM "Wow, that's some house," I said as Fang opened the car door for me.

"It is. Dev's a lucky bloke." Fang slid me a glance. "In many ways."

I was still staring at the house, suddenly a bit unsure of myself. You know how it is—you look forward to a party and then suddenly you're there, and you realize you don't know a lot of people, and your dress has a repaired armpit, and you aren't wearing as much makeup as you should be wearing.

Fang squeezed my hand. "You're not nervous, are you?"

Oh, god, how did he know? "No, of course not. Why do you ask?"

"Because you're cutting off the circulation to three of my fingers."

"Oh." I loosened my grip on his hand, but I didn't let it go altogether. "You should see me when I'm really nervous. You wouldn't be able to feel anything below your elbow."

"I'll keep that in mind." He rang the doorbell and whispered, "Relax, Emily. It's just Devon. And if you need anything, I'm here for you."

"Oh, I'll need you later, when we discuss the benefits package," I said, trying to calm myself enough that I didn't behave like an idiot in front of everyone.

Just then the door opened, and some guy I didn't recognize greeted Fang and waved us in. The hallway was gorgeous, black-and-white tile on the floor, a big curved wrought iron staircase sweeping up to the floor above (first or second, I can never keep it straight what they call it here), a big chandelier, and arty stuff like dingy old pictures, and big urns. Doors opened on either side to show huge rooms. Fang took my coat and dropped it off in a small room at the end of the hall, then shooed me into the room on the left.

"Lalla!" I said, a bit relieved that I knew someone besides just Fang. "And Peg!"

"Hello, hello," Peg said, greeting us. Fang answered a few of their questions as to what he'd been doing with the Irish sheep; then he murmured something about saying hi to some mates, and went off to talk to a group of guys who were standing in the corner laughing.

I was unhappy at being marooned without him for a few minutes, but remembered that he had other friends he hadn't seen in a while, and it wasn't fair to expect him to spend all his time with me. Even if he would be off to Scotland in a few days. So I sucked it up, buttercup, smiled when he glanced my way, and waggled my fingers to indicate it was OK if he chatted with his buddies.

DRU Awww. You are the best girlfriend-with-benefits ever.

EM I try. Lalla looked up from where she was talking to a friend and saw me. "Emily! Oooh, you look ever so nice! That's a stunning brill dress. This is Ronnie, my stepsister."

"Hi, Ronnie. Thanks, Lalla," I said, trying to look like my goal was stunning brill. "I like your leather bustier. It's really … busty."

She stood up and turned around so I could see all of it. "It's fabulous, isn't it? Periwinkle leather. I found it at Garfinkles. Tash helped me pick it out."

Tash. Grr. I knew that since she was Devon's cousin, she was likely to be at the party, but that didn't mean I had to like it.

"Aidan was asking for you."

"Was he?" Now, I'm not the sort of girl who arrives with one guy and leaves with another—OK, I am if he's drunk and tries to force me into sexual situations—so I wasn't going to go hunting for Aidan while Fang was around.

But that didn't mean I didn't want to know what he was up to.

Lalla glanced around. "He's here somewhere. If I know him, he's probably playing bartender. Why don't you go see? Drinkies and food are just through that door."

"OK. Thanks. Nice meeting you, Ronnie."

Fang was still hanging with his buddies, so I wandered to the huge dining room (I'm thinking forty or fifty people could have fit in it), which had a long, long table covered in food, plates, napkins, etc., and at the end was a portable bar with two guys behind it, pouring out drinks. I went back to see if Fang was done catching up, but he was happily chatting away. He cocked an eyebrow at me when I caught his eye, but I felt bad at disturbing him, so I gave them the thumbs-up, and toddled off to do a little reconnoitering. I wanted to see if Aidan really was here with Tash, or if he'd hooked up with someone else. And just why was he asking about me?

DRU Oooh. This is just like a TV show. Go on, go on!

EM It kind of felt like a TV show—at least, the house did. It was seriously dripping with the scent of aristocracy.

It took me a bit, but at least I reached the back of the house. People were wandering all around here, too, everyone laughing and drinking and joking with one another.

"Who knew Devon had so many friends?" I said under my breath as I stepped over a couple of people who were flaked out on the floor playing some card game.

At last I ran Aidan to earth in a room that looked like Brother's library, only a hundred times nicer. Think glossy leather chairs, leather books, dead animal heads on the wall, expensive-looking rugs on the floor, that sort of thing. Aidan was sitting in a big leather armchair with Tash in his lap, leaning over sideways and laughing at something Devon was saying. Devon, oddly enough, didn't have any girls hanging off him. I was a bit surprised, because he usually had at least one girl with him, but this time he was by himself. I gathered that as the host, he felt it wiser to leave himself unencumbered.

"Oh, look, there's your little schoolmate," Tash said, her scratchy voice making my ears hurt.

"Emily!" Devon said, beetling straight for me. "You look lovely. Tash, love, get Emily and me a couple of drinks, would you?"

Tash snorted, but headed to the temporary bar set up in the corner. Devon zoomed in and kissed me.

And not a swift peck, either. It was a full-on kiss, the kind I'd been laying on Fang earlier in the evening.

DRU Hoo! That was unexpected.

EM Tell me about it! I was about to tell Devon he needed to warn me if he was going to do that again, but I didn't want to make a scene in front of everyone. "Hello, people. Happy birthday, Devon. It looks like your party is a roaring success."

"The party is a success now that you're here," Devon said, half-turning to wave at the people in the room. "You know everyone?"

"Not really—"

"Good. Ah, here's Tash with our drinks."

Tash shoved a glass at me with the grimace that passes for her smile. "Evening, Tash," I greeted her, because—you know me—I'm polite as can be.

DRU Uh …

EM Well, sometimes.

DRU Eh …

EM When I feel like it.

DRU I'll buy that.

EM I looked beyond Tash to where Aidan still sat in the chair, watching me with an unreadable expression.

"Drink up, drink up—there's plenty where that came from." Devon nudged my hand before tossing back his own beverage.

I looked down at the glass. It was filled with a clear liquid, and sported one tiny little sliver of ice and a curl of lemon. "Oh. Thanks. I will. It's just that I'm not really fond of … um … vodka."

"That's a gin and tonic," Devon said.

"Ah. Sure." Mai tais aside, I don't like to drink a lot, but this drink didn't look bad. It smelled like there was a lot of tonic in it, too. To be honest, I wasn't very much concerned about the drink. No, what held my attention was Aidan. I felt like there was some unfinished business between us. I wasn't as crazy wild about him and his hipster goatee as I had been, especially if he really had lied to me about being ill, but I wasn't ready to completely ignore him, either.

DRU I know that feeling. You don't want to care, but you do.

EM Bingo.

"Come in, make yourself at home. Aidan's here, but I expect you noticed that?" Devon's eyes twinkled when he said that.

"Oh, Dev, don't pick on her. She's so sweet and innocent, I'm sure she doesn't even drink, let alone understand the sort of complex relationship that Aidan and I have. Isn't that right, love?" Tash kissed Aidan as she said the last part. I waited for a minute to see if he was going to stop her, but he didn't seem to.

That was all I needed to see. I formally struck his name off the roster of potential men with whom I would consort in a sexual manner, and allowed my heart to feel abused even though it probably shouldn't have. After all, Fang was in town for a short while … and when he was gone, there was Devon.

DRU Ah, Devon.

EM Ah, indeed. I gave him a long look when he turned to greet some newcomers. What was with that kiss? Was he trying to tell me something? And if he was, did I want to do anything about it once Fang was off to the wilds of Scotland?

DRU You do if you're half the woman I know you are.

EM And I am! Don't get me wrong—I wasn't about to jump his bones while Fang was there. But Fang wasn't interested in anything beyond scratching some mutual itches, and it appeared he was going to be gone a lot more than I first thought, limiting our itch-scratching time.

In other words, all that introspection went toward whether Devon deserved a place at the top of the Get This Man Naked at the First Possible Moment list.

I considered this possibility. I liked Devon. He was funny, and genuinely sweet even if he was flirty as sin, and we both loved Thai food. But was there more waiting to be discovered than just friendship?

While I was going through all of that, I had a few sips of the gin and tonic. It tasted horrible, so I chugged it down as fast as I could, and wished I had a nice mai tai.

Devon laughed and patted me on the back when I wheezed as the gin hit the back of my throat. "Careful, now! Another one?"

"No thanks, I've had enough," I said, instantly feeling the booze hitting my brain. And legs. I wish I knew why I always feel alcohol in my legs.

"Now, where's the fun in being sober?" Devon asked, putting his arm around me and pulling me with him when he left the room. "It's a party, after all. Here, let's get you another one."

By now, people were pretty well lubricated. Devon shoved another drink into my hands, but I ignored it. What I really wanted was to find Fang, but I didn't see him in any of the groups of people we passed.

Devon pulled me along toward the stairs, and my only excuse for allowing him to do so was that by that time, I was feeling the full effects of the gin and tonic. I thought it was odd that just one little drink could make me so woozy, but I figured it had to do with the fact that I'd never had gin before, and it clearly didn't agree with me.

DRU !!!

EM Yes, yes, I know, my thinking ability wasn't exactly sterling.

DRU I was gonna say! Go on. I'm going to be quiet and let you tell me the rest, because this is just like a Hallmark movie. A really weird one.

EM "Come to my room, sweetheart," Devon said to me, his eyes bright blue and glistening just like your mom's sapphire ring.

"OK. Have you seen Fang? I thought he was talking to his friends, but now I can't find him. Boy, is it hot in here? I'm hot. I'm really, really hot."

He sucked on a spot beneath my ear that made me go all boneless and tingly. "Oh, yes, you are hot. Aidan said you're very, very hot, and I've wanted you to burn me for so long, sweetheart."

"Is Fang in here?" I asked when he opened a door to a room and pushed me inside. "I should find him."

"Why? You and he together?" Devon made a little circle symbol with one finger.

I sighed to myself, suddenly morose. "No. We have benefits, but not very often because Fang has to go off and get practical experience."

"Benefits?" Devon squinted at me. Or at least that's what it looked like to my gin-muddled mind. "So you're not together?"

"No." I mused sadly on the fact that I'd lost him in the crowd. I thought briefly of going to find him, but I was suddenly very sleepy in addition to being hot. I recognized that I was pretty squiffy, and figured a little time away from the crowd would help me pull myself together. "I'll just sit here for a bit if you don't mind."

"I don't mind at all." Devon sat on the bed next to me, and next thing I knew, his hands were all over me.

"You smell so good," he said, kissing my neck. "I wanted to do this ever since I met you, but I thought you were Aidan's girl. I'm glad you're not."

"No, I'm not." I tried to frown, but my eyebrows got tangled up with each other. "I'm not with him at all."

"But you were, right? He said you were a lot of fun, too. I thought of a few things you might enjoy." He slobbered on my neck a bit more.

"Whoa," I said, and got up quickly. A little too quickly, because my stomach made a couple of somersaults. "I think I'd better go find Fang."

"Why?" he asked, his eyes narrowed on me.

"Because he's brought me here, and it would be rude to just disappear," I said, feeling sad at the thought of Fang leaving in a few days. Dammit, I wasn't going to fall in love with him. Not when we didn't really have a future together beyond a little casual (but highly enjoyable) sex.

"If that's all you're worried about—" Devon was suddenly at the door just as I was opening it. And then he was kissing me again, this time letting his tongue in on the action.

"Nooo!" I moaned, and, lurching back from him, managed to make it to the bathroom before I unloaded all the gin and tonic. And the lasagna. And my mom's salad. All over the bathroom floor.

I didn't exactly pass out at that point, but I did slouch down with my face on the wall, enjoying the way it was solid and not at all rolling like the floor. Then something cold touched my face. It felt so good, I leaned into it, wanting more.

"Hot," I said, that horrible barf aftertaste in my mouth. My tongue felt like it had been dipped in wax.

The cold thing went away, then came back again, wetter and colder. I pried open my eyes and saw that it was a washcloth, and thought, for some stupid reason, that part of the problem with England was that the stuff they call things just doesn't make sense.

"It's a washcloth, not a flannel. I don't know why they call it a flannel," I said, a little startled that I said out loud what I was thinking. "It's not made out of flannel, now, is it?"

"They used to be," a familiar voice said. I turned my head and saw Fang. It was his hand at the end of the washcloth.

"Oh, I'm so glad you're here. I couldn't find you," I said. Well, "croaked" might be a better word to describe my voice. My throat burned and I tried to not speak directly at him, because I was sure I had barf breath.

"I went outside to see my friend's new bike. Dev asked me to come up. He said you were a little unwell."

"I'm not drunk," I said, the words coming out a gargled moan. "I hate people who are drunk. I just had one drink, and I didn't like it. It's just that gin hates me, and then I got hot and my stomach decided it had enough of the party, and I couldn't find you. Did I mention I tried to find you?"

"You did," he said gravely.

I realized then that he thought I was the sort of woman who got drunk at parties and barfed all over the host's bathroom. Which, of course, I did. I sniffled, feeling sorry for myself. "I'm sick. I think I have the flu."

Fang didn't even smile. He just put his hand on the back of my neck. "I don't think so."

"I'm hot and I threw up. I believe that qualifies as ill."

"No, that's pissed," Devon said, coming in to check on me.

I eyed him, wondering if I had imagined him kissing me a couple of times, or if he had really tried to hit on me. I wanted to confront Devon, but decided that if I did so in front of Fang, he'd have an even worse impression of me than he already had. "I want to die now, please. Fang, you're almost a vet—would you put me out of my misery?"

"She's pissed all right." Devon's voice was kind of muffled, because Fang was cold-washclothing me again.

"I'm not mad. I'm sick," I told the washcloth. Fang pulled it away.

"All right to sit up now?" he asked. I couldn't look him in the eye. It was too mortifying. He thought I was a drunkard. He thought I was a Boozy McBoozerton, and I didn't have any proof that I wasn't. God take me now, because my life is over.

"I'm OK," I murmured, clinging to the desperate hope that if I repeated it enough, he'd believe me. "Just sick."

"Want to go home?" Fang asked.

I tried to sit up, but the room kept spinning and making my stomach flip-flop, so I lay slumped against the wall, and prayed for death.

"What the hell happened?" I heard Fang asking Devon. "Did you *pour* the alcohol into her?"

"Of course not. She may have had a few before I found her, but I just gave her the one. Well, two, but she only drank one."

"Well, she's clearly had more than just one drink." Fang's face, which was a bit blurry, got frowny. "You didn't slip her anything, did you?"

"If you weren't such a good friend, I'd take your head off for that. No, of course I didn't give her anything. She just started drinking and then the next thing I knew, she's puking all over. It's not my fault if she can't hold her liquor."

"No, but that doesn't excuse this." He waved a hand at me just like I was an object.

"I don't drink a lot normally," I said, trying not to breathe (it made my stomach worse). "Bess and I had a lovely mai tai party, but that was at home, and I only had two whole mai tais before I had to call it quits. Bess says I am a cheap date because I have a low tolerance to alcohol."

There was silence for a minute.

"I guess you shouldn't have been drinking a lot, then," Fang said, and I cringed at the censure in his voice.

I wanted to cry. I had so been looking forward to a couple of nights of sex with Fang, and now I'd gone and ruined it all. I was worse than miserable—I was pathetic.

"I'm not drunk. I'm sick," I insisted for the umpteenth time, suddenly really tired. I couldn't keep my eyes open; I was so tired. Things got a bit woozy again then, but I do remember Fang picking me up and carrying me, because it made my stomach lurch around. Then there was wonderfully cold air, and I could sleep some more, and then Mom and Brother were talking, and Fang was saying something, but I couldn't quite understand him because he sounded like he was talking into a tin can.

I threw up again, sometime in the middle of the night, but at least I made it to the bathroom for that. When I woke up this morning, I thought I had died and was in hell. My mouth tasted like … well, I can't even think of anything bad enough to describe it. My head hurt. My eyeballs hurt. My hair hurt. I felt like I was made out of something really, really fragile, and I had stress fractures all over and was about to shatter.

Gah. I need more aspirin. The ones I took aren't working. Be back in a couple of minutes.

CHAPTER FOURTEEN

DRU HOLY CHEESE AND TOAST! You can't just tell me that amazingly horrible story and then disappear for twenty-five minutes!

EM Sorry. I feel so incredibly bad. I can't even begin to tell you how awful I feel, except to say that the air around me is too thick. I can't breathe it in. It won't fit into my lungs.

Let's see, where was I? … Oh, yeah, this morning. By the time I staggered to the bathroom, I realized what had happened.

I'd been drugged. Tash, that expletive deleted, had put something in that drink she gave me. No wonder it tasted horrible. I don't know if it was a roofie, or something else, but I have never had such an extreme reaction to a drink as I had last night.

I couldn't imagine what Fang and Devon must be thinking about me; it made my brain hurt too much, but I do know this—I don't have any proof that Tash drugged me. I doubt if I ever will. It'll be her word against mine, and everyone will think I am claiming to have been drugged just so they won't think I was drunk as a skunk.

I will never be able to face either Fang or Devon again. Ever. I just can't do it. I would scream, except then my head would splat open and it's not fair to Mom to make her clean up the brain-splat mess.

DRU Oh my god! I was going to say that I just bet you she roofied you! Holy Cheetos, girlfriend! What a horrible night!

EM My eyelashes are way too heavy.

DRU You poor thing.

EM I managed to brush my teeth (I swore they screamed when I touched them) and my tongue and the rest of my mouth to get that lovely après-barf taste out of it, and then I staggered downstairs to see what living human beings looked like.

DRU OMIGOD your parents!

EM Yup. I had a feeling that I'd be getting a lecture from them, at least until I explained about Tash and the nasty-tasting drink. Since my whole body was numb around the edges at that point, I figured it would be better to face the family when I didn't actually have the ability to hear any chastisement.

"Ah, Emily," Brother said, looking over the *Guardian* to cock the Unibrow at me. "There you are. You look ghastly. Doesn't she look ghastly, Chris?"

Mom was pouring herself a cup of coffee. The molecules of coffee in the air pounded my body. I almost fell over. "Yes, yes, she does. She looks as if she feels like she's been turned inside out. I can't imagine it's a good feeling."

"Gah," I said, and sort of slumped into a chair.

"I remember feeling as if a herd of elephants had danced on me once," Brother said. "It was the time I went to South America and got malaria, but even after lying in bed with a fever for two weeks, I believe I looked much better than Emily does. Have you noticed the fact that the flesh around her eyes is red and swollen to the point you can hardly see her eyes?"

I tried to gingerly feel around one eye to see how much Brother was exaggerating, but instead of an eye, my fingers found two big sausage rolls of flesh with a few eyelashes poking through them, so I decided it was better that I not explore any further.

"I did notice that. And the green pallor of her skin—would you say it had the same consistency and color tone that a week-old dead frog has?"

I touched my cheek. It felt green.

Brother tipped his head as he considered my frog flesh. "Oh, I don't know. You remember that dead body they found in the Green River? The one that had been in there six months? I think her skin tone looks more like that than a dead frog."

"Gark."

"The bits that remained, of course. So much of the corpse was eaten off by fish."

I tried to stand, but couldn't get my legs to work. "You're both cruel. Why can't you just lecture me like any other parents? Why do you have to make this worse?"

Mom smiled her evil mom smile. "What are you talking about, dear?"

"I believe she's speaking of the fact that she was brought home last night in a near stupor, smelling of vomit and alcohol, having passed out earlier, according to the man into whose hands we had placed the responsibility for her safety and well-being, a responsibility he had obviously failed to keep."

Oh, god, what had he said to Fang? I wanted to die all over again. "No one is responsible for my safety and well-being but me," I muttered, trying to think of how I was going to apologize to Fang, since I wasn't ever going to be able to face him again.

"I'm glad to hear that you recognize that fact," Brother said drily.

"Not that I did anything wrong."

The Unibrow rose in question.

"I didn't," I said stubbornly, then instantly regretted it as a red wave of pain washed over me. I took a very slow, very gentle deep breath, and figured I'd better get it over with. The Parentals weren't going to let me go without my admitting the worst. "I wasn't drunk last night. I was drugged. By Aidan's so-called girlfriend."

"Drugged?" Mom said, frowning. "Are you sure, Emily?"

I rolled one painful eyeball over at her. "I had one gin and tonic. Just one drink, nothing else. I might be a lightweight with booze, but I'm not *that* susceptible."

"Oh," Mom said; then suddenly she was on her feet. "Dear god, were you raped? Brother, someone slipped her a date rape drug! You have to call the police!"

"No rape," I said, wanting to clutch my head against the monstrous noise of her speaking so loudly. "No police. I got sick and barfed it up before anything horrible could happen, not that Devon would do anything like that."

"I'm relieved to hear that, at least," Brother said. "Do you know what drug you imbibed?"

It was hard to see him clearly through the swollen-eye sausages, but I could see enough to recognize that he was wearing his smug look. "No. It's just a suspicion, but it explains why I got so sick so fast."

"Surely there must be something we can do," Mom said, looking agitated.

Brother's Unibrow did a little up-and-down motion that instantly made me seasick. "I don't see what we can do. We have no evidence to give the police. Emily wasn't violated in any way other than being made sick. I believe we can do nothing other than remind her yet again to be cautious when drinking with people she doesn't know."

"Trust me," I said, clutching the remains of my head. "I'm not going to make that mistake again. At least, not while Tash is around."

"In any case, I think she's learned a valuable lesson, and the resulting punishment has been fitting," Brother said in that pompous manner he gets when he thinks he's got something on me.

I tried to glare at him, but it hurt too much. "I'm not a child who needs to be punished," I pointed out.

"Indeed," Brother said. "One would think you would know better."

"And yet you are both looking at me with identical expressions that say I'm supposed to have learned something from this hellish nightmare."

They smiled. They were just that evil.

"Fine, you want to grind home a learning experience that I didn't need or deserve because I did nothing wrong, you go right ahead." I gently touched my face. "I'll deal with your unrealistic expectations later, after my eyes stop bleeding."

Mom made like she was going to pat me, but I flinched. "Your eyes aren't bleeding, Em."

"They feel like they are." I stood up very slowly and, clutching the available bits of furniture, made my way to the library, where the air molecules were slightly less dense.

DRU I am just speechless. That Tash! What are you going to do about her?

EM I dunno. I probably will never see her again, since I can't ever face Fang and Devon again, so I suppose it's a moot point. Crap. Phone. Must be Holly checking on me to see how the party went. Back in a few.

YOU LOGGED ON

EM Oh, god. Oh, god.

DRU What now?

EM That was Holly, but she wasn't calling to ask me about the party—she told me to get dressed, because she and her non–Russell Crowe uncle are coming by in half an hour to take me to some hospital for terminally ill kids where Chris Hemsworth is doing pictures and signing autographs. Argh. My one chance to meet him and he's going to see me with week-old dead-frog, corpse-like flesh and sausage eye rolls. Kill me now, please. Well, not now. Later, after I get the picture with Mr. Hunkypants.

Must go. Must meet the Hemsworth. Must apply massive quantities of makeup.

I hope I survive the walk up the stairs.

DRU *waves You Can Do It, Emily pom-poms*

CHAPTER FIFTEEN

EM Hello?

FANG What's this, now?

EM It's the way you text when you have a father who insists on a shared data pool and refuses to give you more than one hundred texts per month.

FANG Hullo. How are you feeling?

EM Like I died a few days ago. I'm really, really sorry about last night. Not just the part where you had to haul me home sick as a dog, but also missing spending time with you. Benefitting.

FANG I'm sorry about that, too.

EM For the record, I'd like to state that I was not drunk. I repeat, not drunk.

FANG You did a hell of an impression of it, then.

EM Someone—probably Tash, since she hates me—slipped something into the one drink I had. Just one drink, that's all. And it tasted awful.

FANG Hmm.

EM I did want to thank you for bringing me home. I seem to recall drooling on the inside of the car door. I hope it wasn't a lot to clean up. I'd also like to apologize on behalf of my deranged father, in case he yelled at you for my (drugged, not drunk) state upon arrival home.

FANG He did have a few choice things to say. As for being drugged, I wondered if you hadn't taken something for a little recreational fun.

EM Nope. Not a single thing. Anyway, since I am too embarrassed to ever see you or Devon again, will you please have a really nice life, and remember me with some fondness. Especially how we didn't scare the badgers. That will remain one of my best memories ever.

FANG Don't be silly. You don't have anything to be embarrassed about. It was kind of surprising, since you don't seem like the type to get legless.

EM I'm not. And I'm glad you aren't thinking the worst of me, because Tash is a horrible person who would drug someone just to make her look (and feel) like an idiot, but the fact still remains that I can't see you again. I hope your life as a vet goes swimmingly, and that you name your first child after me. If it's a girl, naturally.

FANG You're making too much over nothing.

EM Am not.

FANG You'll get over it. I'll have a word with Dev, though, and make sure that he knows you were drugged. And stop talking foolishness—my first child is going to be named Galileo. Besides, I'm taking you to the Halloween party in a few weeks. You have to see me, at least one more time.

EM I've changed my mind. Good-bye. I hope you have a really happy life.

FANG What sort of a fancy dress am I supposed to wear?

EM You can't come to the party. Go away.

FANG I'm no different than I was before, and I certainly don't think any less of you because you were drugged at a party, you daft girl! Speaking of doing things, do you want to see the new James Bond?

EM Well … OK. You can take me to the Halloween shindig, but you can't look at me. Ever. Those are my conditions. Oh, and if you have to leave tomorrow, I'd rather not spend tonight in a movie theater. I don't suppose you have any badger-watching to do tonight, hmm?

DRU Will you guys take me off this group message? I don't care whether or not you go see the new James Bond movie, and it's just weird seeing you talk about benefitting each other.

EM You're just jealous because of my fabulous picture with Chris Hemsworth (even with sausage eyes, it was pretty splendid, no?).

FANG ?

DRU Hi, Fang. I'm Dru.

FANG Ah. Emily's friend. I've heard a lot about it. Nice to meet you.

DRU Likewise.

EM Sorry about the group thing. I'll separate Fang out so that you don't see us sexting.

FANG We're going to sext? I thought you wanted to watch badgers again?

EM I do. I just don't want Dru to know that we're going to the land of boink.

DRU Too late.

DRU HAS LEFT THE GROUP

EM See you in a bit?

FANG An hour?

EM Perfect! Smooches.

CHAPTER SIXTEEN

Note to self: really? Still no super-fabulous title for this? Must brain up a good title; else the book will never sell to Hollywood, and Chris "His Cheek Has Touched My Lips" Hemsworth will never star in it.

Fang called me after our little text flurry.

"I'm running a bit late, but I'll be there in forty minutes, all right?"

"Okey-doke."

"I take it that you're feeling well enough to do all the carnal things that I suspect you're planning?" he asked, his voice warm on my ear. "No hangover?"

"If I did have one—and I will admit to not feeling tip-top pippidy squeak, or whatever it is you British people say—then it would be a drugged hangover, not a too-much-booze hangover."

"Now that you mention it, it is a bit odd that you got so drunk in the half hour I'd been talking to my friends. I ... erm ... I wondered if you'd had words with Aidan."

"Aidan didn't so much as say hello to me, not that I did, either. But still."

"Ah. So that's over, is it?"

I sighed. It felt a bit weird talking to Fang about this, but I reminded myself that he wasn't a boyfriend; he was just a friend who I liked to have sex with. Lots and lots of sex, not that I'd gotten it thus far, but a girl could hope. "I don't know that there was much to begin with, to be honest. Devon seems to be more smitten with me than—"

Oh, holy hellballs, what had I done? I stammered to a stop and wished, for the one hundredth time that day, that I was dead.

"Oh?" His voice was neutral, almost flat.

"You can stop ohing right there. There is nothing to oh about. As far as I'm concerned, Devon is just a flirty man who was a bit squiffy himself last night. For one thing, he kept saying something about Aidan talking about how hot I was."

"Ah, that. Yes."

"What do you mean, 'ah, that, yes'?" I asked, rubbing my forehead.

"Evidently Aidan told Devon that you and he—Aidan— had a bit of a fling while I was in Ireland."

"We most certainly did not!" Indignation made me sit up straight. "How dare he lie about me? That little rat!"

"Don't worry about it. I had a word with him about repeating it, even if it was true."

"It's not!" I protested.

"I'm glad to hear that. Now, about Devon …"

"There's nothing there, either. He must have thought I wanted to hook up with him because Aidan is trying to make me look like Emily the Wonder Ho. I am so going to get him."

"That being said, I wouldn't want to make you do something you'll regret later," Fang said, and all of a sudden, I was worried.

"Don't you want to get together tonight?"

"I want to, yes, but not if it will make issues for you and Devon."

A little something inside me twinged painfully, but I reminded myself that Fang, while a wonderful friend and occasional lover, wasn't looking for anything more, and if I told him that I wanted more from him, I risked losing him entirely. "There are no issues to be had on my part. If you're sure that you haven't changed your mind—"

"I haven't."

"Awesome. Then we're good."

With him being delayed, I had enough time to have a nice bath, put some ice on my face to try to deflate the sausage rolls, and generally get myself ready for Sexy Hot Times with Fang.

"What would you like to do first?" Fang said forty-five minutes later, just as I dashed out of the house and threw myself on him. He'd just gotten out of his car, so I took him a little by surprise, a fact that became noticeable when he staggered backward into a flower bed, tripped over a decorative stone border, and fell ass first with me on top of him. Our heads clunked together as we fell.

"Ow. Ow ow ow. Are you all right?" I asked, rubbing my forehead and squinting down at him.

"Yes, although next time, I'd appreciate a warning of your intentions." He rubbed his head as well. I took the opportunity to sit up on him, my hands on his chest, smiling down at how his head was wreathed in flowers.

"Sorry. I just got a little excited."

"So I noticed."

At that moment Brother came around the side of the house, marching past us with a glare so pointed, you could have roasted marshmallows on it. "Would it be too much to ask that you not engage in sexual congress in the front garden?"

"You know how to take all the fun out of life. Oh, don't expect to see me until morning. I plan on having my way with Fang, and it's going to take a while to do everything I want," I yelled after him, but managed to get off Fang before I did, in fact, strip him naked and do wicked things to him.

"I was going to suggest that we have dinner and then go to my place, since my roommate is in Belgium for the month," Fang said as we got into the car. "But if you have other ideas—"

"Sex," I said succinctly. "Lots and lots of it. Then maybe some food. Followed by chitchat, some *Doctor Who* viewing, and then more sex, after which we should probably hydrate, and possibly shower. Then, just to switch things up, we'll have some sex. Sound good?"

He laughed, and gave my knee a quick squeeze. "That's what I like about you, Emily—you are so shy and undemanding."

I laughed with him until the thought struck me: What if he wasn't joking? What if he was couching his real thoughts in a joking manner so as not to offend me? I looked down at his crotch, and gasped, pointing. "You are not sporting wood!"

He looked in a somewhat startled manner at first me, then his groin. "No, I'm not."

"But I was rolling all over you. And kissing your face. And if Brother hadn't come out when he did, I would have gotten my hands on your nipples, and you know how you liked me touching your nipples!"

"I do like you touching my nipples, but it wouldn't be very advisable for me to drive with a raging erection, would it?"

"It wouldn't have to rage," I argued. "No one said it has to rage. Raging is bad. Just a little friendly stiffy would be nice, though. Something that says, *hey there, happy to see you, and I'm really anticipating later on when you go crazy on me with your mouth and hands and lady bits.* Raging doesn't enter into it at all."

"Emily—" Fang started to protest, but I decided to take the matter in my own hands. Literally.

I put my hand on his fly, and gave him a gentle squeeze.

He jerked, both his body and his penis. And then he plowed into the hedge at the side of the road.

"So," I said a good ten minutes later, after he managed to separate the front of his beat-up VW (now, sadly, a little more beat-up) from the hedge. "The lesson we've learned here is that it's not wise to grope the driver when he's a bit skittish."

Fang looked like he wasn't sure if he wanted to yell or laugh. He just looked at me, shook his head, then walked down the road a good twenty feet.

I decided he needed a moment to himself, so I stood next to the car, and worked on an apology. When I had it where I thought it was sufficient, I strolled after him. He was standing with his hands on his hips, staring off into the distance.

"I'm sorry, Fang. I really am sorry. Sometimes I act before I think."

"Sometimes?"

I couldn't see his face in the growing darkness, so I moved around to the front of him. His lips were twisted in an odd half smile. "Forgive me?" I asked.

He grabbed me with both hands, pulled me up against his body, and kissed the ever living breath right out of my lungs. "That," he said when I pounded on his chest to let him know I needed some air, "is how much I missed you. All of me, not just my cock."

"See," I said as we walked back to the car. "If you'd only said that when I came out of the house, then we wouldn't get in these situations."

He roared with laughter, and was still snorting and chuckling to himself some ten minutes later when we arrived at his flat. He lived above a row of shops and shared his apartment with another vet student, named Lars.

"So this is chez Fang," I said, looking around at the room. It was pretty Spartan, with the living room consisting of an old couch, a couple of dog beds, and a flat-screen TV. Attached was a small kitchen, a bathroom, and two bedrooms.

"Food?" Fang said, gesturing toward the kitchen. "I have plenty of frozen fish."

I pursed my lips.

He smiled, and led me to the bedroom.

"I'm not sure what to do," I said as he pulled down the duvet that covered the bed. "Should I strip first? Should I strip you, then take off my clothes? Should I wrestle you to the bed and have my womanly way with you while fully clothed? These are the decisions that face us, Fang. What's your opinion?"

He thought for a moment, then sat down on the bed, scooting so he was leaning against the headboard. His room was almost as Spartan as the living room, but there were a couple of pictures on the wall, photos of his dogs and what looked like his parents. "Why don't you go ahead and take off your clothes, and I'll watch."

"That doesn't seem very entertaining," I said, glancing down at myself. "Besides, the bike riding I did to see Chris Hemsworth didn't do as much for my behind as I hoped. I don't think you need to see it bared in all its dubious glory."

"I've already seen it, Em."

"You did not!" I said, aghast.

"I saw it when we were badger watching."

"It was dark out!"

"Not so dark I couldn't recognize an ass when I saw it."

"And?" I said after a moment's thought.

He smiled again. "I liked it. Would you prefer I take your clothes off?"

"Oooh, yes, please."

In a flash he was next to me, pulling my shirt off, his hands all over my boobs. I decided that turnabout was fair play, and started unbuttoning his shirt so I could get at his chest and nipples, all while he was trying to get my bra off.

"This is … oh, yes, right there, please … this is a bit … ouch. That was my hair. This is very, very—hey." I stopped, staring down at my hands. Somehow, in our frenzy to get both our clothing off, I'd managed to tie a knot in our sleeves. "Now, how on earth did we do that?"

"I don't know," Fang said, laughing again. "But I'm not surprised that you managed to pull my sleeves off of me and get them onto your arms. No, Emily, stop, you're just making it worse."

"But it's … gah … how did that make a knot? OK, you take your sleeve that way, and I'll pull the body of your shirt up and out of the way, and then my collar can go this way, and … oh, hell. That was part of my skirt that got twisted into that bit."

Fang laughed harder and harder as I continued to try to untangle us. In the end, we had to shuffle over to his nightstand to get a pair of scissors and cut his sleeves off his shirt so I could untangle myself from his clothes.

"Do you mind if I try a cowgirl thing?" I asked when we finally got all our clothing off. Fang had sat to pull off his shoes and pants, and I pushed on his shoulders until he rolled onto his back. "I've been dying to try it ever since I saw it in a porn movie."

Fang's eyebrows rose. "I'm surprised you watch porn."

"Why?" I asked, climbing up his legs until I was sitting just shy of his genitals. "Because I'm so shy and undemanding?"

His lips twitched. "Hardly. More like because you're so into feminism and women's rights. I didn't think porn was known for being particularly supportive of either issue."

"Then you haven't heard of porn for her," I said, and put both of my hands on his penis. "Oooh, good, I didn't scare the crap out of Mr. Pokey, here. I was worried that after the scene with the hedge, he wouldn't want to play anymore."

"Oh, he wants to play," Fang said, pulling me down so he could nibble on my breasts. "Condom? I have some, this time."

He gestured toward the drawer of his nightstand.

I gave him my wickedest smile, the one where my fingers go walking through his naughty parts. He sucked in all of his breath and grabbed the sheet in either hand, his back arching just a bit as I slid down a smidgen, and swirled my tongue around some very sensitive flesh.

"Ride me, cowgirl," he said hoarsely, his hips bucking.

"Ah, you poor men," I said as I slid the condom on him with a minimum of fuss, and a maximum of touching. "With all your parts right out in the open where they are so easily pleasured. Whereas we women have more subtle pleasures."

He opened his eyes wide, lifted his head, and glared at me. "Why aren't you riding me already?"

I grinned. "Now who's demanding?"

"Emily!" he growled.

"All right, all right," I said, scooting up and positioning him where he would be assured of a happy welcome to Emily Land. "So impatient. You know, this isn't at all like it was the first time. I couldn't wait to get you naked then, but now I'm much more in control. Don't get me wrong—I'm enjoying myself, but it's not even close to how exciting it was—hoobah!"

I sank down on him, the sensation of him invading my body enough to make my breathing stop dead, and my intimate muscles begin a song and dance routine about how happy they were to see Fang's penis again.

"Now," Fang panted, pulling me forward a bit so he could slather one of my nipples with his tongue. "Now who's excited?"

"Oh dear god, I am, I am!" I moved awkwardly at first, not quite sure what I was doing differently from the movie I'd watched with the cowgirl actress, but Fang helped out by grabbing my hips and helping me pick up a rhythm that had us both moaning nonstop.

Fang pulled me down to kiss him, and the change in angle was enough to send me over the edge, my body tightening around him so tightly, I saw stars.

I collapsed down on him, his shout of happiness echoing in my ears as I lay inert on his heaving chest, feeling him buried so deep inside me, I couldn't tell where he ended.

After an eon or two, when I managed to get my brain functioning again, I propped myself up on my elbow and looked down at him. "So. Are we 'go' on cowgirl?"

He laughed and flailed his arms helplessly. "Most definitely so."

I smiled. I'd watched enough of the movie with the cowgirl to stockpile a few suggestions of alternate methods that I'd like to try in future sessions. "Maybe in a bit we can do the Tangled Spider. Or, if you're really pooped, Reverse Wild Stallion. Or maybe even Rainbow Arch, although I'd need to do a little yoga first to loosen up my back."

"Assuming I survive, yes, we can try your wild spider. Although I make no claims that I will live through the night if you continue to do that hip swivel you started right before you pushed me too far."

I smiled, and snuggled down against him. I'd give him a bit of time to recover; then I'd show him just how much swivel my hips could do when they put their mind to it.

I did not, in fact, return home the next morning. Fang decided he wanted to go check on his dogs, so we drove out to his cousin's house, played with the dogs for a bit, and then took our time going back to Piddlesville. We had a nice lunch in a dark little pub where he got me hot and bothered by repeatedly sliding his hand up my leg until I was ready to jump him right then and there. I got my payback on the way back to his flat by telling him in exquisite detail just what Tangled Spider consisted of. By the time we got into his apartment, we were literally pulling the clothes off each other, and didn't make it to the bedroom before we were licking, nibbling, and touching each other, rolling around on the living room rug until we couldn't stand it any longer, and he performed a perfect Tribal Dance.

By Sunday, when we reluctantly parted—me to try to do a last-minute paper for college, and Fang to head up north to continue his practical experience—Fang had dark circles under his eyes, rug burn on his butt, and a particularly colorful hickey on his left pectoral (where I slipped off him while trying to show him how to do Wild Rodeo), and I just downright walked funny.

Brother emerged from his study when I collapsed onto the hall bench. "Do I—"

"No," I said, interrupting him with a wan hand. "You don't. Because if you ask, I'll tell you. Everything, even though, as Fang says, it's none of your business. In detail so complete, it'll haunt you to the very end of your days. And before you make the objection that I see you're about to make, I'll remind you that I'm of legal age, of sound mind, and yes, we took precautions. So it's your choice. Either ask the question that's trembling on your tongue, or let me stagger to my room, where I'll take a nap for ten or twenty hours, and emerge with a smile on my lips, and a song in my heart."

Brother thought for a moment, then wisely returned to his study without saying another word.

CHAPTER SEVENTEEN

EM Putting this here for you when you get back from wherever you're at. Again, this is edited to remove smutty bits, although I left in the titles of the porn positions in case you want to look them up.

DRU Hello!

EM Oh! You're here.

DRU Yes. Oooh, a new smutty story?

EM No smutty parts, no. Just the prelude and conclusion to smutty bits.

DRU Sigh. You know I have read erotica, right? I can take smut.

EM You'll have to wait for the book and movie deal. Then I'll let you read it.

DRU You're such a diva now that you're writing your sexual memoirs.

EM Back later. Smooch.

YOU LOGGED ON

DRU I just got the picture you sent me. I can't believe you actually told the Hemsworth that you wouldn't marry him if he was available, but that you would put him at the top of your bucket list. And to kiss him! OK, it was a cheek kiss, but still! I would never have had the nerve to do that.

EM For the record, that was the remainder of the party drugs talking, and not normal, sane me, who would never tell a Handsome Movie Star that she wouldn't marry him, but she would shag him. No sir. I'd never do that in my right mind.

DRU Mmmhmm.

EM The kiss, though? It was pure me, baby, pure me.

DRU Are you still walking funny?

EM No, but I do have some pretty damned good memories stored up. Although …

DRU ???

EM Nothing. Just kinda sad.

DRU I get that. We can be sad sisters together.

EM Have you heard anything from Mr. Package?

DRU No, and at this point, I don't expect to. I think he'll probably go back to his ex.

EM Poor Dru. What can I do to make you less sad?

DRU Nothing, unless you want to ship Devon to me.

EM Ha! I would if I could. No other guys looming on the horizon?

DRU Nope. I'm counting on you to cheer me up.

EM Oy. Things are rather bleak around here now. Fang is gone for two months or so—with the exception of the weekend for the Halloween party—and although we both agreed that what we have now is perfect, I feel … I don't know. Depressed, kind of. Maybe a little rejected, which is stupid, because both Fang and I went into this relationship knowing it was nothing more than what it is, and to now feel bummed out because he's gone off to do his own thing … it's not fair to him, and I know it.

DRU Doesn't make you feel any better, though.

EM Nope. I have a horrible feeling that the benefits part of our friendship isn't working out. Not literally, because holy hellballs, does that man know how to … yeah. But maybe it's not as perfect a relationship as I thought it was. Maybe it's him being all free and easy and not seeming to mind that he's away for several months.

DRU Dude.

EM I know, I know.

DRU He told you!

EM He did, he said he didn't want a long-distance relationship, and that's exactly what I think I want—a real relationship, not just itch scratching. I'll have to think about this. Maybe I'll call him this weekend so we can talk about how things are going for each of us.

DRU That might not be such a great idea. I've had more boyfriends than you, and in my experience, no man ever wants to talk about relationships.

EM Siiiiiiiiigh. You're right. Hokay, time to pull myself out of the self-pity patrol. Fang is what he is, and I am what I am, and if we aren't meant to be together in any way but casual funsies, then so be it. There are other men available, ones who wouldn't mind having a full-time partner.

Change of subject time.

DRU Oh, good. I think we both need that.

EM You should enjoy this, then.

The Duff Creature turned me in for showing up to Holly's French class without my uniform. You'd think by now she'd give up trying to get me into trouble (since it's clear to everyone else that I have Russell Crowe immunity), but no, she keeps trying. Naturally, I blame her sister, Tash.

Speaking of French, the teacher, Madame Grayson, is growing more and more suspicious of me. I think it was the claim of tuberculosis that did it, but I'm not sure. It might have been the glandular fever I was supposed to have had last week. I knew I shouldn't try to describe my illness using Google Translate. It never gets the words quite right. Anyway, she demanded that I go see Russell Crowe.

"Mrs. Grayson tells me that you've not been participating in French," RC said, all nice and friendly-like. "I'm afraid that given your record, I shall be forced to expel you. Again."

We both looked at each other, and laughed.

"Sorry," he said, plopping himself down on the corner of his desk. "I couldn't resist. How is Holly doing? Her mother tells me that you've made great progress with her, and I see from attendance records that you're down to just the one class with her now."

DRU Wow, really? She really has come far!

EM She has. I'm so proud of her.

"She's actually doing really well. I got her to volunteer for the web project—" I coughed, having forgotten for a moment about that. "Well, you know about that."

"Yes," he said slowly, cocking an eyebrow.

"Sorry," I said, clearing my throat. "But the good thing is that Holly is starting to volunteer for things on her own, without me having to shove her into them. And she hasn't talked at all in the last month or so about feeling alone and isolated, and like there's no hope for ever feeling normal. I think between her therapist and the time we've been hanging together, we have her past the worst of it."

"I hope so. She has a bright future if only she'll allow herself to see it through. And how are your classes going? Still hating diversity?"

I grimaced. "Don't get me started."

He got up, glancing at his watch. "Well, now that you've been duly chastised for not wearing your uniform to school, we shall have to address the French issue. You don't, by any chance, want to learn the language, do you? I could assign you a tutor if you liked."

"I wouldn't be opposed to learning it, but not right now," I said, and gathered up my things.

"Let me know if you change your mind. And as for the tuberculosis … would you please pick a slightly less communicable disease next time? Madame was quite upset at the thought that you were contagious, and I wouldn't want word to get out to the parents that there is an epidemic."

"Sure thing. I'll tell Madame I was wrong about the tuberculosis so she stops freaking out. And on the bright side, at least I don't have to continue trying to cough up my lung in class."

DRU Really, Em? Tuberculosis?

EM It was all I could think of. After talking to the Crowe, I had to go turn in the paper that I was late writing due to Fun Time with Fang, which was meh. The paper, not Fun Time.

And who should I run into while trotting through the library at the university, but your favorite Tash-kissing hipster and mine, Aidan.

DRU Oooh, drama!

EM "Emily!" Aidan caught my arm as I was passing by a table where he was sitting. I had decided not to see him, since he couldn't be bothered to notice me at Devon's party, but I had to stop when he wouldn't let go of me.

"Oh, hello," I said coolly.

"I was looking for you this morning. Your father said you should be in today, and I was hoping to see you."

"Really?" I waited, deciding that I had made my point, and that from here out, I'd be chilly but polite. "I was busy earlier. I had to discuss my eighteenth expelling from Holly's school."

He smiled at me, really smiled, with his eyes and mustache and everything. "Trouble in scholastic paradise?"

"Not really, no." I steeled myself to be immune to that smile. His goatee could go soak its head in a bucket of water so far as I was concerned.

"Good. I thought you might like to come with me to the club again. Friday?"

I stared at him, wondering if he was insane, or if I had suddenly gone mental.

DRU Is he insane? Wait, you just said that. Never mind, it should be repeated.

EM "Wait a minute," I said after thinking about whether to call him on his previous behavior. "Wasn't it you who just three nights ago sat in a chair in Devon's house and stared at me without so much as blinking in my direction? I could swear it was you who was quite happy with Tash mauling your face with those faux-plumped lips of hers. Wasn't that you, or do you have a doppelgänger that I don't know about?"

He made a sad face. "I'm sorry about that, I really am. I was more than a few sheets to the wind by the time you got there, and Tash was making a fuss, and it just seemed better if I played it cool with you in order to keep her from making a scene on Devon's birthday."

DRU Ha! Likely story.

EM I frowned a little, watching him closely. His eyes met mine without the slightest indication of deception. Could I have totally and completely misjudged him? Was I being swayed by a pretty goatee? Was I finding excuses for him because I was blue over the situation with Fang?

DRU No. Yes. Yes.

EM I hesitated a few seconds before answering, deciding to be cautiously optimistic. "That sounds like fun, but I can't. I'm going to London with my folks on Friday. They're going to see a show, and I'm doing a little shopping for the Vampire Ball."

His smile became more … ugh. The only word I can think to describe it is "intimate." Language: it still beats the crap out of me. Anyway, his smile was quite warm. "Why don't you stay home, instead? I'd be happy to keep you company if you are … *lonely.*"

"That sounds very much like a proposition," I said bluntly, feeing it better to lay our cards on the table, so to speak. I glanced down the table to see if Lalla and Peg could overhear us. Lalla was talking to a woman who was showing her a pretty purse, but Peg … Peg was staring openmouthed at Aidan.

Clearly, she overheard.

DRU I am appalled. Tell me you're not falling for this!

EM "It's whatever you want it to be, as am I." He stroked one finger down my arm. "Come on, Em. I won't believe you've forgiven me for behaving so badly at Devon's if you don't say yes. Give me a chance to show you just how sorry I am."

"Thanks, but I'm afraid not," I said, still confused as to which was the real Aidan. "I really have to go to London this weekend. Perhaps we can go to the club another time."

"Sure," he said, putting his hand over mine and squeezing my fingers, crushing the little package of chocolate bits I had just bought from the vending machine. "Whenever you like. Just let me know. What about Sunday?"

I looked over at Peg. She chewed the end of her pen and watched us closely. "Sunday?"

"Maybe we could go to the cinema?"

"Oh, sorry, I can't. I have a paper due that I haven't started on."

"Ah." His eyes got all squinty for a minute; then he smiled again and rubbed his fingers over the top of my hand. "Busy girl! Well, there is one thing I know I can do—I can take you to the Vampire Ball."

"Well," I said, and tried to think of how best to say that Fang was going with me. Then I had to pause at that thought, because maybe by the time Fang and I had our Relationship Talk, he wouldn't want to go with me. "Well, as it happens—"

"Good," he said quickly, not waiting for me to finish my sentence. "It's a date, then."

I stared at him, stunned into silence for a few seconds. "But—" I started to say.

"Must run. Your father is waiting for some essays I graded for him, and I wouldn't want to get on his bad side, now, would I?"

He grabbed his messenger bag and hurried off.

"I have a date already, Aidan!" I yelled after him.

DRU *clutches head* Oh, Em. Em, Em, Em.

EM The row of people on the big tables all turned to stare at me.

Aidan lifted his hand to show he heard me, but didn't bother turning around.

I made a frustrated noise, turning back to Peg. "Do you think he heard me?"

"Oh, he heard you," Peg said, giving me a questioning look. "He just didn't care."

"Is he that mental that he thinks I'll dump someone else in favor of him?"

"No," she said with a little smile. "He just doesn't think any other man is real competition."

"Hmm." I thought for a moment. "Do you think Tash hates me enough to want to drug me?"

Peg raised an eyebrow. "With what?"

"I'm not sure. A roofie, maybe?"

She considered this for a moment, then shrugged. "Wouldn't say no, but I wouldn't say yes. It's hard to call."

"You're already a lawyer," I told her, and, with a smile, headed off.

And there you have it in a not-so-nutshell: the horrible mess of emotions, desires, possibly treacherous men with goatees, and one very lickable soon-to-be vet who would rather be off on his own than letting me romp on his body.

DRU You're not going to believe him, right? Right?

EM I don't think he's being honest, no, but I also think that maybe I'm being a bit too harsh on him.

DRU Oh, Emily.

EM I know, you don't agree. It's because you're not right in the middle of it. It's different when you have to face someone and they are really trying to make it up to you.

DRU Just don't do anything stupid.

EM I won't. And I should go tackle the other paper that's due. Are we good?

DRU Sad, but wiser. And good. Smooches.

EM Backatcha.

CHAPTER EIGHTEEN

PERSONAL AND PRIVATE JOURNAL OF EMILY WILLIAMS

Note to self: not smutty at all. Just want to get this out, but can't show it to anyone.

I called Fang tonight. I couldn't stand the worry of not knowing if I was blowing everything way out of proportion, or if my gut feeling was right.

"I miss you," I told him after we'd finished with the catching up on all the news. "I mean, I really miss you."

"I miss you, too, sweetheart."

"When … uh … how much longer are you going to have to do this traveling-around stuff? Not that I'm bitching or anything, but isn't it kind of odd for a vet student to do so much stuff away from school?"

"Not really, no. We have to have practical experience before we graduate. I'm just doing mine while the offers are open. Emily, what's this about? You knew I was going to be away from the area when we started our benefits package."

"Yes, but I didn't realize it was going to be quite so much. It's just … I *really* miss you, Fang. And I was thinking that since we have such a good time when we're together, that maybe we want to drop the friends-with-benefits thing and just … you know … be together. A couple."

He was silent for a few minutes; then he said, "I told you how I feel about long-distance relationships."

"Yes," I said miserably, my heart feeling trampled on, but that didn't stop me from going on. "But I kind of feel like what we have is special."

"It is special. And that's why I don't want it destroyed. Em." He sighed. "When I was younger, I went out to stay with a cousin in Australia one summer, and fell for his neighbor. It was great while I was there, but once I came back home, the relationship fell apart. We just couldn't maintain it when all we did was talk on the phone and text each other."

My heart turned to lead. "That's all we seem to do."

"Exactly. It's why I don't want to take what we have, what I feel for you, and ruin it."

"I see." I didn't know what to say. I wanted to cry, but I hate playing the emotional-blackmail card, and I'd never do it to Fang.

"I'm sorry, Emily."

"Well, you can't say you didn't warn me going into it," I said, pulling up my big-girl pants, and putting aside the need to yell at him, to cry, to make him promise to be something he wasn't. "But I have to say that I don't think I can cope with having you as an occasional lover anymore. Can we just be friends, Fang? Without the benefits?"

He was quiet for a long time. "I'll always be your friend, Emily. No matter what happens, I will always be your friend."

I did start crying then, but silently, so he wouldn't know. I talked about nothing then, just chitchat for a few minutes to show him that I was totally on board with that, because, stupid, stupid me, I'd agreed to the terms of our relationship at the outset.

After he hung up, I sat for a while having a big pity party, facing all the ugly truths about what I'd done, how idiotic I'd been about Fang, and how I'd set us up to fail.

I swore to myself that I would never go into another causal relationship. If I wanted to be with a man, it was going to be with all of him, all parts of his life, not just the sexual bits.

"Buck up, Sad Emily," I told myself at the end of the pity party. "Count your blessings—Fang still wants to be your friend, and that's worth more than anything. Dru's your bestie forever. You have a good friend, if a bit weird, in Holly. Your dad has a hair horn, and your mom is obsessed with becoming the next

Grandma Moses. And there're possible more-than-just-sex men on the horizon: There's Devon. And possibly Aidan, if he stops being such a dick. And who knows what man is just around the corner, waiting to be Mr. Fabulous?"

It didn't do much good, that pep talk, but at least it stopped me from feeling like I wanted to hide for a few months until my heart healed up.

"You weren't in love with Fang," I told my aching heart the next morning when I was getting ready for class. "You were just on the verge of it, so it's good you put the brakes on now, before it really did get too far."

"You saying something?" Bess poked her head into the bathroom, where I was brushing my teeth.

"Yes. I was saying I was smart to end things with Fang before I fell wholly, madly, and completely in love with his puppy-dog brown-eyed self." I took a deep breath. Just saying the words out loud made them hurt a little less. A tiny bit less.

Bess watched me a for a second, then surprised me by nodding instead of flipping me shit, as she was wont to do. "I never did think that was going to work. Much less heartache this way."

"Right," I said, looking back at my reflection. My eyes looked like Holly's used to look. "Much less heartache."

CHAPTER NINETEEN

EM So, it's over. No more benefits with Fang. We decided it wasn't working. We'll still be friends.

DRU Oh, Em. I'm so sorry. Are you OK?

EM Sure. It was only just about the sex anyway.

DRU Honey, it was never just about the sex. Sex you could have had with anyone. You waited all those years until you met Fang for a reason, you know. Let yourself grieve, Em.

EM No grieving, because I haven't lost him—he's still my friend. Hell, he even said he'll be at the party later this month. Only a real friend would do that, don't you think?

DRU I think that sometimes being an adult sucks donkeys' balls.

EM Yeah.

EM This is one of those times.

YOU LOGGED ON

EM As if my life couldn't get any worse.

EM I know it's about three in the morning your time, so I'm going to dictate and go to class. The whole family went up to London for the weekend. Brother sprang for a suite— you'd think this would be a good thing, wouldn't you? But that's when I realized that Mom and Brother were flirting with each other, which meant they would be having Parent Sex while we were there, and that just put me right off my dinner.

"I'm going to bed," I said when Mom giggled and stuffed a chocolate-dipped strawberry into Brother's maw. "I don't think I can take much more of this."

"What's wrong with a little romance now and then?" Brother asked around the strawberry, waggling his Unibrow at Mom. "It makes the world go round."

"Emily is a bit heartsore at the moment, dear. She and that nice Fang parted ways. ..."

I closed the door on Mom explaining just how pathetic my life had become. Bess, who I was sharing a room with, had gone off to visit a group of hedgehog radicals (that's radicals concerning hedgehogs, not actual hedgehogs being radicals), so I had the room to myself, which I put to good use by moping around and feeling sorry for myself.

Then I texted Fang to see what he was doing, figuring I could at least cheer myself up that he was working or studying or something like that. Here's how that went:

Me: Whatcha doing? Working? Studying?

Fang: Done working for the day. Did immunizations until I was dead tired. Now out with a friend.

Me: Ah. One of your vetty friends? I didn't realize you knew peeps up there.

Fang: Not vetty, just a friend. You OK?

Me: Fine. Just ... wondering how you were.

He didn't answer that, which at first made me want to go all weepy, because I can read between the lines as well as anyone. He was out with a woman. He'd found someone up there who he could hook up with, someone who wasn't clingy and demanding and wanting a relationship even if we couldn't be together. *They! They* couldn't be together.

And then I got mad. I mean, if I meant so little to Fang that he could immediately go out and hook up with someone, then why couldn't I do the same?

I marched out of the bedroom intending on telling the 'rents that I was going out to find myself a man, any man, but they were gone. So I told the empty room, and then I went downstairs to prowl the lobby, since it was a nice hotel, and I'm not stupid. If I was going to pick up a man, then I wanted to pick up a nice man. One who wouldn't be a deranged sex fiend. Although I suppose they stay at good hotels, too.

Regardless, just as I was eyeing a guy who was flirting with another man (no, I was not desperate—sometimes, a man you think is gay is actually bisexual), I spotted a beauty salon.

"Makeover!" I said to myself, and, deciding that's what just I needed to move past the Fang Experiment, I toddled in and plopped myself down in a stylist's chair.

"Hullo," the woman said. "I'm Samantha. What may I help you with?"

"I just broke up with my friend with benefits, the only other men I know are dubious or players, and he—my friend now without benefits—is at this moment out with another woman."

"Oh, dear," she said, narrowing her eyes in thought as she combed through my hair. "It sounds like you need a pick-me-up."

"An industrial-sized one," I agreed.

"You know, when I get down, I always think a spot of color brightens life. What would you say to lifting your color to a new level?"

"I have dishwater-blond hair," I told Samantha. "I'm down for anything. I was thinking maybe dark and dramatic. Raven black? Navy blue?"

"You have the skin tones of a redhead," she said after some consideration. "Why not go red?"

"That might be kind of fun," I said, thinking about it. "It would certainly be different."

"We all need an attitude adjustment from time to time, and a nice color will do wonders to perk you up. People will see you anew. And men! Men love redheads."

That sold me on it. "Let's do it," I said, and settled back.

"Just look through here, and tell me what shades you like," she said, handing me a book of fake hair snippets in all ranges of red, from maroony pink on down to strawberry blond.

"This one," I said, tapping on a pretty copper color. The Brits call it ginger, but it was a deep, rich color that I thought would signal the New Emily, the Emily on the Prowl for a Man. Sexy Emily. Emily Without Borders ... oh ... wait, that's something else. "I like this. Copper Sunset Splendor. Even the name is nice."

"Oh, that's ever so pretty," Samantha said, stroking her fingers through my hair. "It'll do wonders for your skin tone, and since your hair hasn't had color on it in a long time, it should take well. We'll just do a little trim to get rid of some of these split ends, yes?"

I agreed to the trim, and let her go to town on my head, trying to figure out just how I was going to balance my budget when I had planned on spending money only for the costume, and not a hair session.

For once, I was glad that the judge garnished my wages, so I wouldn't have to figure out how to add in the payment for the car repair.

"Well, now, that turned out just lovely," Samantha said a good hour later when she took the towel off my hair after washing the goop out. "It's so bright and vibrant, isn't it?"

"Yeah," I said, examining my head. It was more a dark auburn than copper, but I decided that was OK. "It's a bit darker than I thought, though."

"That's just because it's wet. Wait until I get it dried."

And she was right. Once it was dried, heat treated, flat ironed, and coiffed within an inch of its life, it looked gloriously copper. And sunsetty. And most definitely splendid.

"Now, you just go out and forget that man who dumped you."

"He didn't really dump me—"

"—and you find yourself a good man, one who will value you for who you are." Samantha twirled me around in the chair, and whipped off the protective cape. "I just know you'll find true love. Redheads always do."

I wasn't so sure about that, but I figured she had more experience with hair-color-related romance than I did.

It was too late to go man hunting by the time I was done (in fact, Samantha had to stay late at the salon just to deal with my hair, which made me tip her more than I would normally have, thereby cutting into my meager savings even more, but sometimes, you just have to treat yourself), so I just went back up to the room, and went to bed.

The next morning, I strolled out to the living room, where Bess was up reading the paper and having breakfast.

"So, what do you think?" I asked her.

"I think the world is going to hell," she answered, her nose still stuck in the paper.

"No, what do you think about my hair?"

She looked up. Her eyes widened. "You look like Lucille Ball."

"I do not!" I glared at her. "You take that back."

"You look like you'd be right at home as Lucy's double."

"You have the soul of a misanthrope," I exclaimed, plunking myself down on a chair and pulling the basket of rolls from in front of her. "My hair is gorgeous. You're just jealous."

She stood up and walked around me, examining all sides of my head. "I'll be damned. You went and dyed your hair orange. Rebound orange."

"I am not rebounding from Fang," I snapped. "I texted him just last night. You can't rebound from someone if you are still friends with them."

"Uh-huh." She picked up a strand of hair and examined it.

"Besides, it's not orange—it's copper. Copper Sunset Splendor, to be exact, and it's going to drive men wild with redheaded lust."

"Well, if you were looking to have hair that can be seen in the dark, you certainly succeeded."

"Jealousy does not become you, sister."

"Mom's going to pitch a fit, you know."

"No, she won't," I lied, knowing full well she would, but not caring. "What I do with my hair is my own business."

"Yes, but you know how weird she is about that sort of thing. It comes from her having fundamentalist parents, I think."

"I dyed my hair two years ago and she didn't say anything," I pointed out.

"That's because you weren't living at home, and she didn't know until you came home for Christmas. If you don't remember the incident where she read you the riot act and ended up dropping the turkey on the floor, which Brother tripped over when he came in to see why Mom was yelling, then you're in denial. Because it happened."

I grimaced. "I remember. I was just hoping that she'd get over that little peccadillo. I mean, everyone colors their hair."

"Not Mom," Bess said with a knowing look, and picked up her newspaper again.

"I admit she's a bit odd about things like that, but the turkey thing was just an accident. Besides, she let me get my ears pierced when I was fifteen."

"That's only because you threatened to quit school if she didn't say yes."

"So?"

"And you didn't get them all done at once. It took you a good year to get all the piercings. Mom didn't notice they went all the way up your ears until you got the last set."

"Dammit, Bess, I'm an adult! I am not beholden to my mother's dictates, especially when those are just downright unreasonable and bizarre—"

The door to the Parentals' room opened up. Brother paused in the doorway, took a good long look at me and my Copper Sunset Splendor, then turned around and closed the door again.

"See?" I said, feeling nervous all of a sudden. "Brother didn't say a word."

"Brother is not Mom," Bess said from behind her newspaper.

"*She what?*" came the muffled cry from the bedroom.

"That, on the other hand, *was* Mom," Bess pointed out.

"I heard," I said, making mean eyes at her.

"Doesn't sound like she's going to be too happy with the new you."

I straightened my shoulders. I was an adult, dammit. If I wanted to color my hair, then by god, I had every right to do so.

"If I were you, I'd start thinking up reasons they shouldn't shave your head, because you know Mom. She's going to go—"

"EMILY MARIE WILLIAMS!"

"—ballistic."

Mom stood in the doorway of the bedroom, her eyes blazing. Behind her, Brother stood looking slightly worried.

Mom stalked out, stopped, then glanced back at Brother. "Dear god, she looks like she should be starring in *I Love Lucy*."

"That's it," I said, standing. I had decided the best defense was an offense. "I disown all of you. I am going to get my costume and then go back to Piddlesville, where people are reasonable, and polite, and don't say mean things about Copper Sunset Splendor!"

"Well, you have to say one thing for it," I heard Brother say as I grabbed my purse and stomped my way out of the door. "Now you can find her in a crowd just by the glow around her head."

I picked up my costume, and then I did, in fact, go back home. The Infuriating Ones stayed on in London for another day, which was fine by me, because it meant by the time they got back home, Mom would have worked out the worst of her unreasonableness. Bess took off to do some art project in Cornwall, taking my digital camera with her, so you have to make do with crappy phone pics of my hair.

I started up a new Sims family. Well, just one person, SimEm, who lives by herself, and moons around the yard talking to everyone who walks by her house. There's a guy in town who looks a bit like Fang, but every time SimEm tries to talk to him, he makes an excuse and runs off to work.

Sigh.

Hugs and Copper Sunset Splendor kisses.

CHAPTER TWENTY

DRU I hate my life. HATE MY LIFE!

EM Oh dear. What happened now?

DRU BTW, your hair is … intense.

EM Intense good, or intense bad?

DRU Good. I like it. You should be able to have neon orange hair if you like.

EM It's not neon!

DRU I hate my life!

EM You said that already. What's up?

DRU Richard. He wants to have a ménage. Just me, him … and his ex.

EM Whoa. I didn't see that coming. No pun intended.

DRU !!!

EM What did you say?

DRU I said no!

EM And then?

DRU I hung up on him. And then I cried, because the only man I can get nowadays is gay or bi or I don't know what, and likes his ex better than me.

EM That's not true. Why don't you try one of the dating apps and find yourself another man? Wait, I'm not sure that's the answer. I think you're going to have to talk with Richard about why you're feeling the way you do. Maybe just talking with him will make you feel better. Or not. What do I know? I messed up my own good thing, so really, don't listen to me. Do what makes you happy. That's my new motto.

DRU I just wish I knew what would make me happy right now. But I suppose I should at least talk to Richard. If I tell him I don't want to do a threesome, maybe he'll dump the ex. But then I don't know if I really want him. This is so infuriating! Why isn't this shit easy?

EM I got no answers, babe. As you can tell by the sorry mess that is my life.

DRU Speaking of your sorry mess …

EM Hey!

DRU What's going on with Devon? Did you ever talk to him?

EM Yes, I saw him a couple of days ago, as a matter of fact. I had taken Holly shopping to get some makeup for her costume (I managed to talk her out of the wraith, but she decided to go as an emo fae, whatever that is). Just as I was expounding the virtue of glitter fingernail polish for all fae beings, who should stroll into the drugstore (called a chemist here) but Devon, and a woman I'd never seen before.

"Whoa," I said when they sauntered past the end of the aisle. "I wonder who she is."

"Who?" Holly asked, fingering black sparkle polish.

"Black won't show the glitter—go with white. All fae wear white nail polish," I told her, shoving a bottle into her hands before scurrying down the aisle so I could crouch down and peek around the end.

"Who did you see?" Holly asked, scurrying, crouching, and peeking with me.

I pointed.

"Oh! It's Devon."

We watched as Devon and the woman (waist-length hair, skinny enough to be a model, big feet) browsed in the aisle that contained products of a feminine nature.

"She must have the painters in," Holly said, looking uninterested.

"Assuming that means she's having her period, I'm going to have to disagree. They aren't on the tampon side of the aisle. They're on the side with the …" I stopped and eyed Holly.

Sometimes—despite being an undercover tutor at her high school—sometimes I forget she's only sixteen.

"Condoms?" she asked in a shocked whisper.

"Looks like. I'd make a reference to him being a dawg here, but I would like to stress with you just how helpful condoms can be, and if you ever need any, just let me know. I'd buy some for you, but I don't need to. My mother and sister are forever shoving boxes of them onto me. Honestly, they must imagine I have sex four or five times a day, seven days a week."

"Are you going to talk to him?" Holly asked, nodding toward the condom aisle.

"I suppose I could say hi. I have to admit, though, I'm a bit embarrassed about the party, so I don't really want to."

"He's your possible boyfriend's best friend," she argued.

"Ex–possible boyfriend, I'm afraid," I said sadly.

"No, not Fang—Aidan. You said he wants to take you out again, right? That means he wants to be in the picture."

"Hrmph. What he wants and what I want aren't necessarily the same thing. But you have a point. Devon is Fang's buddy, and I should say hi. I'll just stroll down the aisle and look surprised to see him."

"I think you should, although how you can face someone who had his tongue in your mouth is just too hard to imagine."

I patted her on the shoulder. "That's because you aren't as old as I am. I talk to guys whose tongues I know intimately all the time."

"Wow," she said, clearly eyeing me in a new light.

I peeked around the corner to see what Devon was up to. The condom aisle was empty.

"Rats!"

"What?"

"They're gone."

"Oh. Good, that means I can stand up. I'm getting a cramp in my leg crouching like this."

"Who're you looking for?" a man's voice behind my shoulder whispered.

I shrieked and fell backward onto my butt, looking up to find Devon squatting behind me.

"Sorry, didn't mean to startle you, but when I saw you hiding from someone, I thought I'd offer my assistance."

I shot Holly a look as I got to my feet. "Um … yeah. It's no one important."

"Ah." He eyed me up and down, then winked as he wrapped one of my curls around his finger. "You look much better than the last time I saw you. I like the hair; it glows. I guess we get to call you Ginger now."

"The last time you saw me, I was passed out after having barfed on your bathroom floor."

"That's what I mean—you look much better. Although as I recall, you were feeling pretty fine before that." He waggled his eyebrows at me. "At least, you felt damned fine to me."

I looked pointedly at the woman had just stopped next to him. "Really, Devon?"

He laughed. "It *was* a hell of a party, wasn't it? I had a buzz for days. So did Pier, didn't you, sweetheart?"

The dark-haired woman gave us a crooked smile. "You always do throw the wildest parties, Dev. I passed out before I made it back to my flat."

I stared at her for a couple of seconds, wondering if it was normal for people to pass out after they'd been to one of Devon's parties, or if she, too, had been drugged. "As we're talking about it, Devon, I think we need to have a talk about that party—"

"If you like, but another time. We have plans for the evening. This is Pier, by the way." Devon grabbed the skinny model around the waist and growled into her neck, making her giggle.

Holly and I murmured hellos.

"That's Holly," Devon said, nodding toward us. "And this ginger beauty is Emily, who can outdrink a sailor when it comes to G and Ts. Well, ladies, we have to be on our way. Pier has promised to give me a massage, haven't you?" He wiggled his eyebrows at Holly and me, and followed Pier when she giggled her way down the aisle to the checkout stand.

I let out a breath I didn't know I was holding. "Well, now, what do you make of that?"

"You were so calm," Holly said, her eyes still round. "You were like, blasé almost."

I straightened up my shoulders and adopted a nonchalant expression. "There are things I can teach you about handling men, when you get to that point in your life," I said, heading off to the mascara. Holly had the palest lashes I'd ever seen on a person. "One of them is how to face a flirty, flirty man. To them, kissing you means nothing. So you just have to treat things the same way. Yes, he tried to get busy with me, but to him, that was probably just instinct, nothing more."

"Wow," Holly said, obviously thinking about that. "I don't think I'd like someone to be instincting me like that."

DRU Oh dear god. Please tell me you're not going to give that poor girl dating advice.

EM Hush, you.

"Well, I didn't say it was pleasant," I admitted to Holly. "Right, enough man talk for the day. Let's get the rest of your makeup, and then I have to go finish a paper on animal rights."

"Ugh," Holly said, scrunching up her nose. "I wouldn't like that."

"I don't either, which is why I'm writing my paper on why it's OK for wacky old people to leave their pets money in wills."

"But is that animal rights?" she asked as we hauled the basket of goodies up to the checkout.

"They're animals, and someone used his or her right to give them a fortune. Sounds good to me."

And now I really do have to go finish that paper. I couldn't find any good examples of animals who used their inherited fortunes for the good of the world, so I'm going to make up a couple. Because honestly, at this point, I don't really give a hoot about diversely ethical animals.

DRU I don't blame you. I do think you handled Devon well. Do you have any more mai tai stuff?

EM Maybe. Why?

DRU I was thinking we could have a long-distance drinking pity party.

EM Aww, sweetie, I'm sorry you're so upset. I'll be back as soon as I can, OK?

DRU Sure.

EM Back.

DRU Good. What are you up to?

EM Same five foot five as always.

DRU Heh. What would you think if I told you I was going to become a nun?

EM I'd think you were crazy, because you aren't Catholic.

DRU There are other kinds of nuns.

EM You also aren't religious in the least little bit.

DRU A girl can change, you know.

EM Do you feel that a religious epiphany is on the threshold for you?

DRU No, but it's the only thing I can think of where I can be cloistered away from men, and live a peaceful and useful life amongst my fellow celibate sisters.

EM Oh dear. No progress with Mr. Out of the Closet?

DRU No. He has issues. Lots of issues.

EM One being he likes men at least as much as he does women?

DRU Sigh.

EM Did you talk to him?

DRU I tried. He made an excuse that he had to go to a fitting for a drag queen beauty contest, and that he'd talk to me later about my suggestion that if he wanted us to be a couple after all, we go to couples counseling.

EM OH, HONEY. WE SO NEED TO HAVE A LONG CHAT.

DRU Not if it concerns Richard. And I didn't ping you to talk about myself. I wanted to know what you're going to do about your party.

EM What about the party?

DRU You are going with two men.

EM Like hell I am.

DRU You said Fang is still taking you to it, right? And then Aidan kind of confiscated you despite you saying you had a date already.

EM Oh. That. Yeah, I guess I do have to make sure that Aidan understands he's not taking me to the party.

DRU I had an idea that might help you.

EM I wait with bated breath.

DRU Shouldn't that be baited? Like you bait something so you can catch it?

EM No, it's bated.

DRU How do you know for sure?

EM People whose private sexual journals are someday going to make it into film pay attention to details like that.

DRU Oh, is that what it is? And here I was thinking it was just you being smug because you are wordier than me.

EM What was your idea?

DRU Well, this is going to be a smidgen complicated, so you'll have to pay close attention.

EM That sounds ominous.

DRU It's going to take some doing, and you'll need a helper monkey. I thought maybe Holly could help you.

EM Do what?

DRU Here's the thing: You know how at parties everyone mingles and dances and talks and noms the foodstuffs?

EM Yes. What about it?

DRU Well, it's hard to keep track of people. So if you have Holly dancing with whichever man you aren't dancing with, then you can dance with the one you … uh … are dancing with.

DRU Somehow that sounded better in my head.

EM I'm glad it sounded good somewhere.

DRU Regardless of my ability to write, Madame Expert on the English Language, I'm sure if you have Holly rotating to the man you aren't dancing with, then neither one of them will notice.

DRU It'll be fine, trust me.

EM I seriously doubt that. For one, this dance is for the high school kids. I won't be doing much if any dancing. OK, it's open to the public, but mostly it'll be the high school kids dancing away like the little [trying to come up with a nice word and not having any luck, so just going to leave this blank] they are.

Second, I am not going with Aidan to the party, no matter what he thinks. Fang asked me, I accepted, and even though we aren't doing the horizontal hokey-pokey anymore, we're still friends.

I repeat, still friends, and one doesn't dis a friend by dumping him to go with another (potentially jerky) friend.

DRU Fine, be that way! I was just trying to offer you some of my expert advice. You know full well that I am known for attending our senior ball with not only one, not two, but three different boys.

DRU At the same time!

EM And they all got pissed when they found out what you were doing, right?

DRU Trivialities.

EM Crap.

DRU Thank you very much!

EM No, that wasn't directed at you. I just noticed that I'm shedding a lot, big handfuls of hair. I'm going to go the local hair place and get some good shampoo. Try not to stress over Richard. Keep the lines of communication open. You never know what can happen when you do that.

DRU LOGGED ON
YOU LOGGED ON

EM OMIGOD!

DRU Ohai. What horrible thing has happened to you now?

EM The woman at the Leading Edge (POTW hair salon du jour) says it isn't my shampoo—it was the hair color used by the London hotel salon. It was too harsh, and stripped something or burned something or I don't know what because I couldn't listen to her explain it. My mind shut down when she said that it's likely a lot more hair is going to fall out before my follicles recover.

I'm going bald! Wah!

The hair woman said I shouldn't color my hair again for a long time, which means I'm going to have roots, and it'll look awful, and holy hand grenades, my mother was right! She said

I'd live to regret coloring my hair, and now look at me! Baldy McBalderson!

DRU Eep. OK. So, here's what my mom did when she got a perm that made her look like that guy who painted the happy little clouds: cut it short.

EM Are you insane? Dru, I look like one of my mom's old Cabbage Patch dolls with my hair cut short. It makes my nose look stunted, *and* gives me chipmunk cheeks, and you know full well I've been cursed with the Williams Forehead, which I couldn't possibly bare at unsuspecting passersby.

DRU I'm telling you, cut it short; then cut it again once the roots start to show. That way people will be used to you having short hair and they won't think anything of it.

EM No, the only thing for me to do is to start buying hats now, because that's all I'll be able to wear once the rest of my Copper Sunset Splendor falls out.

Mom said she'd pay for me to have as much of the color removed as possible (but only after lecturing me for twenty-five minutes—honestly, the woman has a mania about hair color), but the Leading Edge woman said it might damage my hair even more, so it's all over as far as I'm concerned.

"Upon speaking to the local hairdresser, I have come to a conclusion," I told Brother, marching into his library, and spinning his chair so he had to look at me and not the book he was reading. "You can go ahead and just give me the money you're paying Oxwills for my classes, because once all of my hair falls out, I'm never leaving the house again."

He just squinted up at me. "I'm sorry, is that you, Emily? The glow from your head is rather blinding, and obscuring my vision."

"Ha ha," I said, only just remembering in time that I wasn't fifteen and therefore couldn't stomp my foot. "Ha. Go ahead. I know you want to lecture me just like Mom did."

"Actually ..." He set his book aside. "No, you're right, I do want to. But I suppose I won't, because your mother tells me the only reason you dyed your head Day-Glo orange is because you've parted ways with that man with whom you insisted on copulating all over the front flowers."

"I was greeting him, not having sex, but that's not important. What am I going to do, Brother?"

He looked wary. "About the man who put his hands and I shudder to think what other body parts all over you, or your hair?"

"The latter."

His Unibrow rose in contemplation. "Live with it, I suppose. It'll fade with time. And if it doesn't, you can hire yourself out to the town council to stand on dark intersections during times of fog."

At which point I left him, naturally.

DRU Naturally.

EM Later on, Holly texted me that one of the projects she had worked on (a gaming stream with chat for the fifth formers at her school) was live, and did I want to go in it with her while she was doing moderator duty?

"The very last thing on this earth that I want to do at this moment is watch a gaming stream and its attendant chat filled with a bunch of grotty little fifteen-year-old pimply boys," I said while texting that I'd be happy to.

So I logged in (I'm Skipley, BTW) and here's what I saw:

Pinkfluffyhandcuffs: u fancy me?

Maximus: fancy who?

R-O-M-E-O: how r ya?

Pinkfluffyhandcuffs: not bad cud b better

Docman: my throat is hurty

Throbbing_Gristle: Skip, I wan u 2 know dat our friendship means a lot 2 me.

Docman: boring bean.

Skipley: Huh?

Throbbing_Gristle: U cry i cry. U laf i laf. Skip.

Skipley: Um …

Maximus: Rom, do you fancy me?

Throbbing_Gristle: Skip u jump out of da window …

Skipley: Sorry, it wasn't me who jumped out of THE window.

Docman: boring bean

Skipley: What exactly does that mean? Boring bean?

Throbbing_Gristle: dat wuz a pome Skip.

Throbbing_Gristle: Skip I saw ur game n luk here nw palya da dks on u!

Skipley: Does anyone have a dictionary that I can use to translate whatever it is Throbbing_Gristle is trying to say?

Maximus: u fancy me, Skip?

Skipley: Not in this or any other lifetime, Maximus.

Docman: boring bean

Skipley: You know, that's really annoying, Docman. Does your vocabulary include any other words?

Throbbing_Gristle: u nva luved me u nva will bt evn so I luv u Skip

Skipley: You are too strange for words, TG. I think you need mental help. No, seriously, don't be afraid to admit you need help, and get it.

Docman: boring bean

I left after that. It was just too idiotic.

DRU I like some of the streamers, but not the ones that have obnoxious chats. They get negative so fast. Or they're full of brown-nosers.

EM So, that's pretty much my life right now—I'm going bald, I have no male company in my life, and now some guy named Throbbing_Gristle is sending me private messages through the streaming client, and asking me to show him my boobs.

DRU He's probably a forty-four-year-old FBI agent looking for child molesters who hang out in streamers' chats.

EM *headdesk* Laters.

DRU Night.

CHAPTER TWENTY-ONE

SUBJECT: FWD: RE: DETAILS OF THE GHOST AT 249 BASQUE CLOSE
FROM: THEEMSTER@OXWILLS.GOBBOTTLE.CO.UK
TO: DRU@SEATTLEBIKERCHIX.COM
DATE: 30 OCTOBER 6:33 A.M.

Dear Miss Williams:

We at the Psychic Research Society appreciate your offer of 8 October to investigate the possible haunting of your underwear drawer, but at this time, our investigative team is booked through this year, and most of next. We will keep your request in our files, however, and should a team be in your area and have time to investigate the unusual activity in your knickers, they will contact you.

Thank you for your interest.

Best,

Ken W. Kittenshanks

PRS Vice President

YOU LOGGED ON

DRU I had a talk with him.

DRU He said that he wanted a relationship with me, but that he wants the freedom to also explore experiences with his ex. He said he felt like I was strangling him with my demands on his masculinity, and that he thought it would be good for both of us to be open to new experiences.

EM Morning. Well, for you it's last night, since it's only six here.

DRU Hi. I was just going to bed. I thought I'd update you.

EM I see that. What do you think of what he said?

DRU I was going to ask you the same thing.

EM You know I'm never short of opinions, and I'll gladly give you mine, but what I think doesn't really matter. It's what you are comfortable with.

DRU I am so not a ménage à trois girl.

EM Me either. So tell Package Man that.

DRU *sigh* It's not that easy.

EM It never is.

DRU How did your day go?

EM Oh lord.

DRU That good?

EM That typical.

DRU Good. *pulls up comfy chair* OK, I'm settled. Fill me in on the latest soap opera happenings of your life.

EM You wouldn't enjoy it so much if you had to suffer through this shit.

DRU Of course not! Dish, sister.

EM Well, today's episode is the Saga of Aidan the Hun and Hitlerina Tasha.

DRU You should totally write that as a screenplay. Netflix would pick it up superfast.

EM I was doing a little shopping in Piddles, picking up an ivory silk shawl that I'd ordered for Mom's birthday, when a car honked at me. I figured someone was going to yell something gingery out of the window (which they've been doing of late—that Samantha has a lot to answer for, getting my hopes up that men find redheads irresistible), when to my surprise, Aidan stuck his head out and whistled.

"Niiice," he drawled, giving me the old once-over. "Very nice. Color suits you."

"Thank you," I said, ever polite. "What are you doing here?"

OK, so maybe I'm not as polite as I could be.

DRU Was gonna say! Go on.

EM "Going home," he answered. "You need a lift?"

I hesitated a couple of seconds. Part of me (Sane Emily) wanted to be haughty with him, while the other part (Impulsive Emily) pointed out I have no men friends but platonic ones, that everyone makes mistakes, and that Aidan *had* apologized. The only polite thing would be to give him another chance.

I have a very talky Impulsive Emily.

DRU I have another word for her, but whatevs.

EM "That would be nice," I said, giving in to IE. I got myself and my shopping settled in his car (Audi, and one that's seen better days), and off we went.

At first, everything was fine. He told me about the project he was working on with Brother, and how he was firing his stockbroker for messing up something (I tuned out at that point, because I was trying to figure out how much of my next paycheck would be left after the car deduction had been taken out), and finally, I realized that he was talking about how hard it was to be a man in today's world.

DRU That noise you heard was me snorting in disgust.

EM "What?" I said, looking around and realizing that we were down a country lane I didn't recognize, surrounded by nothing but empty fields and pastureland. "Your sexuality is repressed? By who?"

"You birds. You have ideas from the media of what a man should be, and how he should act, and when we don't conform, you go mental. You have no idea how difficult it is to be sensitive to what women want, and yet show the strength they demand. It's like we can't win for trying."

"I … I just don't know what to say to that."

"That's because you know I'm right," he said, pulling up next to a chestnut tree.

"I don't know anything of the sort, and why are we stopping?"

"I thought we could have a little talk. You never seem to have time to talk anymore." He turned and, with a move that I wasn't at all expecting, pulled me over so I was half on his lap, his mouth glued onto mine. I struggled to get free, but he had a painful hold of my waist, and it wasn't until he was done checking my tonsils that he let me breathe.

"Jesus Christ, Aidan," I gasped, just barely keeping myself from wiping my mouth. "Give a girl some warning before you do that."

"Come on, Emily. You can't expect me to resist the opportunity to kiss you like I've been wanting to kiss you for weeks." He slid a hand over to one boob, and did a little gentle stroking. "Tell me you forgive me for the other night at Devon's."

"There's nothing to forgive," I said, conflicted as hell. I didn't really want to deal with this, not now, but at the same time, if he was sincere about his feelings ... "Now, Tash is another subject. Did you know she slipped something into my drink?"

"Why would she do that?" he asked, trying to get a hand under my shirt.

I slapped his hand away. "Because she hates me? I don't know—ask her. Unless you already know."

"I don't know anything other than you're the sexiest thing I've seen in a long time." He smooched his way along my neck, nibbling on my ear, and getting his other hand into the boob action. "I've missed you, Emily. I've missed talking to you. Missed the way you look at me. Missed the way you make me hard just by looking at me."

Whoa, now. That came out of the blue! I slid a glance down to his crotch, but the way he was sitting, it was hard to see if he was unduly bulgy.

"Wow. That's ... I had no idea you felt that way, Aidan. I had the idea that you were happier with Tash."

DRU Sorry, swallowed wrong at that line of bullshit he's trying to feed you, and had to choke for a few minutes. You're not buying that complete and utter fabrication, are you?

EM Of course not. I want to be fair to him, but I'm not stupid.

Aidan said, "She's a bit psycho, if you want to know the truth. She got it into her head that we have a thing going, and won't let it go, no matter what I do. But it's you I really want."

I was speechless for a few seconds. "I appreciate that, Aidan, but right now, I'm kind of ... well, not celibate, per se, but kind of taking things slow relationship-wise."

DRU Wait, you're celibate now?

EM Fang broke my heart.

DRU He did not.

EM No, he didn't, but I have to cling to something to make the hurt inside feel better. Where was I?

Oh, Aidan. He kissed me again and, to my relief, let me go. "Don't play games with me, Em. You don't need to. You've got me, all right."

"I'm not playing games, Aidan. I wouldn't do that to you. I honestly thought you were happy with Tash."

"Well, now you know different," he said, smiling like he thought I was lying. He started the car up again, whipping around in a U-turn to head back toward the area the Haunted Mansion was in.

"That's … that's nice to know, Aidan," I said, at a loss as to what to say. I felt like if I'd give him any encouragement, he'd jump me again, and I just wasn't ready for that.

"You're a beautiful girl, ducks. We could have some fun together. More fun than you've had recently, eh?"

"Pardon?" Was he talking about Fang? I felt all sorts of ew thinking about him knowing about Fang and me. I mean, we hadn't gone out of our way to keep it secret, but neither of us talked about it to any of our social group.

"Devon."

"What about him?"

"You know."

I shook my head. "I have a feeling we're talking at cross-purposes. I'm not sure what it is you're asking."

"I'd just like to know what you see in him. Is it the money? I know other women are like that, but I hadn't pegged you that way."

"What on earth are you talking about?"

Aidan shot me a look, his lips curled into a smile that made me feel itchy. "I'm talking about you and Devon. You know, the bloke you were with the other night—you *do* remember the night of the party, don't you?"

"Yes, of course I remember it."

Hmm. That was curious, him asking me if I remembered the party. Perhaps it was Aidan, and not Tash, who had drugged me.

DRU I wouldn't trust either of them.

EM But why would he do that? He hadn't even so much as spoken to me that night, let alone try to take advantage of my drugged state.

I decided that a change of topic was in order, since I had no idea what it was he was trying to get at. "Speaking of keeping things in mind, you did hear me when I told you that I am already going to the Halloween party with someone, right?"

"I heard. Dev says you were planning on going with Fang, so that's all right."

"Not planning on going, I *am* going. Aidan, look, this is kind of awkward, especially after you just said so many nice things about me, but we aren't going to the party together."

"Sure we are," he said, just like I wasn't even speaking.

DRU I hate that. I HATE THAT! Guys think they can can totally ignore anything we say, and they can't! So fucking annoying!

EM "I'm going with Fang," I said slowly and carefully.

"Exactly. Fang's a nice guy, but he's too focused on his work to pay proper attention to a bird. So stop making that face— I'm not asking you to get rid of him. You can let him think he's taking you, and we'll both know who'll really be around ready to take care of you."

I was going to tell him that Fang was more than able to take care of me, but that wasn't any of his business (not to mention that it wasn't true anymore). "I hope you have fun while you're at the party; just don't expect me to be able to spend much time with you. I'm running the whole shebang, so I'll be busy with that."

He hummed a song to himself, but I caught him flashing a look at me from the corner of his eye that I couldn't read. I thought about asking him just what the hell he was playing at, but reflection (and the fact that we were coming to my house) kept me quiet. Instead I thanked him for the ride, and got out of the car before he could try to kiss me good-bye.

DRU I don't know how you could sit there and not punch him in the gooch.

EM It was an effort, but then I started thinking that maybe I damaged his frail male ego, and he had to talk big in front of me to try to make himself feel better. If that's all it is, I can live with it.

DRU Hrmph.

EM Oh! Before I go, I have to mention that I think Holly is showing signs of life at last. And by that, I mean while we were waiting for the bus to go to our respective homes, she was watching a thin black guy with a gold earring who stood a little way off, reading *War and Peace*. I kid you not, *War and Peace*!

"Now, there's a man who commits himself to reading," I said lightly.

"Hmm? What do you mean?" she asked, blushing a little and immediately looking away from him.

"The guy over there. He's reading *War and Peace*, which is a notoriously long book. Actually, I've read it twice, but I have a love of Victorian lit."

"Oh, him." She busied herself with the canvas bag she wears slung across her chest. "He's OK, I guess. Kind of nice to look at."

DRU Riiiight. Like we both haven't heard that before.

EM Yup. Needless to say, I'm delighted to see that she's interested in someone, but I don't think I'll mention it to her parents. Poor kid is kinda smothered by them (as evidenced by them hiring someone to watch over her at school).

Fang texted me that he'll be at the party as a vampire, so I expect he'll show up in black with a cape or something. He doesn't really like the costume part of the party, I think, but it's still nice that he's willing to come all the way down just for the party. Especially as we aren't … sigh. Never mind. Not going there again. Time to move on, right?

DRU Well …

EM RIGHT???

DRU Right.

EM Gotta run, Mom is doing yet another English dinner tonight (steak and kidney pie, which sounds gross, but Mom took out the kidney, so it's really just a giant steak potpie), and she wants me to go with her to some farmers' market that opens up at the crack of dawn.

If you need to cry on my shoulder, go ahead. I might be half a world away, but I'm still here for you, girlfriend.

DRU You are the bestest bestie.

EM Lots of hugs and kisses.

YOU LOGGED ON

DRU For once, I have something positive to tell you. Ohai.

EM Hiya.

DRU You're up late again.

EM Planning for the party tomorrow. What good thing do you have to tell me?

DRU Well, at Richard's request, I met his ex, Timothy.

EM *blink*

EM You did?

DRU We went to a little tapas place that's down by the lake, and had a three-way ... dinner! Ha!

EM You're not considering a ménage, are you?

DRU Not sexual, no.

EM Whew. I was trying to think of how to be positive and supportive about that when it kind of squicks me out.

DRU Timothy isn't at all what I thought he'd be like. Turns out he's Timothy McNeil from grade school! Do you remember him? He's bi, just like Richard! Isn't that interesting? We had a long talk while Richard had a little lactose-intolerance issue in the bathroom, and I have to say that Timothy seems so much more mature. And he likes binge-watching all the same shows I binge on! I think that's a sign it's kismet.

EM I'm not sure that kismet applies to your bisexual wannabe lover and his equally bi boyfriend who just happens to be addicted to *Black Mirror* like you are, but hey, who am I to naysay a relationship if it makes you happy. Except ... just be careful, Dru. A threesome always sounded to me like someone is going to be left out in the cold, and I'd hate to see you hurt if Richard decides he likes his boy toy better than you. Or worse, is jealous because you and Tim get along so much better than they do. You did say Tim was his ex, right?

DRU Right. They aren't formally together again. They are exploring their options. I like that.

EM That sounds reasonable, but just be careful of your feelings and such. Although I will say that Tim is a really nice guy even if he did used to pants all the girls (never me, though, because he knew I'd beat the crap out of him if he did).

DRU I forgot about that. I'll have to remind him. What's left that you have to do for the party?

EM Oy. So much. I went to a theatrical rental place today and I rented an awesome fog machine. It's going to be a surprise—I haven't told anyone about it—but everyone is going to be so impressed when the fog starts rolling out of the equipment room and fills the gym.

DRU Um.

EM Stop throwing shade on my fog machine.

DRU All I said was um!

EM Yeah, but that wasn't all you were thinking!

DRU Meh.

EM I think I told you the local bakery is doing the cakes and tortes and pastries, right? The pastries will be in the shapes of bats, and we'll have chocolate-covered strawberries, punch and coffee and tea, and some cheese-snacky things. I thought the cheese ruined the ambience, but Russell Crowe (at our last meeting, when I was sent to him because I answered Madame La Frawnch in Russian) said, "We really should have something for people who don't care for chocolate."

I snorted. "As if that's humanly possible?"

"There are some people out there," he said with a little head bob.

"Uh-huh. Have you ever met one?"

"No, but I've heard of people who don't like sweets. Just make sure there is a selection of cheeses in for those people, and the food should pass without comment."

"Well, I hope there're comments. I'm not having bat-shaped pastries made for nothing, you know." I got to my feet and checked my tablet. "All right, I think we can conclude this meeting of my nineteenth expulsion and party planning."

He chuckled. "I will certainly miss your visits once Holly moves past having need of you here."

"Well, we're down to just the French class, so hopefully that'll be soon," I said, gathering up my things.

"Did she mention anything to you about the work-experience month in January?" he asked. "I believe her mother wishes for her to go somewhere away from Alling in an attempt to broaden her horizons."

"She said she wanted to talk to me about that, but we haven't had a chance yet. I've been busy with my own school things, and of course this party."

"Ah. Well, I'll let Patricia speak to you about it, then. And let me know if you need the gym opened early this afternoon."

"We should be good so long as everyone does what I tell them to do," I said with a blithe unconcern that you just know will come back to haunt me.

DRU Yeah. So many comments about possible disasters.

EM Nothing I haven't already thought of a thousand times.

The plan is to have all of the tables done in a gorgeous dark red crushed-velvet material, with two huge candelabras from the theater rental place that look like they're straight out of *Dracula* (the good version, not the sucky one), cobwebs, and, per the request from the high school kids, dried roses scattered around the table. Yesterday we draped the walls with cobwebs and black gauze, and set up a bunch of little round tables with candles and more black gauze. It's not my idea of a grand party, but the kids seem to be happy with it, so all is well.

Really, really have to go. Stop making me type at you! I have a to-do list that's a million items long for tomorrow, and I have to get some sleep.

DRU Happy almost Halloween!

EM Gah!

CHAPTER TWENTY-TWO

EM I hope you're sitting down.

EM Oh no, you aren't here?

EM Dru?

EM *sigh* I have the evening to end all evenings to tell you about, and you're MIA. OK. I'm going to start narrating it now because if I don't, I may never do it.

I'm so pooped. No, beyond pooped and into the land of downright comatose. I'm so tired I don't know what to feel, whether I should be looking for a rock to crawl under, or happy, or mad, or all of them. I suspect it's all of them, but in order to explain it, I'm going to have to start at the beginning; otherwise it'll be too confusing.

Ready? OK, let's dive right in.

Yesterday evening, Holly and I and the three other girls on the committee finished setting up for the party. I set the girls to work on the food, and got Holly to help me move the fog machine behind a stack of mats in the equipment room. The plan was to wait until the party started, then turn it on and let the fog slowly trickle out across the floor. We tried it out in the equipment room, and it worked fabulously.

"You're sure this will be OK? Uncle won't be mad that you're doing this without his approval?" Holly's just not happy unless she's worrying about something.

"Of course he won't be mad. He approved everything else for the party, didn't he? And the school isn't paying for the machine—I am—so there's nothing he can complain about. Turn it so the fog is a little thicker, will you? I want to see if it hangs around the floor like it does in the movies."

She twisted a knob and the fog came out thick, spreading out until it covered the floor. I walked through it and it swam around my feet perfectly. "Oh, man, this is going to be so great!"

"It is very eerie," Holly said, running through it so long tendrils of fog snaked after her.

"Yeah, well, you're in charge of watching the level of fog, OK? We'll have to turn it on much higher, since it will have to fill a much bigger space. What setting do you have it on now?"

"Three. It goes up to eleven."

"Great, it sounds like there'll be more than enough power to cover the whole floor. Okey-doke, let's go out and see how the snack arrangement is going."

Once the last touches were laid out (cheese was packed on dry ice; chocolates were arranged; drinks were ready to be poured into a couple of punch bowls), we turned out all the lights except the black lights that the girls insisted we have, and they ran around the gym shrieking and generally having a blast until the janitor came and turned the regular lights back on.

I shooed them out after that, and reminded them they had just an hour to get dressed and get back to be on hand to take tickets.

Holly ran home to get into her emo fae costume, and I hitched a ride with Russell Crowe so I could don my own fabulous outfit.

You're dying to hear about the costume, right? Yes, there's a reason I didn't describe it to you—I wanted you to be surprised. I didn't get a picture of me in it because … well, I'll get to that. You'll just have to make do with a description until I get a picture.

I told you I was going as a fallen angel, yes? Well, the dress was white satin with a square neck, and tight sleeves to my elbows, at which point they flowed out in the medieval style. The material was really beautiful—it had this delicious white-on-white embroidery with a plain front panel (that went all the way to the floor). Attached to the back of the dress was a pair of soft, feathered wings (short ones, not the long ones), made up of that fuzzy kind of faux-ostrich-feather stuff, not big feathers. The wings went almost to my waist. So that's the angel part of my costume. The fallen part was the black studded dog collar and matching wristbands, a long, long rope of black shiny beads that were knotted just below my boobs, and a big black crucifix that hung down to my stomach.

"What are you doing?" Bess asked when I was in the bathroom slicking back most of my hair into a bun at the nape of my neck.

I made a face at her. "What does it look like I'm doing? I'm dancing on the ceiling, of course."

"Don't be so rude," she said, sitting on the little bathroom bench. "I came in to offer my help with your makeup."

I gave her my patented Look of Utter Disbelief. "Like I need help with makeup?"

"You said you wanted really dramatic eyes, and I do have a degree in art. I'll do it better than you."

I thought about that for a minute, then realized she was probably right. "All right, but if I don't like it, I'm taking it off. I don't need to look like one of your weird impressionistic art projects that no one understands."

"Heathen. What are you doing to your bangs?"

I held up the spiking gel. "Spiking them in soft, swoopy curves."

She chewed on her lip for a minute as she looked at my bangs, then jumped up. "Stay here, I've got something better."

"Something better than spiking gel?"

She came back with a small bottle in her hand and showed it to me. "It's not permanent color, so it'll wash off, but I think it'll look good with your orange hair."

"It's not orange. It's Copper—"

"Sunset Splendor, I know, but that's just another name for orange. Oh, don't get all huffy on me. Just spike your bangs. This is going to look really great, and it has the added bonus of making you a walking advertisement for Halloween."

"Huh?"

"Black and orange!"

Once I got my bangs spiked, she carefully applied the temporary black coloring to the ends of the spiky bits. I hate to admit that she was right, but she was. It really did look dramatic, although my hair is *not* orange.

"Now, let's see. For your eyes, I think the kohl will be best."

"I was going to use some plum eye shadow—"

"No, no color. Just black and white and your hair. That'll be all the color you need."

"But my lipstick—"

"Black. You have black lipstick?"

I started to nod, but she *tsk*ed and grabbed my chin, tipping my head back. "Sit still. I think an exaggerated Egyptian look is what you want."

She did my eyes, darkened my eyebrows, and then did the lipstick last. "There you go, all done. You look like an angel who's been up to all sorts of trouble."

I looked in the mirror and did a little dance. "Thanks, Bess. It's very cool."

"Told ya."

I stuck my tongue out at her and started to leave the bathroom. She grabbed my arm. "I know you're limited on money. … You need condoms?"

Why is everyone in this family trying to give me condoms? I mean, how many condoms can a girl use? "No, I still have the last batch you gave me, and then Mom insisted on giving me two more boxes once she got a good look at Fang."

"OK, just checking; don't get your knickers in a twist."

I snorted and went downstairs. Brother came out of the kitchen and did a double take at me. He turned to Mom, who was following him, and said, "You told me girls would be easier to raise than boys."

Mom smiled at him. "I lied."

I did a twirl for them, holding out my arms so the sleeves would flutter. "Well? What do you think? Do I look like a fallen angel?"

"Er …"

"You look very nice, dear. Doesn't she look nice?" Mom said.

"Er …"

"I did her makeup," Bess said, coming downstairs.

"Er …"

"Very striking, Bess."

"Er …"

I rolled my eyes and whapped Brother on the arm. "Oh, stop it! You know I look fabulous. Now come on, I have to be there early so I can show the DJ where to set up, and to make sure that no one has touched anything they weren't supposed to touch. Quickly, people!" I clapped my hands. "We have a party to put on!"

Brother drove me to the school and managed not to lecture me on the way, although as I got out of the car, he maneuvered his hair horn out of the window and said in a near whisper, "Do you need condoms? I don't condone you conducting sexual acts, but as you keep reminding me, you are old enough to make those decisions for yourself. I took it upon myself to purchase you a couple of condoms in case you find yourself faced with a rampant penis."

I was actually touched by such consideration, and leaned down to kiss him on the forehead. "You're really annoying sometimes, but on the whole, you're not a bad father."

He looked surprised for a minute, then appeared to get a little weepy-eyed. "Thank you, Emily. Such words of praise are rare, and thus worth their weight in gold."

I smiled and headed into the school, feeling all warm and fuzzy. I wonder how long Mom and Bess will let him wear the black lipstick kiss on his forehead.

Drat. BRB. Phone.

EM Still not here?

EM Phone was Holly calling to see if I was going to kill myself or not. OK, slight exaggeration, but she did say she wondered if I was going to go home to Seattle. I have to admit, the thought is tempting.

DRU I'm here, I'm here! I was in the shower. Wait, what? You're coming home now? Let me read back.

EM *sips water to warm up throat for next round of narration*

DRU I don't see any reason for you to come home.

EM I haven't gotten to it yet.

DRU Is this going to be an epic story?

EM Yes.

DRU OK. Proceed. I'm going to dry off and do my hair and get dressed, but that will give you time to talk without me interrupting.

EM Sounds good. Back to last night. Everything started off really well. The kids did a good job pushing the cheese twiddles, approximately seventeen types of Stilton, cheese crackers, cheese puffs, and cheese-something with mayonnaise that looks like what our dog used to ralph up after he'd been eating in the compost heap.

I had told Fang that I had to be at the gym early, but couldn't help but keep an eye out for him. "Any sign of him?" I asked Holly when she rolled up to see if anything else needed doing.

"Not yet, no. Emily …" She looked nervous, almost like she was going to be sick. "You're not going to go off with Fang, are you?"

"Go off? Go off where?"

She shrugged. "I know you will want to be with him. I just … I just hoped you wouldn't go away for the whole evening."

Poor kid. She's been so improved at school lately that I'd forgotten how much social anxiety she had in situations like this. "I promise I won't disappear on you, OK? You remember our signals, yes?"

"Um …"

I made a circular signal with my left hand. "If I do this …?"

"Erm … left hand, make sure the DJ isn't playing crappy remixes."

"Right. And this?" I did a zigzag with my right.

"Tell you if something runs out on the buffet table?"

"You got it. And what about this?" I grinned really wide and made a backward-and-forward motion with my forefinger.

"Uh ..."

"Do I have any lipstick on my teeth?"

"Oh, that's right, that's the teeth-check signal. Sorry. I won't forget again."

I patted her on the shoulder. "Just relax and have fun. I'll be here if you need a breather from the Snickerers, and you can always dance with Fang if you want a Safe Dance."

"Relax!" She heaved a really big sigh. "Dance with Fang! How can I relax with that hanging over my head?"

"Oh, come on, you've known him for two months, and he likes you. A lot. He won't bite, and you know he won't do any-thing"—I wiggled my fingers at her—"grabby-handsy."

She nodded but still looked worried, and declined to go mingle with the other kids, so I set her on door watch. "Just let me know when Fang arrives. Or, for that matter, Aidan. And if you see someone you want to go talk to, or dance with, do it. Remember what I told you."

"You have to take the bull by the balls in order to get ahead," she parroted, then frowned. "Are you sure it's not take the bull by the horns?"

"Balls, horns ... same difference."

"Not really, no ..."

"Just do whatever feels right, OK? And if some guy gets a bit too intense, let me know."

Her smile was so watery it was more of a grimace than anything else, so I decided to cool it on the warnings. They were clearly frightening her more than bolstering her spirit.

"Devon's here," Holly said about fifteen minutes later, pop-ping up while I was chatting with some parents who'd been roped into helping supervise.

"Is he? Good. Who does he have with him?" I asked.

"No one," she said, surprising me.

"Huh. He's such a flirt, I figured it would be impossible for him to come to a party alone. I guess I'm wro—holy moly, Batman!"

I finally spotted Devon. He strolled into the gym, flipped off a long dark green cape, and turned to face us.

Holly's eyes were huge. "He's dressed as a knight!"

"Hoo!" I blew out a breath and just about ate Devon up with my eyes. He had on a seriously awesome costume, with black leggings, boots that cross-gartered up his legs (I'm not Brother's daughter for nothing), a dark green hauberk, chain mail that reached to his knees, and a broadsword belted at his side.

"He looks just like that guy from Lord of the Rings," Holly said, all breathless-like.

I cocked an eyebrow at her, but didn't point out he was almost six years older than her. Devon might be a flirt, but he wasn't stupid—he wouldn't encourage a sixteen-year-old. Her little crush on him would probably be safe enough.

"Yeah, he's all shades of gorgeous, that's for sure," I agreed. "He could definitely give Viggo a run for his Aragorn money."

"You don't expect me to dance with him, do you?" Holly asked, kind of panicky.

I laughed and gave her a little nudge. "You don't have to dance with anyone if you don't want to, silly. But if you did want to, Devon would be totally safe, just like Fang. It's up to you what you want to do."

Empowerment, empowerment, empowerment … that was the name of my game for Holly. Sometimes, it seemed like an uphill battle.

Just then Devon saw us and smiled, which made something inside me melt; then I melted even more when he came over to where Holly was clinging to me. I pried her cold fingers off my wrist and struck an *I'm not slobbering over him in that gorgeous outfit* pose. Or I tried to—I'm not absolutely sure I was successful, because Devon's smile got bigger the closer he came.

"My angel! How wonderful you look. Positively dripping with all sorts of delicious sins. And Holly—what a charming elf you make."

"I'm an emo fae," she whispered, her eyes still huge as she looked him over. You know, Dru, I've never understood Brother's fascination with medieval stuff, but if this is what those knights looked like, I'm going to have to rethink my policy of avoiding everything Middle Ages.

"You look great, Devon. That's a fabulous costume."

"Had it made up last year when a girl I was with was into the Ren Faire scene. Now, you told me you want me to mingle, but before I do, you have to promise to dance with me. Both of you," he said politely, and I did a little swoon inside.

"Sure thing, although I can't speak for Holly."

Holly gasped out something that sounded like a yes.

"Excellent. Ah, I see a friend of my mum's. I'll just go say hello. ..." He wandered off, but it wasn't to speak to a middle-aged lady. I noticed he found one of the younger, prettier teachers and hightailed it over to her to work his moves.

"Wow," I said, watching him as he strolled off, one hand on his sword. "He's really something, isn't he?"

"Aidan's here," Holly said, nodding toward the door. "At least, I think it's him."

I looked. Aidan had whited out his face, then painted on three long slash marks that went from above his eyebrows down across his nose and cheek. It was quite effective.

"Hello," I said as he sauntered over to us. "That makeup is amazing."

"Should be, it took long enough to get right. You look good."

I opened my mouth to say that the rest of his costume was wonderful as well, but just then he pulled me forward, and slapped his lips on mine in a blatantly sexual kiss. His tongue was everywhere, as were his hands, a fact that had me shoving back on him.

"Aidan, for heaven's sake, there are kids here! Let's try to keep the boob-grabbing and full-tongued snogging to a minimum, OK?"

He laughed, and made a fancy bow that left me wanting to giggle. "Apologies, my angelic one. I'll try to restrain myself around you, although it won't be easy." He leaned forward, saying softly, "But don't expect me to be so patient later on. Especially not if you're going to continue to be such a tease."

I stared at him for a few seconds. "I'm not being a tease, Aidan. I wouldn't do that."

He smiled then, but I have to say, it wasn't a very nice smile. It was more of a sneer. "That's not what I hear."

"What—" I started to ask, but he lifted his hand in greeting to someone who called out at him.

"Later, ducks, later," he said, moving off.

I narrowed my eyes on him, but was almost immediately distracted when Holly nudged me. "He's here."

"Fang?" I spun around to face the doors.

"Yes. And wow."

"Where? I don't see—holy cow! What happened to him and Devon? Did they drink some sort of super-sexy potion or something?"

A small clutch of people moved to one side, revealing Fang, where he was being greeted by a man in black with huge horns curling back off his head, but I ignored Horn Man (who I suspected was the janitor) to give Fang the eye.

And boy howdy, was he worth the time to look over. He was dressed in a Victorian frilly-front shirt with lace cuffs, a black, really tight-fitting frock coat, tight black pants, and a gorgeous scarlet vest embroidered in gold. He'd evidently let his hair grow a bit, because it was tied back in a little ponytail. He looked … elegant. It was so un-Fang-like, I couldn't help but stare.

"Man, if this is what happens when they go to a costume party, we're going to have to start having them every month," I said, trying to remember to breathe.

Holly giggled.

"Well?" she asked, when I continued to stare.

"Hmm?"

"Go say hello, silly."

"Oh. Yeah. Good idea. It's only polite, after all." I hustled my way over to him, possibly elbowing a teen or two out of my way, stopping when I got to him. He turned, saw me, and smiled.

Just like with Devon, my innards melted. "Hullo, Emily."

"Hi, Fang. You look beyond gorgeous. If we weren't in public, and hadn't decided to cool things down, I'd jump you where you stand."

He grinned, then walked around me, making a show of examining my costume, stopping in front of me to tip his head to the side and say, "That suits you."

"What does? The crucifix? The black and Copper Sunset Splendor? The medieval gown with fwoofy sleeves?"

"The wings. You look like an angel." He took my hand and turned it over; then he kissed my palm.

I didn't know how to react to that. Part of me (Susceptible-to-Fang Emily) went all melty.

"Thank you," I said, then decided what the hell, so I turned my hand around in his, and kissed his palm. Holly made kind of a gasping noise behind me.

Fang's eyebrows rose. "Why did you do that?"

I have no idea why I did it other than impulse, but I wasn't about to tell him that. Evidently there is a limit to how stupid I'm willing to appear. "Same reason you did."

Holly *eek*ed.

Fang's eyebrows lowered. "I doubt that."

Holly grabbed my arm.

"Just a second, Holly. Really, Fang? Why did you—"

"There you are. Fancy dress suits you, mate—you look like something out of Jane Austen. Maybe you should stop grubbing around vet school and go apply at the BBC. Bet they'd snap you up. Doesn't my little Emily look stunning sexy tonight?" Aidan came up and put his arm around me, pulling me up next to him.

Oh, crap!

"*Your* little Emily?" Fang looked first at Aidan, and then at me.

"Jealous? You needn't be, old man—there's enough birds to go around. Just keep your hands off mine."

Fang gave me a long, long look, and said slowly, "I think I understand."

"No, you don't—" I started to say, but Aidan laughed and interrupted me.

"Had a thing for my girl, did you? I'm sure you'll survive the loss."

"And that's just about enough out of you," I said, worming my way out of Aidan's grip.

I was just opening my mouth to give him a piece of my mind—as well as reassure Fang that the situation wasn't what he thought—but Fang took that moment to say, "You always were a lucky sod, Aidan. I hope you appreciate what you've got this time."

Then he gave me a little nod and turned to Holly and asked her if she wanted to dance. I stared after them, my stomach knotting into a painful ball.

I had hurt Fang. No, not me … Aidan.

Aidan massaged the back of my neck, murmuring, "Don't mind him, duck. He's just a bit green because I've got the bit of goods tonight."

I was consumed with guilt until Aidan's words sank in. "Bit of goods? Did I hear you right? First I'm a tease and now I'm a bit of goods?"

I looked at Aidan, really looked at him. He just laughed and pulled me toward the dance area, making sure to rub his crotch against me. "Don't be such a twat, Emily. Let's dance."

Why hadn't I ever noticed that his eyes were so hard? Why hadn't I seen through that shallow, attractive surface to the man underneath? Why hadn't I remembered that I never did get on well with hipsters?

He had hurt Fang. Deliberately. And he'd used me to do so.

"Don't want to dance?" he breathed into my ear, his mustache tickling me. "I can think of something else for us to do, something perfect for my luscious little fallen angel."

I jerked my hand away from him and only just kept myself from punching him in his smug face. "Whereas I can't think of anything I want to do with you that doesn't involve a gelding knife. Go away, Aidan. I really do not want to see you anymore."

"Emily—"

I jerked away when he tried to grab me, and raised my voice so he could hear me over the music. "You're a nasty little man with a nasty little mind, and I don't think you should be around vulnerable teens, so why don't you just take your bad self off."

"Emily—" he said again, only this time he kind of snarled it.

"And stop being mean to Fang. I don't like it," I said loudly, aware I was losing my temper and making a scene, but unable to stop myself.

"Will you stop—"

"And to top everything off, you're a horrible kisser, and your tongue feels like a slimy slug!" A couple of people around us turned to look.

"For Christ's sake, you slag-faced cow, shut up!" he yelled.

Everything might have been OK if the music hadn't stopped right then, and his words echoed off the gym walls so everyone could hear them.

"Out," I said, pointing to the door. "Go away, Aidan. Just go the hell away."

"Stupid little slut," Aidan hissed at me. "No bit of pussy is worth this!"

"Watch your language," I snarled, making a fist with my right hand. "There are kids who can hear you."

Beyond him, Russell Crowe (wearing, by no small coincidence, a gladiator outfit) hustled toward us.

"Is there a problem?" he asked.

"No problem. This man was just leaving," I said, and then turned on my heel. "I'll be right back. I just need to turn on the fog machine."

"Fog machine?" Russell Crowe asked, looking confused. Aidan looked like he wanted to kill me. "What fog machine? Emily—"

I pushed my way through the crowd in the dance area, past Snickerer Ann (tight red dress that showed she had no boobs, and long black wig) and Snickerer Bee (dressed like a shepherdess, of all things), both of whom laughed really loudly when I passed them; past Mrs. Spreadborough (pumpkin, complete with little green vine hat), who looked shocked; past Miss Horseface (not wearing any costume), who flared her equine nostrils as I ran by; past Devon, who was leaning up against the wall, laughing (no doubt at me); past a horrified Holly, standing really close to Fang, who watched me with an odd look on his face; past everyone else, who ignored the fact that the DJ had started the next mix.

They watched me, the idiot American who hurt a really nice man because of an asshat.

I bit my lip hard, refusing to let anyone see me cry. I'd done enough to bring the party down, and just wanted it to go on so it would be over, at which point I could crawl into a hole and die, or immediately fly home to Seattle. I wasn't sure which I wanted most.

The fog machine sat at the ready. I flipped the switch that turned it on, and cranked it up so it thumped and hummed loudly, belching fog out of the end of the long hose that snaked out the door and around to the edges of the DJ's stand.

Once it was going, I slumped against a mound of mats, taking stock of my shredded ego.

"Emily?" Holly stood in the door, Fang behind her. "Are you all right?"

"Fine. I'm just fine," I said, turning just enough so she wouldn't see me wiping away tears.

"Are you going to come out?"

"In a few minutes. I'm just making sure the machine is working OK."

"Oh. All right. I'll see you when you come out."

"Sure," I said, still facing the wall.

There was silence for a few seconds, and when I glanced back, Holly was still standing in the doorway. "I … I'm sorry, Emily."

"I know. Thanks."

She left quietly, and I felt even worse because Fang just stood there, leaning against the doorframe and watching me.

I swallowed back a big lump in my throat and said, "I am not with Aidan."

"So I gathered from your comments."

I bit my lip for a few seconds, then blurted out, "That night I texted you. When you were out with a friend. It wasn't a male friend, was it?"

"No," he said quietly. "It wasn't."

I nodded, fighting back another wave of tears. "I'm glad you found someone," I lied.

He tipped his head a bit to the side. "It's not the ideal situation."

"No. But life seldom gives us that."

"Emily—"

"No," I said, raising a hand to stop him. "I've had about as much emotional turmoil as I can stand in a night."

"I just wanted to say that I would have told you. I was afraid …"

"Don't be." I swallowed back yet another lump of tears, and smiled. Dru, I actually smiled at him. I should have won an Oscar for my acting, I really should have. "We're friends, remember? And friends don't have to be afraid to tell each other how they feel."

He was silent for thirty seconds; then he gave a sharp nod and left me alone.

I let myself cry then, feeling I deserved it, but only for three minutes. Then Empowered-Woman Emily pointed out that it was pathetic and weak to hide away at a party I was responsible for running, so I gathered my tattered dignity and headed for the door.

"Emily?" It sounded like Russell Crowe calling for me. I sighed.

The fog machine gave a sympathetic gurgle and continued to thump and hum away.

"Emily? Where are you? Emily, this—Oh, I beg your pardon. Yes, I'm very sorry, I'm trying to stop it. Emily?"

I took a deep breath, and opened the door into the gym.

There was no gym to be seen. Everything was sucked up into a wall of whiteness.

"Well, at least I know I'm getting my money's worth for the fog machine," I said, peering through the white to see dark shapes flit back and forth. "Guess I turned it on a bit too high."

"Emily?" Russell Crowe called again. I couldn't see him, but he sounded fairly close by. "Emily, turn the machine—"

Just then the fire sprinklers went off. I heard later that they were overly sensitive ever since the school had a fire the year before, but I say that fake fog shouldn't have set them off no matter how sensitive they were. Evidently I was wrong, though, because they went off, dumping water on everyone.

The DJ started yelling and throwing stuff over her equipment. Russell Crowe yelled for me to turn the damned machine off, and everyone else screamed and shrieked and ran around in the fog trying to find a way out of the gym.

By the time I turned off the machine and ran back to the gym, someone had found the doors and thrown them open. Fog rolled out the door, twisted and torn as partygoers stampeded through it to get out of the indoor downpour.

I ran across the floor, too, slipping and sliding on the heels of the last of the crowd, my dress soaked, my cute little fluffy white wings sodden, and, as I found out later, my black eye makeup streaked down my cheeks all the way to my jaw. As I came through the door, I stopped. I didn't want to stop, but I had to. Everyone was standing outside, wet, teeth chattering, hair dripping, and all of them, every single one of them, had turned to face me as I came out the door. OK, "glare" would be a better word. They all glared at me.

"Um ..." I swallowed hard. I had a feeling no one would see the humor of the situation. "I think there was a little problem with the fog machine."

Have you ever heard a crowd growl? It's not pleasant, Dru. In fact, it scared the crap out of me.

"Sorry, everyone," I added, trying to edge my way past them.

They growled even louder; then the janitor came up behind me, his horns trembling in agitation. "I've turned the bleedin' sprinklers off, but there's a hell of a mess to be cleaned up, not to mention three coats of my best varnish ruined. It'll cost a pretty penny to repair, I'm thinkin'."

Russell Crowe, who was standing in front of me, shook his head, and walked past without saying anything. I knew, though.

Oh, I knew what he was thinking, and sighed. I'd never be out of debt if now I had to pay for the new school floor in addition to my ex-boss's car.

All the teachers filed past me, none of them saying anything, but all of them giving me the same look.

"Sorry," I told the fifth- and sixth-form kids, who stood around wet, most of their costumes ruined, shivering in the cold. "It was an accident."

None of them said anything to me, either. Not directly, although a lot of them muttered stuff that made me flinch. Some of them left; others went back into the gym, until the only three people left standing on the steps were Holly, and Aidan, and me.

"What are you still doing here?" I asked Aidan, too tired and beat up to be anything but irritated with him.

"You may think I hang on your every word, but I don't. I was talking to Devon." He gave a couple of golf claps. "Bloody brilliant, Emily. Bloody brilliant. I thought after Dev screwed your brains out that you might be worth my time, but I was wrong."

"What are you talking about? I've never had sex with Devon."

"Oh, get off it. We all know you spent the night in Dev's bed after his party. I saw you going with him, and I know my Dev—there's no way he'd get a bird in his room and not screw her silly."

I lifted my chin, wondering why I ever considered him as a potential boyfriend. He was just a slimeball, really. I guess maybe it was the accent that threw me, because normally I'm pretty good at spotting slimeballs. "Not that it's any of your business, but I didn't spend the night in his room. Fang took me home. And while we're on the subject of you and Devon, just why did you imply to him that you and I had hooked up?"

He snorted. "I don't know what you're talking about."

"Sure you don't. It's all starting to make sense—if it's not Tash drugging me and being a general pain in the ass, it's you telling lies about me."

"That's your story. Tash was right—you are a stupid little bint who doesn't know her arse from her elbow. And now you're whining because you've gotten what you deserve."

"You know what's wrong with your costume, Aidan?" I asked.

He squinted his eyes at me and sneered again. "Nothing?"

"Nope. It's the blood. It's fake."

He blinked at me.

"What it needs is real blood." I smiled at him, made a fist the way I'd learned in a self-defense class, and punched him as hard as I could in the nose. He screamed and fell backward through the door. Holly stood at the end of the stairs, her hands gripping the metal railing, her mouth an O of surprise as I rubbed my sore knuckles.

"I hate to run away from a bad situation, but my raging headache just got a hundred times worse. I think I'm going to go home and die now. Are you OK to get home?" She nodded. "All right. Don't stand out in the cold too long, or you'll get pneumonia or something. Sorry I got your fae costume wet. It looked awesome."

I headed off toward the road, then decided that as long as the entire school hated me, I might as well compound my sins, and walked across the front lawn that students were strictly forbidden to walk across.

"Emily!"

Someone called my name behind me. Someone male. I ignored him.

"Emily, wait."

I walked even faster. I was shaking with cold, and nerves, and my stomach was churning, but I felt really good about punching the Slimeball's nose. I hoped I gave him another nosebleed. Or broke his nose this time. That would be some pretty sweet justice right there.

"Emily, stop!"

That was a second voice. I stopped and looked back. Fang and Devon were running toward me, Devon holding the cape

I'd worn over my costume, Fang with one of the emergency gym blankets under his arm.

"Fang, you remember when I barfed at Devon's, and you took me home, and I said I couldn't ever see you again because I would die of embarrassment? Well, this is a hundred times worse, so if you don't want me to curl up and die right here, don't come any closer."

Devon laughed, and punched Fang in the arm. "Don't be stupid. If I had a pound for every time I tossed my cookies, I'd be a rich man."

"You *are* a rich man," Fang told him as they stopped in front of me; then he punched Devon in the arm, too.

"Why are you doing that?" I asked, momentarily distracted from my horrible, ghastly, depressing, miserable existence to wonder why they were punching each other.

"Fang and I had a little bet." Devon smiled, and put my cape around my shoulders. "I bet him that this party wouldn't go off without some sort of disaster, and he bet me that it would be a party to remember, because you were running it."

Fang put the blanket around me as well. I looked between them, then punched Devon in the arm. It hurt a lot worse than Aidan's nose because of the chain mail, but I just rubbed my knuckles and glared at him. "Why did you tell Aidan I slept with you?"

Devon's smile melted. "I didn't. I wouldn't tell him that, Emily. It's just … well, I have a bit of a reputation, and he didn't see you go home, so he assumed …"

"You could have told him that we didn't do anything!"

"I did. He didn't believe me."

I turned to Fang, and thought about punching him in the arm, too, but my knuckles were too sore. So I pinched him. Hard.

"Ow!"

"You could have told me the truth about Aidan! You could have warned me! Aidan is your friend."

"I didn't know he had his eye on you until tonight. You said before that you weren't interested, and I assumed that was still the case." He tipped his head to the side and looked at me. "Would you have believed me if I had known and said anything?"

I clutched my blanket and the cape tight across my chest. "Yes. Because we're friends, dammit. Friends believe friends."

"Then I apologize," Fang said.

"We told you he was a mixer," Devon pointed out.

"Oh, right, so all of this is my fault?"

"Some of it, yes," Fang said.

I pointed at him. "Just because you're a friend doesn't mean I can't pinch you again. Stop being right, and show me some sympathy, dammit. Do you have any idea how much that school floor is going to cost me?"

Devon threw his arm around me, turning me around so we were headed back toward the school. Fang walked along on my other side.

"I'm not going back in there, Devon."

Devon squeezed my shoulders. "We're not going back to the party."

"Then where are we going?"

"Fang and I are going to take you home. My car is parked over this way."

"Good. I really do not feel like facing the headmaster or the teachers again. I'll do it in the morning, when I can beg for mercy."

Devon laughed.

"Don't let it bother you. Dev did the same thing at our school," Fang said.

"Really? You set the sprinklers off during a party?" I asked Devon.

"Not during a party, during the awards ceremony at the end of the year. I was in the fifth form, and having a smoke behind a screen, and next thing I knew, the sprinklers went off and soaked everyone, kids, parents, teachers. It was a right bungle. My mum still talks about it."

"Sounds like something you'd do. I assume you did not quit that school because you couldn't face anyone afterward?"

Devon's arm jiggled when he laughed. "Not likely. I became the hero of the school. Some of my mates offered me money to do it again, just for a lark."

We were in front of Devon's car by then. Fang held the door open, and I scooted into the back. "Even if I could afford to pay for the damage I caused, there's still the fact that I punched Aidan in the nose. If he wanted to, he could file assault charges against me, and given my luck, I'd end up in prison."

Devon and Fang grinned at each other.

"We knew you'd done something of the sort. Aid came in spurting blood, yelling about you attacking him. Fang pointed out that given the way he'd been groping you earlier, you could probably hit him up for sexual assault charges. That shut him up."

"Little bastard had it coming," I said, shivering. "I know he's your friend and all, but he really had it coming."

"Don't worry about it." Fang smiled. "We'll have a thing or two to say to him as well."

I sat back and let myself relax a little, warmed by the fact that they both cared enough to come after me. "Don't beat him up on my account."

"We'll be having a few words," Devon said. "But I doubt if we'll thrash him. For one, he's got a mean right hook. And for another … well, he is a mate. Of sorts."

I thought about that for a bit. "Understandable. Would you mind telling him something for me?"

Devon smiled at me in the rearview mirror. "Anything you like."

"Would you tell him I've got a pair of big shoes my friend Dru calls ballbusters, and if he spreads any rumors about me, I'll show him how they got that name?"

Both Fang and Devon laughed, and I felt a tiny bit better, enough that I could contemplate the miserable future before me without

CHAPTER TWENTY-THREE

DRU Without what? WITHOUT WHAT?

DRU OMIGOD, Emily, how can you log off without finishing? Here I've been very good and not interrupting you AT ALL because I've been utterly and completely riveted to what happened to you, and you just log off? YOU CAN'T DO THAT … ohai.

EM Sorry. Phone did an update.

DRU OMIGOD, girl! OH. MY. GOD.

EM I know, right?

DRU I can't … so many things … I don't even know where to start. … Wait, what were you going to say when you dropped off-line?

EM Um. Oh, that I could contemplate the future without changing my name and moving to Brazil.

DRU Why Brazil?

EM Why not Brazil?

DRU Point taken. I can't believe Aidan said those things to you. It's totally not fair you have to pay for the floor. It was their system that was defective, not the fog machine! And finally, can I have a little swoon at Devon and Fang for being so there for you?

EM Why not? Neither of them is mine.

DRU You sound so down.

EM I am, kind of.

DRU Let Dru cheer you up with her Reasons to Be Happy!

EM Oh lord.

DRU 1. Worry gives you ulcers, so try very hard not to worry.

EM How is that a Reason to Be Happy?

DRU Work with me! It's a pre-reason. Also, you don't have an ulcer now. That's something to be happy about.

EM I guess.

DRU 2. You'll work something out with the school.

EM Do they still have debtors' prison in England, do you know?

DRU A what, now?

EM It was in that Dickens book we had to read in high school.

DRU Oh, that. No, I'm sure they don't. So that's point 3: no debtors' prison.

EM I bet they bring it back for me.

DRU 4. You'll get a good job when you go back home, and pay off your ex-boss's car in no time, so then you can pay for the school damage. In a few years, you won't owe anyone anything!

EM Ugh ugh ugh.

DRU And finally, 5. You're only going to be in England for another ten months.

EM I wonder how much debt I'll owe by the time we go home.

DRU You really are a Grumpy Gerta today, aren't you?

EM Sorry. You're right, a couple more years paying off debt won't kill me, although they may well if I have to spend them living with my parents. I really need to get a well-paying job when I get home so I can be sane again.

Holly told me that the kids at school say they had a blast at the party despite the sprinklers, and that it'll go down as the party to remember.

DRU See? You're probably a hero in their eyes.

EM I doubt that. I'm not sure I like being remembered that way, but whatever.

One good thing has happened: Holly decided that she can get by for the rest of the semester without me in French class, so I've done some good there.

DRU Brava, Holly! And go, you, for getting her to that point.

EM Oh! I didn't tell you because I was so caught up in everything, but Holly's mom called me the other day to talk about January. It seems it's a thing in Holly's school for the kids to go away for a month and get some practical work experience, and Holly told her mom that I have an aunt who lives in Scotland on a sheep farm.

"Do you think," Mum A. asked in that breathy voice that always made me feel like my ears were being tickled, "that your aunt and uncle would allow Emily to conduct her work experience with them?"

"I'm not sure, but I don't see why they wouldn't," I said, confused. "But why does she want to go to a sheep farm? She's not interested in becoming a farmer, is she? I thought she wanted to be a poet."

Mum A. laughed. "No, not at all, but Dr. Alton and I thought it would be a good thing for Emily if she were with you for the month away from home. She's shown much improvement under your tutelage, Emily, but there is still a long way to go before I'm comfortable that Holly will be thrive on her own."

"Wait … with me? I'm not going to Scotland. I have classes at Oxwills."

"I'm sure you can take them online, can't you? Almost all the classes are available online. We had a meeting about that."

"Yeah, but—"

"Naturally, we will compensate you for your time."

That stopped me dead. "Oh. Just how much compensation are we talking?"

"I'm sure we can work something out," Mum A. said coyly.

"Yeah, well, about that. I just happen to have a bill from Holly's school for the little contretemps that happened at the Halloween party. Your brother said something about me working it off as a chaperone during some trip to France, but if you wanted to pick up the tab for that, I suppose I could go stay with my aunt for a month. Although that would depend on them agreeing to the proposal."

"I'm sure we can work something out to our mutual satisfaction," Mum A. said, and I knew that my aunt Kathie wouldn't stand a chance.

So, it looks like I'll be going to Scotland after Christmas. To live on a sheep farm. Oh joy.

DRU I had forgotten about your aunt! A sheep farm sounds kind of … muddy.

EM In January in Scotland? I bet it's up to its elbows in mud.

DRU Yeah, but it's still kind of fun. I mean, men in kilts! Castles! Um … what else is Scottish? …

EM Whisky.

DRU Ick. Hate the taste of it.

EM Me too, to be honest.

DRU Are you feeling better about your future?

EM I guess so. I'll have a long-distance friendship with Fang, and a closer-to-home one with Devon. And Lalla and Peg, and of course Holly. They'll keep me sane. I hope.

Bess said she knows of a real psychic, so I'm going to have a séance held in my room to contact the spirit of my underwear drawer. I can't tell you how much I'm looking forward to getting my drawer back.

DRU You have to video it and put it on YouTube.

EM Will do.

All in all, it's been a hell of a couple of months, hasn't it? You dumped the weasel and met a man who appears to love everyone. Literally. And then you meet his boyfriend and hit it off even better with him.

DRU Tim and I are going to have a Netflix and Chill night tonight.

EM …

EM And I hope you have a good time.

DRU Thank you. I shall ignore that loaded ellipses.

EM And I … well, I'm here in a land of men with lovely accents, and not a single one to keep me warm at night. Sooner or later, I have to find one of them who wants to be with me, don't you think?

DRU Absolutely.

EM And until then, I'll just keep on doing what I have to in order to get by.

I mean, it's not like anything worse can happen to me, right?

YOU LOGGED OFF

AUTHOR'S NOTE

Sharp-eyed readers who dipped into my Emily YA series years and years and years ago (we're talking 2003, people!) may find a few passages of this book familiar. That would be because I took the original book, *The Year My Life Went Down the Loo* and rewrote most of it, bringing Emily up to date with modern times, and more importantly, making her an adult so she could explore having adult relationships.

I had so much fun updating Emily, allowing her to have a relationship with Fang, and giving her more grief than she ever thought possible, I decided to continue updating all the rest of her series in the near future.

I hope you enjoyed this brave new Emily as much as I did!

Katie Mac

ABOUT THE AUTHOR

For as long as she can remember, Katie MacAlister has loved reading. Growing up in a family where a weekly visit to the library was a given, Katie spent much of her time with her nose buried in a book.

Two years after she started writing novels, Katie sold her first romance, Noble Intentions. More than fifty books later, her novels have been translated into numerous languages, been recorded as audiobooks, received several awards, and have been regulars on the *New York Times*, *USA Today*, *Wall Street Journal*, and *Publishers Weekly* bestseller lists. Katie lives in the Pacific Northwest with two dogs and a very elderly cat, and can often be found lurking around online.

You are welcome to join Katie's official discussion group on Facebook, as well as connect with her via Twitter, Goodreads, and Instagram. For more information, visit katiemacalister.com

OTHER BOOKS BY
KATIE MACALISTER

Dark Ones Series
A GIRL'S GUIDE TO VAMPIRES
SEX AND THE SINGLE VAMPIRE
SEX, LIES, AND VAMPIRES
EVEN VAMPIRES GET THE BLUES
BRING OUT YOUR DEAD (novella)
THE LAST OF THE RED-HOT VAMPIRES
ZEN AND THE ART OF VAMPIRES
CROUCHING VAMPIRE, HIDDEN FANG
CUPID CATS (novella)
IN THE COMPANY OF VAMPIRES
CONFESSIONS OF A VAMPIRE'S GIRLFRIEND
MUCH ADO ABOUT VAMPIRES
A TALE OF TWO VAMPIRES
THE UNDEAD IN MY BED (novella)
THE VAMPIRE ALWAYS RISES

Aisling Grey Guardian Series
YOU SLAY ME
FIRE ME UP
LIGHT MY FIRE
HOLY SMOKES
DEATH'S EXCELLENT VACATION (short story)

Silver Dragon Series
PLAYING WITH FIRE
UP IN SMOKE
ME AND MY SHADOW

Light Dragon Series
LOVE IN THE TIME OF DRAGONS
THE UNBEARABLE LIGHTNESS OF DRAGONS
SPARKS FLY

Dragon Fall Series
DRAGON FALL
DRAGON STORM
DRAGON SOUL

Time Thief Series
TIME THIEF
THE ART OF STEALING TIME

Matchmaker in Wonderland Series
THE IMPORTANCE OF BEING ALICE
A MIDSUMMER NIGHT'S ROMP
DARING IN A BLUE DRESS
PERILS OF PAULIE

Contemporary Single Titles
IMPROPER ENGLISH
BIRD OF PARADISE (novella)
MEN IN KILTS
THE CORSET DIARIES
A HARD DAY'S KNIGHT
BLOW ME DOWN
IT'S ALL GREEK TO ME
Noble Historical Series
NOBLE INTENTIONS
NOBLE DESTINY
THE TROUBLE WITH HARRY

THE TRUTH ABOUT LEO

Suffragette Historical Series
SUFFRAGETTE IN THE CITY

Paranormal Single Titles
AIN'T MYTH BEHAVING
DEATH'S EXCELLENT VACATION (short story)
MY BIG FAT SUPERNATURAL HONEYMOON
(short story)

Mysteries / writing as Kate Marsh
GHOST OF A CHANCE

Steampunk Romance
STEAMED

Emily Series (2018 Reboot)
YOU AUTO-COMPLETE ME

Young Adult / Writing as Katie Maxwell
CONFESSIONS OF A VAMPIRE'S GIRLFRIEND
EYELINER OF THE GODS

Emily Series (Original)
THE YEAR MY LIFE WENT DOWN THE LOO
THEY WEAR WHAT UNDER THEIR KILTS
WHAT'S FRENCH FOR "EW"?
THE TAMING OF THE DRU
LIFE, LOVE AND THE PURSUIT OF HOTTIES

www.ingramcontent.com/pod-product-compliance
Lightning Source LLC
Chambersburg PA
CBHW050603190726
48283CB00007B/2259